"ONE OF THE RISING STARS OF
HISTORICAL ROMANCE."
—*Booklist*

"THOMAS . . . HAS MADE A NAME FOR HERSELF
WITH HER EXQUISITE USE OF LANGUAGE."
—*Library Journal*

PRAISE FOR THE NOVELS OF SHERRY THOMAS

"Ravishingly sinful, intelligent, and addictive. An amazing debut." —Eloisa James, *New York Times* bestselling author

"Enchanting . . . An extraordinary, unputdownable love story."
—Jane Feather, *New York Times* bestselling author

"Sublime . . . An irresistible literary treat." —*Chicago Tribune*

"Sherry Thomas's captivating debut novel will leave readers breathless. Intelligent, witty, sexy, and peopled with wonderful characters . . . and sharp, clever dialogue."
—*The Romance Reader*

"Thomas makes a dazzling debut with a beautifully written, sizzling, captivating love story . . . Her compelling tale of love betrayed and then reborn will make you sigh with pleasure."
—*RT Book Reviews*

"Deft plotting and sparkling characters . . . Steamy and smart."
—*Publishers Weekly* (starred review)

"Thomas tantalizes readers . . . An enchanting, thought-provoking story of love lost and ultimately reclaimed. Lively banter, electric sexual tension, and an unusual premise make this stunning debut all the more refreshing." —*Library Journal* (starred review)

"Historical romance the way I love it." —*All About Romance*

"Big, dramatic, and romantic." **DISCARD** —*Dear Author*

Berkley Sensation titles by Sherry Thomas

BEGUILING THE BEAUTY
RAVISHING THE HEIRESS
TEMPTING THE BRIDE
THE LUCKIEST LADY IN LONDON

The Luckiest Lady in London

SHERRY THOMAS

B

BERKLEY SENSATION, NEW YORK

THE BERKLEY PUBLISHING GROUP
Published by the Penguin Group
Penguin Group (USA) LLC
375 Hudson Street, New York, New York 10014

USA • Canada • UK • Ireland • Australia • New Zealand • India • South Africa • China

penguin.com

A Penguin Random House Company

THE LUCKIEST LADY IN LONDON

A Berkley Sensation Book / published by arrangement with the author.

Berkley Sensation Books are published by The Berkley Publishing Group.
BERKLEY SENSATION® is a registered trademark of Penguin Group (USA) LLC.
The "B" design is a trademark of Penguin Group (USA) LLC.

For information, address: The Berkley Publishing Group,
a division of Penguin Group (USA) LLC,
375 Hudson Street, New York, New York 10014.

ISBN: 978-0-425-26888-9

PUBLISHING HISTORY
Berkley Sensation mass-market edition / November 2013

PRINTED IN THE UNITED STATES OF AMERICA

10 9 8 7 6 5 4 3 2 1

Cover art by Gregg Gulbronson. Cover hand lettering by Ron Zinn.
Cover design by George Long.
Interior text design by Laura K. Corless.

To X, whose company—
and output—I enjoy tremendously.

ACKNOWLEDGMENTS

Wendy McCurdy, my generous editor. Katherine Pelz, her capable assistant.

Kristin Nelson, my inimitable agent, and everyone at the Nelson Literary Agency.

Tiffany Yates Martin of FoxPrintEditorial.com, whose vision shaped this book.

Janine Ballard, my wonderful critique partner, for the fastest turnaround ever.

Courtney Murati and Shellee Roberts, for their general awesomeness.

My production editor at Penguin, for her endless patience.

My family, for being my bedrock.

My readers, for making it so rewarding to be an author.

PROLOGUE

For as far as he could trace back in time, Felix Rivendale had spent half an hour each day with his parents before teatime. And as far as hazy childhood memories could be trusted, he had always looked forward to and feared that time equally.

Every afternoon, his governess brought him to the door of the parlor. He'd scratch timidly at the heavy oak panel and be told to enter. His beautiful mother, seated in her favorite chair, would put aside her embroidery, rise, and open her arms to welcome him.

He always crossed the room as fast as his legs could carry him, and always stopped just short of the huge perimeter of her skirts. It wouldn't do to run smack into Mother. Her hoops would fly up behind her, he had been told, and that would be a very awful thing to happen.

Felix was careful. He didn't want anything awful to happen. Gingerly, then, he navigated his way around the tricky skirts and up the chair. This was his favorite part of the day, to be ensconced beside his mother and enveloped in her heavenly scent. She'd ruffle his hair and kiss his cheek and call him, to his delighted embarrassment, "muffin cake."

Immediately, however, came his least favorite part. His father, who had been observing them keenly, would storm to a far window and stand with his back to the room. His mother, so affectionate until that moment, would smile an odd, rather chilling smile, cease all her petting, and return to her needlework. Felix was allowed to watch her quietly, which he did, a little miserably, constantly aware of his father's turned back.

By his fifth birthday, he had decided that there was something wrong with him. He must be the cause of all the tension, which became more palpable, more breath-crushing when his parents were forced into close proximity with him. The daily half hour before tea was bad enough, but Sunday mornings, with all three of them sitting side by side in the front pew of the parish church, while the sermon droned on and on, were pure torture. Their desire to get away from him was a palpable weight upon his chest; every breath felt like inhaling needles.

At six he came to a shattering conclusion: His parents hated each other.

But after two more years of stealthy yet intense observation, he revised his previous verdict. It wasn't quite true that his parents despised *each other*. His mother could not stand her husband, but the latter didn't find her as loathsome as she did him. In fact, the marquess was always the one who started conversations, which were usually cut short by the marchioness's chilly replies that barely fell short of discourtesy. He also bought her gifts, which she tossed into the bottom of her trunk without opening. Felix knew because he liked to sit in her rooms and touch her things when she was out of the house for her daily drive, imagining that she was sharing her time with him, imagining that the scent of her came not from lingering molecules of perfume in the air, but from the very fabric and folds of her gown as she let him snuggle next to her.

One afternoon, not long after he turned eight, he found a new packet in the trunk, a large, square black velvet box. Inside, nestled against cream satin, a magnificent necklace of rubies sparkled like crystalline drops of blood. He set the necklace next to the long strands of black pearls, the diamond earrings, the many rings and bracelets and brooches and jeweled hair combs—beautiful, exquisite things, each and every one.

Why wouldn't his mother forgive his father?

Once, belowstairs, Felix had seen a footman give a chambermaid a small ring, saying that it wasn't real gold, only made to look so, but he hoped to be able to afford a better one in the future. The maid had jumped into his arms and kissed him with great abandon.

Not even real gold, and the girl had been in seventh heaven. Why didn't his father's gifts please his mother in the same way? He decided to find out from the marchioness's maid.

The story she told flabbergasted him.

Once upon a time, ten years ago to be exact, Mary Hamilton had been the most beautiful debutante in London. She had many admirers, Gilbert Rivendale, the Marquess of Wrenworth, among them. But she preferred another gentleman, who unfortunately had not a sou to his name. The marquess proposed and was politely turned down. Undaunted, he went to Sir Nigel, Mary's father, and offered him an astonishing sum for his daughter's hand.

Sir Nigel had a weakness for the gambling table; his gaming debts had pushed him to the brink of bankruptcy. The marquess's offer was readily seized upon. Sir Nigel commanded Mary to marry according to his wishes. When she refused, she was locked in her room, with no means of reaching her beloved.

She capitulated after four months of house arrest, living

on only water and bread. Two months later, she became the Marchioness of Wrenworth.

The marriage, however, was doomed from the start. She abhorred the marquess passionately for his part in derailing her dreams. Since her father died not long after the wedding, she decided to dedicate the remainder of her days to making her husband forever rue the day he laid eyes on her.

The marquess was first given to believe that he had finally attained the sweet wife of his dreams. Then, bit by bit, she began to chip away at the happiness she had bestowed upon him, until in a great strategic blow, she let slip that Felix might not be his.

Felix did not run from the room, but it was only because he had become incapable of all movement. Jess Jenkins, the maid, had related the story as she cleaned the marchioness's combs and brushes. When she was finished, she said, "Don't feel so bad about it, young master," and left to join the other upper servants for their own tea, served in the housekeeper's parlor.

Felix, on the other hand, did not eat the rest of the day. That night he woke up from a nightmare. In his dream, he was being sent away from home. He couldn't sleep again, even after he had made his way to the kitchen and wolfed down two stale scones for his gnawing tummy.

The next day his nightmare was confirmed. His father spoke of sending him to a preparatory school, now that he was fully eight years of age. Felix's stomach roiled with fear. He kept beseeching his mother with his eyes. She said nothing.

He lived in a state of terror for the next month, checking his wardrobe twice a day to make sure his things hadn't been packed yet. But nothing happened. No more was ever said of boarding schools. His tutor, Mr. Leahy, showed few signs of imminent departure. And at last, Jess Jenkins told him that his mother had refused to let him go.

He was incoherent with relief and gratitude.

The bad dreams, however, did not cease. He awoke always around half past eleven and could not go back to sleep before three. So instead of tossing and turning in his bed, after his midnight snack, he took to walking the grounds of Huntington and looking at the stars.

Soon he was learning the constellations with the help of Mr. Leahy's books. There was something marvelously soothing about the movement of the stars, progressing through the firmament solemnly and predictably with the march of the seasons, unaffected by the human tumults that had Felix in their relentless grip.

The domestic situation deteriorated slowly and steadily. The years did little to mellow the marchioness's icy rage. The marquess plunged into ever-deeper despair.

Felix tried to placate both of his parents. He gave presents— bouquets of wildflowers for his mother, rocks bearing fossilized leaf prints for his father. The marquess barely glanced at his gifts; the marchioness cooed over the bouquets and Felix himself.

And then the tension between all three would turn more poisonous than ever.

Gilbert Rivendale was squatly built, with pale hair, pale eyes, and indistinct, forgettable features. Felix, on the other hand, was often praised as an uncommonly beautiful child, his mother's spitting image: dark hair and deep green eyes, tall and slender of build.

Felix desperately wished he had something of his father, be it the bulbous nose, the weak chin, or the scant eyebrows, so that the poor man wouldn't search his face day in and day out, looking for some proof that Felix was a product of his loins.

The marquess would be plagued by doubts to the end of his days. But Felix became convinced of his paternity. In the marquess's absence, Felix never got so much as a nod from his mother. The displays of affection and indulgence were only that—displays, intended to fire jealousy and discontent in the marquess, to make him think that a man she liked better had fathered the boy.

Felix hated her heartlessness, that she regarded her only child as but a pawn and used him with no concern for his welfare. He hated his father's gross stupidity, that he could not understand it *was* a game and that she would never have dared drive a wedge between father and son had Felix actually been the result of adultery.

When he reached thirteen, he couldn't wait to be sent away to a public school, to god-awful food and drafty residence houses where boys beat one another and were flogged in turn. Anywhere to be away from home, away from his mother's machinations and his father's unmanly wretchedness.

But somehow she prevented that, too. She wanted him around to plague her husband. Two more tutors were hired, and at home Felix was stuck.

So he learned to play the game.

He began to make demands, always at their gathering before teatime, to his mother's beaming countenance as she looked upon her husband's spawn with counterfeit tenderness. He asked sweetly for the best portable telescope yet built, for subscriptions to scientific journals, for classics on astronomy— and for exorbitant increases in his quarterly allowance to purchase whatever else he wanted.

He spun tales to undermine her smugness in her power. *I'm so sorry, Mother,* he'd say innocently when they were thrown together accidentally, alone.

Why? she'd ask.

Oh, you didn't know? Nothing then! he'd exclaim, pretending to be distraught. But then, under her persistent probing, he'd let slip that he had heard that Father had set up a young mistress in town and was quite wild about her.

He milked the phantom mistress for nearly two years, watching with cynical amusement his mother's fruitless search for the shameless tart who dared to ensnare the husband for whom she had no love and even less use.

She realized at last it was a hoax. And that her son had become, at age fifteen, a formidable player on his own. The last pretenses of maternal affection promptly disappeared.

And yet her unexpected death, two years later, devastated him. They had been engaged in a war of attrition, but he came to understand, as he sat by her lifeless body, his eyes burning with unshed tears, that for him, at least, the struggle for the upper hand had been only a front. He had never stopped trying to gain her love—or at least her admiration. All along he had been trying to show her that they were so much alike they could be great friends and allies, if only she would let it happen.

To his shock, when his father died within months, he was no less shattered for the obtuse, ungainly man who paid for his one great error with almost two decades of suffering, and who, according to the family physician, passed away of a broken heart.

And he realized at last, as he watched the late marquess's casket being lowered to the ground, that though father and son had looked nothing alike on the surface, underneath they had yearned for love with the same intensity, the same stubborn hope that even years of antipathy could not completely erase.

*F*elix would recast his entire life.

At seventeen, he had become a peer of the realm, one of the richest at that. But just as important, the isolation of his early years afforded him a blank slate on which to create a whole new persona for himself.

It did not take him long to decide that, of course, he was

his mother's son. The late Marchioness of Wrenworth, despite her insidious domestic tyranny, had maintained an unblemished reputation as a perfect lady, a shining example of all that was good and pure in a woman.

He planned to eclipse her in both acclaim and influence—a fitting tribute from the son for whom she had so little regard.

As for his father, Felix's tribute to him would be to never repeat the man's great mistake of loving with all his heart and soul. Friendship he would permit, and perhaps some mild affections. Love, however, was out of the question.

Love made one powerless. And he had had enough powerlessness to last ten lifetimes. In this new life of his, he would always hold all the power.

And he succeeded remarkably.

He was extremely popular with his classmates at Cambridge, where he read mathematics and physics. He conquered London society with equal aplomb and became, in no time, one of the country's most eligible bachelors.

In the beginning, he worried that he'd meet a girl who would enslave him. But Seasons passed, ladies he met by the gross, and not a single one caused the slightest ripple in his heart. It was as if his capacity to love had been buried six feet under, alongside his parents.

Once in a blue moon, when he was alone at night with the stars, he missed it: the ability to feel and feel deeply. But the rest of the time, he was all too glad to be in absolute control over every aspect of his life, particularly his heart.

In 1885, when he turned twenty-five, he let out the word that he was ready to settle down with the right girl. The matrons heaved a collective sigh of relief. How wonderful. The boy actually understood his duties to God and country.

He had no intention of marrying, of course, until he was at least forty-five—a society that so worshiped the infernal institution of marriage deserved to be misled. Let them try to matchmake. He did say the *right* girl, didn't he? The right girl wouldn't come along for twenty years, and she'd be a naive, plump-chested chit of seventeen who worshiped the ground on which he trod.

Little could he guess that at twenty-eight he would marry, out of the blue, a lady who was quite some years removed from seventeen, neither naive nor plump-chested, and who examined the ground on which he trod with a most suspicious eye, seeing villainy in everything he said and did.

Her name was Louisa Cantwell, and she would be his undoing.

CHAPTER 1

*L*ord Wrenworth might not have heard of Louisa Cantwell until the spring of 1888, but ever since 1883, years before he'd declared his hand available, his name had sat atop her list of eligible young men.

But while Louisa maintained and frequently revised her list of the rich bachelors of the realm, she rarely thought of the almost mythical Lord Wrenworth. He was an abstract concept, too lofty and perfect to figure into the calculations of a pragmatic girl under no illusion that she was good enough for The Ideal Gentleman.

To begin with, the Cantwells were poor. Louisa, her four sisters, and her mother subsisted on an annuity that had been settled on Mrs. Cantwell long ago. Once Mrs. Cantwell drew her last breath, the Cantwell girls would have little more than the clothes on their backs.

In addition, the family was somewhat scandalous, due to the late Mr. Cantwell having once been a fortune hunter. He was not particularly evil: When he realized that his pretty new wife was nowhere near as wealthy as he had thought, he shrugged and made peace with his failure. But Mrs. Cantwell was not received by her family and old friends as long as her husband lived. And while her daughters were respectable, their respectability was as threadbare as some of Louisa's petticoats.

And even if a prospective bridegroom could overlook both Louisa's empty purse and her dubious parentage, he must still deal with the fact that she was something of a bumpkin. She could not paint, play the pianoforte, or speak a foreign language. She had only the faintest grasp of art, history, and literature. And of her penmanship, the less said the better.

Her lack of fortune, pedigree, and accomplishments did not particularly bother Louisa. She was, however, greatly frustrated by the fact that for someone who needed to marry a great deal of money, she was not a singular beauty—as great a handicap as setting out on safari without a working firearm.

Her two elder sisters were both exquisite, but Frederica had not left her room since becoming mildly pockmarked after a bout of smallpox, and Cecilia was determined to kiss only her best friend, Miss Emily Milton.

Of her two younger sisters, Julia was of completely the wrong temperament for the wooing of gentlemen, and Matilda, dear, dear Matilda, was an epileptic and therefore out of the question.

All the other Cantwell sisters were able-bodied, capable of working as governesses or ladies' companions to support themselves—even Frederica, Louisa was sure, would abandon her reclusive ways if she were actually starving. But Matilda must be looked after at all times. She needed a man of means. Since Matilda could not handle the rigors of a London Season herself, Louisa had to be the one to try.

On the day Louisa realized this, when she was sixteen, she walked three miles from her house so she could despair without anyone seeing her. She gave herself one hour. Then she returned home, opened her notebook, and turned to the last page.

Everything I want.

1. *A small cottage*
2. *Books, as many as said cottage can hold*
3. *A good telescope*
4. *Messier's Catalogue*
5. *A tutor in higher mathematics*

When it had seemed that both Frederica and Cecilia might make brilliant matches, Louisa had dreamed of being a happily independent spinster. But dreams were for girls who could afford them—and she was no longer one of them. She crossed out the list and started a new one.

Everything I need to win a man with five thousand pounds a year.

 ouisa would have liked to win that rich man when she was nineteen—Lady Balfour, Mrs. Cantwell's cousin, had promised to sponsor one of Mrs. Cantwell's daughters to a Season. But first Lady Balfour had to marry her own daughters; then she had to refrain from going out in public during her mourning period for Sir Augustus, her husband.

When Louisa finally arrived in London, in the spring of 1888, this was how the list looked.

Everything I need to win a man with ~~five~~ seven thousand pounds a year.

(Being impecunious herself, Louisa had quite underestimated the kind of expenses a man with a large income would have, as well as the number of relations who depended on his largesse.)

1. *Bust improvers*
2. *Recipes for shiny hair, bright teeth, and soft skin*
3. *An understanding of fashion, fabrics, and the styles and cuts of garments that best flatter figure*
4. *Familiarity with French, as commonly seen on menus*
5. *The ability to dance passably well*
6. *Deftness at flattering a gentleman*
7. *Deftness at flattering said gentleman's mother and sisters*
8. *The understanding that no matter how much interest a man professes in a young lady, he is still more interested in himself*
9. *The understanding that if a young lady is seen to be having a good time, she is much less likely to be thought of as scheming*
10. *A coherent strategy before the beginning of the Season and tactics in place before each engagement. Time is limited. Preparation is critical.*
11. *The understanding that—God help me—I must not fail*

By the time Louisa walked down the grand staircase at her first ball, she was twenty-four, well past the first bloom of youth. But all her extra years of practice—she didn't simply make a list and consider her task done—had paid off and London was quite taken with her. Or rather, with the Miss Cantwell she presented to Society. She was warm but not overfamiliar, sweet but not cloying, and appreciative of her moment in the sun without the least whiff of graspingness or, worse, desperation.

Best of all, Miss Cantwell, it was generally agreed, was a beauty.

For a beauty, one hauled out a different set of adjectives. Her neck was praised as sylphish or swanlike. Her eyes, hitherto simply blue, were now either azure or aquamarine, and sometimes nothing less than cerulean. And apparently no one in London had ever heard of that decent, hardworking word *brown*. Her admirers insisted her hair was mahogany, chestnut, or any other arboreal hues that struck their fancy. A few, bent on ever more poetic rubbish, called it Titian or coppery, preferring to give emphasis to the flecks of reddish gold embedded therein.

All this linguistic extravagance sometimes made Louisa laugh at night, under her blanket. And it sometimes made her quake—for surely the illusion couldn't last the entire Season. Soon people would realize that her hair was glossy only because of all the mayonnaise she'd put in it over the years, that her trademark closemouthed smile was to hide several crooked teeth, and that, of course, the bodices of her dresses would look awfully concave if it weren't for the artful and stalwart bust improvers in her wardrobe.

But all in all, things were going very well for this early in the Season.

Gentlemen flocked to her, as attentive and eligible a group as she had hoped for in her most ambitious dreams. Perhaps too much so: Among them were a number who paid court to popular girls by habit; a few were in her vicinity simply because it was where their friends gathered. This crowding of the field worried her, as the two gentlemen she most wished to encourage were not forward enough to compete with the more exuberant swains who did not interest her, and she dared not be any more obvious in her encouragement when surrounded thus.

Viscount Firth and Mr. William Pitt, the latter heir to Baron Sunderley, were her choices. Both were prosperous, kind, solid country gentlemen. Both were earnestly looking to settle down. Lord Firth was in his midthirties, more rugged than handsome, but not displeasing to view. He was, by all accounts, an excellent fellow, if rather straitlaced in his views. But he seemed to be of the nature to be open to a woman's persuasion, provided he believed that the woman essentially agreed with him.

Mr. Pitt, bespectacled and a bit rotund, was an even greater favorite with Louisa. In him she sensed a much more malleable nature. His income would be less than Lord Firth's. But in the end, what mattered most was not the gross amount, but the percentage she could command.

Mr. Pitt would make a supremely acceptable spouse, Louisa was certain. Unfortunately, he happened to be a most awkward suitor. He didn't dance, lacked a commanding presence, and was minimally accomplished at the art of small talk, which relegated him to the periphery of her circle, a place he uncomfortably yet obdurately occupied.

Her heart rather went out to him. There was much she could do to help him better negotiate a crowd, if she were his wife. Or, once they married, they could settle in the country and he wouldn't have to socialize at all, if he didn't wish to. But before any of those ameliorations could take place, she must *become* his wife.

So toward that noble goal, she redoubled her effort on the night of Lady Savarin's ball. "Will we have a wet summer? What do you think, gentlemen?" she asked as thunder boomed audibly in the distance.

"That won't be fair," a young fop protested. "Rain, if it must come, might as well come in winter, when it's miserable anyway. The English summer is short enough as it is."

"Right-ho," his friend seconded. "A crying shame."

"What do you think, Mr. Pitt?" Louisa reached out to her quarry. "I understand that you take a keen interest in meteorology. Have you observed any signs of soggy months to come?"

Mr. Pitt cleared his throat with flustered happiness. "As a matter of fact, I have. I have been going over some records.

The current atmospheric conditions, I believe, combined with . . ."

"What is this? A session at the Royal Society? Did I stumble upon the wrong gathering? But lo and behold, Miss Cantwell, it is you. Why do you let fellows bore you with such trivia? Who gives a tuppence for atmospheric conditions?"

Mr. Pitt shrank promptly before this onslaught of delighted ignorance. Louisa groaned inwardly. But it wouldn't do to openly offend Mr. Drummond. He was, incomprehensibly enough, one of the so-called "arbiters" of Society, presumably because everyone cringed to be on the receiving end of his ostentatious rudeness.

"Mr. Drummond," she acknowledged him with unexceptional cordiality. "We are having a discussion on the weather and Mr. Pitt was just about to give us some very informative—"

If she had hoped to subtly chastise him, she failed utterly, for he interrupted her, too. "I say why talk if you can't do anything about it."

Poor Mr. Pitt was now flame red. Louisa gritted her teeth. Mr. Drummond didn't so much court her as he displayed before her his skills at the game of courtship. And to everyone's detriment, he was of the belief that to make himself appear superior, others must suffer in comparison.

"Well, I for one do believe there is intrinsic value to the study of meteorology," said an unfamiliar voice somewhere to Louisa's right.

Interestingly, Mr. Drummond, instead of dispensing with yet another one of his acerbic remarks, accepted this rebuff without any protestation. "Oh, if you say so, Wren."

Wren? Could it be . . .

Mr. Pitt exhaled with relief. "Thank you, my lord Wrenworth."

The Ideal Gentleman, in the flesh. To say that he would

make an excellent husband for Louisa was analogous to declaring that a Thoroughbred stallion qualified as a four-legged beast of burden. His income was in excess of two hundred thousand pounds a year. In addition to that stagger-ing wealth, he possessed good looks, charisma, athleticism, and tact. Not to mention that his character was so far above reproach that reproach would need a telescope to observe his universally lauded conduct.

Prince Charming, absolutely. The Holy Grail, almost.

Louisa had not been in a particular hurry to meet the marquess—a sensible woman who could afford only a gig did not spend her days dreaming of barouches. But now that Lord Wrenworth was in her vicinity, she was not going to pass on a detailed survey of this paragon of masculine virtues.

She would, however, be discreet about it. Lowering her eyes, she started from his shoes.

They had seen at least two Seasons, possibly three. Yet they did not appear worn, only comfortable. The leather, shined and buffed to a high sheen, was as supple and luxuri-ous as a courtesan's caress.

In contrast, Mr. Pitt's spanking-new evening pumps looked as if they pinched his toes *and* chafed the backs of his ankles.

Her gaze traveled up Lord Wrenworth's expertly pressed trousers to the flute of champagne at his side, dangling from his fingers. Many of the guests at the ball had such crystalware in their hands—Lady Tenwhestle, for one, held hers decorously before her person; Mr. Drummond, for another, idly turned his round and round. Lord Wrenworth's champagne glass, however, gave the impression that it had leaped off a table of its own will into his hand, because it would never fit better elsewhere, or emanate a quarter so much ease and aplomb.

On that same hand he wore a signet ring, a coat of arms engraved upon a crest of deep, rich carnelian. The white cuff of his shirt extended a perfect quarter inch beyond the dark sleeve of his evening jacket. The cuff links were simple gold studs—or perhaps not so simple studs, for she could see lines and patterns, too fine for her to make out the design from where she stood.

She was stalling, she realized, lingering in the same spot because she was . . . not afraid, exactly, but rather apprehensive about looking higher. But really, what could he possibly do to a woman as practical as herself? Her soul was devoid of romantic yearnings; if she didn't need a husband she would have happily embraced spinsterhood.

All at once she lifted her gaze—she might as well get it over with. She was presented with a head of thick black hair and an aristocratic profile. Then, as if sensing her attention, he turned to her.

A pox on everyone who had ever told her that The Ideal Gentleman was handsome. He was not handsome—he was extravagantly gorgeous. One look into his serene yet hypnotic green eyes, and all the romantic yearnings she had never before experienced struck her at once, like a bullet to the heart.

"Miss Cantwell," said Mr. Drummond, "allow me to present my esteemed friend the Marquess of Wrenworth."

Lord Wrenworth bowed slightly, his motion fluid, his manners commendable—an open amiability with no arrogance or condescension. "Enchanted, Miss Cantwell."

The not-quite-smile of his lips threatened to turn her into a gelatinous mass, like a clump of beached sea nettles. How could she defend against such perfection? How could anyone defend against such perfection?

She must. She had a task here in London. She could not trail Lord Wrenworth all about town in the wretched hope that he would notice her. She had no doubt he would, perceptive man that he must be, and he would treat her lunacy with great kindness, sparing her any embarrassment if at all he could, while gently steering her toward less unobtainable gentlemen, thoughtfully reminding her that much depended upon a judicious marriage on her part.

But how could she continue? She was only mildly fraudulent, not profligately so. She could not pursue Lord Firth or Mr. Pitt while her heart burned for someone else, while she compared them to the peerless Lord Wrenworth and found them woefully inadequate at every turn.

"My lord Wrenworth," she croaked, sinking into a curtsy.

As she straightened, their eyes met again. She managed a few meaningless words of small talk—*Yes, I am enjoying my first Season. Alas, my family cannot be here with me. No, I do not find London's air more noxious than I have been told to expect*—heroically holding herself upright, while her spine liquefied vertebra by vertebra.

It was difficult to draw breath. Her heart palpitated in both pleasure and panic. And she flushed furiously, too much heat pulsing through her veins for her to control or disguise.

A heartbeat later, however, she was cold.

She could not say how she knew it, Lord Wrenworth having been nothing but flawlessly courteous. All the same, she was suddenly dead certain that on the inside, he found her patently ridiculous, perhaps even laughable.

Introductions completed, Mr. Drummond began to talk about himself again. Lord Wrenworth appeared content to let his friend garner all the limelight and was soon engaged in conversation with Lady Tenwhestle, Lady Balfour's daughter and Louisa's chaperone for the evening.

So civil, so gracious, so gentlemanly—yet Louisa could not shake off the pins-and-needles sensation of his secret, if slight and casual, contempt, as if he viewed her as a toad trying to kiss a prince. And not the sort of toad who was in fact a cursed princess, but just a plain, warty amphibian who didn't know any better.

She had no idea it was possible to be this mortified when there was no public humiliation involved. Or that it was possible to be this crushed when she ought to be thrilled that she would not, in the end, abandon her fortune hunting to stalk Lord Wrenworth all over London.

So much for her long-delayed romantic awakening, such a starburst of emotions and such a lot of nothing.

She fluttered her fan, if rather too vigorously, and pretended to listen to Mr. Drummond.

Lord Wrenworth did not speak to her again and barely looked in her direction. But as the minutes wore on, she grew more and more acutely aware of his observation, of everyone about her and of herself in particular.

Had she realized this earlier, she would have been in a state of ferment, turning herself inside out with dizzying conjectures of his possible interest. But now she understood that his scrutiny was wholly clinical; he was not curious at all about her, except perhaps as an exercise to keep his mind sharp.

And by this impersonal inspection, he made her feel as if she wore her bust improver on the outside of her bodice for the world to witness. As if he had already seen through her entire facade, from her lack of true beauty to her fundamentally scheming ways.

Had she gone mad? It had to be madness on her part to have fabricated this hysterical response to a cordial greeting followed by little else. No one else seemed to share her disquiet. The gentlemen, Mr. Pitt included, were delighted with Lord Wrenworth in their midst. Lady Tenwhestle positively glowed.

Whereas Louisa felt only unsettled, as if he'd seen her reach into someone's pocket and she had no choice but to wait to see what he'd do with that incriminating knowledge.

Lord Wrenworth didn't stay long—no more than ten

minutes, given that Mr. Drummond had yet to finish bragging about the chances of *one* of his horses at the races. When his lordship politely excused himself, saying he was expected elsewhere, she breathed for what seemed like the first time in years.

Mr. Drummond also took to fleeing soon thereafter, upon the arrival of his former mistress, from whom he had severed relations in a most acrimonious manner, according to all reports.

Louisa forced herself to rally, to not waste a moment of her precious London time. Even though she made very little headway with Miss Jane Edwards, Lord Firth's sister, who sent her poisonous looks, she danced twice with Lord Firth and sat down to supper with him. She was even more gratified when she at last managed to get Mr. Pitt to speak in detail about the hygrometer that he'd commissioned, based on the latest Italian designs.

It was not, however, how others perceived her accomplishments that evening.

"Oh, but I'm excited for you, Louisa," Lady Tenwhestle said as soon as the carriage door closed behind them. "To have made Wrenworth's acquaintance. We should have a toast to that."

His very name tasted acrid.

"That would be premature, wouldn't it, ma'am? Lord Wrenworth is hardly about to look to me for a wife," Louisa said, trying to make sure she sounded pragmatic, rather than bitter. "Besides, he expressed no interest in my person."

"Well, I should think less of him if he did. Considering who he is and how much he is worth, he would be a fool to go around expressing interest. It would cause a stampede," said Lady Tenwhestle. "He spent ten minutes in your company. That should make Mother quite happy when I tell her."

"But he spent that time in *your* company, ma'am, not mine."

"Commendable discretion, that; the man has the most beautiful sensitivity to etiquette." Lady Tenwhestle nodded approvingly. "It would only make your hand more desirable if it is perceived that Lord Wrenworth himself might be interested."

The queen would abandon her widowhood before Lord Wrenworth proposed to Louisa, for whom he felt nothing but a blasé disdain. Therefore any *perception* of his interest would serve only to set her cause back. How would poor Mr. Pitt react if he were to be told, erroneously, that one of the most eligible gentlemen in the land now numbered among her admirers? It was the last thing she wanted.

Or was it?

She could not deny that as Lady Tenwhestle bent Lord Wrenworth's action to fit her own interpretation, she had felt a tremor of hope. Perhaps she truly had been out of her mind. Perhaps Lady Tenwhestle's explanation, however convenient and sanguine, was the correct one. Perhaps despite his less than kind opinion of her, he did find her appealing in some way.

Listen to yourself, came the stern voice of her inner taskmaster. *Lady Tenwhestle is overly optimistic and you know it. Do not fictionalize Lord Wrenworth's sentiments: He has none—none for you, in any case. Now concentrate on the achievable.*

She stood for a long time before the small window of her room, gazing up at a thoroughly overcast sky, going over her plans, and praying for a proposal from Mr. Pitt. But just before she left the window, a single star appeared high overhead, and she was suddenly thinking of Lord Wrenworth, a flare of incandescence in her heart.

*   *   *

Felix stood before the much larger window of his bedroom, examining the same dark clouds, thinking of Miss Cantwell.

Savoring, almost, this unanticipated interest on his part.

Eleven years ago, such a flicker of curiosity would have alarmed him. But eleven years ago he was still a child, his wounds fresh, and his confidence largely a thing of smoke and mirrors.

But now he was The Ideal Gentleman, admired by men and desired by women, his opinions ardently sought, his style eagerly copied.

And it intrigued him that she had turned away from him. Somebody should, but he hadn't expected it of a woman as insignificant as she—hardly the most impressive debutante he'd met in his life, or even in the course of the current Season.

Granted, she had fine eyes and a good bosom, but the best one could say of her was that she was pleasant. She possessed no remarkable beauty and no particular wit. Nor did she emanate that sometimes mysterious power of the fairer sex, the dark, potent allure that struck a man directly in the groin.

Over the years, he had met a few clever girls who thought they could better intrigue him with a cooler reception. Miss Cantwell was acting, too, of course, a young lady of no wealth and no consequence carrying on as if she had no ulterior motives for being in London. She wasn't so good an actor that he couldn't see through her pretense at fifty paces. She was, however, good enough that he'd been slightly surprised at the transparency of her infatuation. When their gaze had met for the first time, he had almost heard the wedding bells ringing in her ears.

Then it dissipated into thin air—not just the look, but the infatuation itself.

And *that* had firmly caught his attention.

He enjoyed being The Ideal Gentleman—he would go on enjoying it for the remainder of his natural life, he was sure. But there were times when he found himself restless and vaguely dissatisfied. Was it really so easy to fool the entire world? Could no one see the cynicism and amorality underneath? And would anyone ever have the audacity to tell him that he was hardly a gentleman, let alone an example to which others should aspire?

Miss Cantwell would probably prove to be a mirage, just another young lady who couldn't see an inch beneath his surface.

But he would give her a few chances to prove otherwise.

CHAPTER 2

$\mathcal{W}$e must find out to which places he has been invited, my dear. Or, more usefully, which invitations he has accepted. The man is always drowning in requests for his company and he is very good about not spreading himself too thin," Lady Balfour said authoritatively, as she and Louisa drove in the park.

Louisa fidgeted. It had been three days, but the subject of Lord Wrenworth would not go away. It did not help her resolution to put him behind her, once and for all. Nor did it help matters on the practical front—a proposal from him was a far-fetched notion that didn't merit any in-depth discussion, let alone motivated efforts. It would be so much more productive if she could convince Lady Balfour to invite Mr. Pitt to one of her dinners.

"Wouldn't Lord Wrenworth prefer to marry a lady with a loftier pedigree or a greater fortune?" Louisa tried one more time.

Lady Balfour snorted. "So he would. But that's what a magnificent catch is all about: gaining the hand of a man who *should* make a more ruthless choice."

Had her moonier sentiments concerning The Ideal Gentleman continued unabated, Louisa probably still would have protested, hoping someone would bring her back to her senses, but at the same time, she'd have been secretly thrilled that she had her sponsor's backing to go boldly after the man of her dreams.

But she no longer wanted to be anywhere near him, a man who made her feel transparently greedy and social-climbing.

"Speak of the devil!" Lady Balfour whispered urgently.

Lord Wrenworth emerged from a bend in Rotten Row, the very image of a dashing gentleman charioteer in his nimble calèche. And in spite of Louisa's wariness, her heart skipped a beat. There was no arguing with beauty of such magnitude.

"I thought bachelors didn't come for these afternoon drives," she muttered, annoyed with herself.

"So they don't." Lady Balfour spoke out of the corner of her mouth, busy nodding at Wrenworth. After all, he couldn't approach a phaeton driven by ladies unless his presence had first been acknowledged.

To Louisa's surprise, he didn't merely nod and move on, but pulled up against their vehicle.

"Good afternoon, Lady Balfour. Good afternoon, Miss Cantwell. Enjoying a drive out before the rain comes again?"

Try as Louisa did, she could not detect any special inflection in the pronunciation of her name. But as soon as his gaze landed on her, she felt as if she were being peeled like an onion, layer by layer—an experience not the least erotic, but clinical, something done with gloves and forceps.

"But of course. And you, young man, what brought you here?" Lady Balfour inquired.

"A wild whim." He smiled.

A man who could smile charmingly at toads, Louisa thought unhappily.

He drove abreast of them for no more than a minute. Perfectly appropriate, not a hint of impingement on their time.

As soon as he left, Lady Balfour began to berate herself for not asking after his itinerary while she had him at her disposal. But even she did not suggest that the meeting was anything other than coincidental.

Louisa, however, felt a certain prickling at the base of her spine.

*L*ady Balfour would not have agonized over her missed opportunity had she known that Felix had already bestirred himself to seek them out. He had a good view of Miss Cantwell across a crowded drawing room at Mrs. Conrad's house. Miss Cantwell pointedly—or so it felt—did not look at all in his direction.

He saw her again toward the end of the week, in the midst of a rowing sortie on the river. He wasn't part of their merrymaking party, of course. Rather, he glided by on a yacht with a company of his own. She frolicked and laughed until she became aware of him. The mirth on her face slipped away, replaced by wariness.

So it was no fluke.

She truly saw something the matter with him.

He was oddly pleased—and stumped. What was one to do in such a situation? Certainly he could not walk up to her and say, *Brava, old girl, for having the sense to be wary of me.*

He put down the book on Asiatic travels he had been browsing. It was nearly four o'clock. He'd be expected at his club, his opinions eagerly anticipated on the day's occurrences. As he exited the bookshop located a little way from Piccadilly Circus, however, he almost bumped into the subject of his preoccupation.

Miss Cantwell.

He ceased flicking book dust from his otherwise immaculate gloves.

She had just alighted from a Balfour victoria, clad in a green velvet walking gown. "I'll be but a second picking up her ladyship's order," she said sweetly to the footman and the driver.

She turned around, and stilled in shock as she saw him, as if she had the misfortune of finding herself directly in the path of a sharp-fanged wolf.

Half a second passed before she recovered her composure. She smiled at him, a smile that radiated no warmth. "My lord Wrenworth, how do you do?"

"Very well, thank you. And you, Miss Cantwell?"

He took off his glove and offered his hand. She shook it uncertainly.

Then it happened. Her face colored. "Very well, too. I'm running some errands for Lady Balfour. Please do not let me keep you."

It dawned on him as she disappeared into the dim interior of the bookshop that she wasn't wholly unaffected by him, as he had assumed. Quite to the contrary. Somewhere deep inside her, the infatuation that he'd thought short-lived still simmered. And at this close range, she had been flustered by his presence.

It was an entirely new experience for him, to be physically appealing to a woman who otherwise did not care for him.

Until this moment, Miss Cantwell had been an intellectual, almost impersonal riddle. Now for the first time he became sexually aware of her.

And a rather ferocious awareness at that.

*M*y dear Louisa," cried Lady Balfour, "you will not believe what good fortune has just befallen us."

Louisa, who had a curling iron in her hair, wielded by Lady Balfour's maid, did not dare move. "Yes, ma'am?"

"Tenwhestle was at his club this afternoon. And guess who

should come to him full of regret and apologies? Mr. Pitt. He must leave London immediately."

"Oh, no. Is everything all right?"

Louisa had been looking forward to sitting next to Mr. Pitt for hours on end. Lady Balfour still thought him too homely, but Lady Tenwhestle was sympathetic to Louisa's cause and had gone ahead and invited him to dinner, so that Louisa could deepen their acquaintance and, she hoped, hasten the arrival of his proposal.

"Nothing serious—something to do with the family estate," said Lady Balfour. "That put Tenwhestle in a quandary—with Mr. Pitt's absence, we'd be thirteen at the table. So Tenwhestle turned to the gentleman next to him and asked whether he happened to be free this evening."

Such delight Lady Balfour's reflection in the mirror radiated—an unhappy suspicion began to coalesce in Louisa's head. "Which gentleman?"

Lady Balfour ignored her question. "The gentleman answered in the affirmative. And he was so amiable as to tell Tenwhestle that there was no need for the lady wife, at this late hour, to rearrange seating to suit his superior rank. He would, literally, take Mr. Pitt's place at the table."

"I see."

"Do you, my dear?" Lady Balfour all but twirled. "You are going to sit down to dinner with Lord *Wrenworth*. I can't tell you how many mamas have tried to arrange the same for their daughters—to think this should just fall into your lap. You must be the luckiest lady in all of London."

More unnerving words Louisa had seldom heard.

Lady Balfour went to fetch her fan, leaving Louisa to stare at her reflection in dismay. Her entire toilette had been oriented toward making herself look as fetching as possible, with an ingenious bust improver that cantilevered her small breasts to the point of spilling over the cusp of her décolletage.

And it was too late to change into a different dress. Or a less excessive bust improver.

The moment Lord Wrenworth's gaze met hers across Lady Tenwhestle's drawing room, before the ladies and the gentlemen had even been paired for their procession to the dining table, Louisa already felt the heat of her utter mortification.

He knew.

He knew that she'd dressed and coiffed herself for Mr. Pitt—the blinding white silk of the dinner gown, the flirty curls in her hair, and the blasted décolletage that made her chest look like the twin cheeks of a baby's upturned bottom. He knew that she'd meant to appear girlish and pure, while leading Mr. Pitt toward resolutely impure thoughts. And he even knew how exasperated she was for all that detailed effort to have gone to waste.

All this—and a hundred more vexed thoughts—washed through her before he'd even said, "Good evening, Miss Cantwell."

What was it about this man that made her lose her mind?

And then lose her mind a little more when she had to walk beside him, her hand on his arm. Because he smelled delicious—like that first lungful of fresh air after a good summer shower. Because though her fingers barely touched his sleeve, she could still feel the shape and strength of his forearm. Because when he leaned toward her and murmured, "You look lovely tonight, Miss Cantwell," she sprouted goose bumps everywhere.

"Do you come to London often, Miss Cantwell?" he asked halfway through the first course.

She watched as he broke a piece of the bread passed around by the servant, his fingers strong and elegant. "No, sir. I visit quite infrequently."

"And where is home, if I may ask?" He spoke without glancing in her direction, busying himself with his butter knife.

"I live in the Cotswold, not far from Cirencester."

"The Earl of Wyden's seat is somewhere in the vicinity, is it not?"

"Yes, the estate is about ten miles away."

When he didn't say anything else, she felt obliged to add, "But we do not know the earl's family very well."

The impoverished relations of a mere baronet's wife did not call upon Lord Wyden at will.

Others had asked similar questions when she'd related her place of origin, and she'd cheerfully admitted to a lack of intimacy with whichever family they'd inquired about. But it was difficult to do anything cheerfully before Lord Wrenworth: He had seen how dazzled she was by him.

Her besottedness had meant nothing to him, she was sure. But she was not one to share her sentiments. She didn't mind letting it be known that she liked the neighbor's new puppy or that she thought three weeks of continuous rain verged on bothersome. But anything strong enough to be labeled an emotion—fear for Matilda's future, fear of a failed London Season, fear of another inexplicable bout of romantic idiocy—those she could bear only by keeping them locked away, far from prying eyes.

But there was no concealing anything from his ridiculously beautiful prying eyes.

She felt cornered.

"A shame," he replied softly. "I know the earl's sons very well. We'd have met much sooner had you been acquainted with them."

She was staring down into her plate, but at his tone, which made her feel strange things, she could not help turning her face, looking into his eyes for the first time since she saw him across the drawing room, before the start of dinner.

Instantly a fierce heat swept over her. Had she thought that there was nothing erotic in the attention he directed her way?

That must have been a different lifetime altogether. For this gaze of his made her think of . . . skin. Flesh. And, God help her, unnatural acts.

When she had assessed herself for her chances on the marriage mart, it had been immediately apparent that her décolletage needed help. A great deal of help. But did bust improvers, in this regard, constitute flagrant cheating? She'd agonized over that seemingly minor decision.

Then she had overheard Lady Balfour gossiping to Mrs. Cantwell about her black-sheep brother-in-law's new mistress. *A flat-chested little thing, and not even that pretty—but I hear she is willing to take part in the most unnatural acts in the bedroom.*

Growing up, Louisa had occasionally been allowed to visit her paternal great-aunts, two sisters who lived in a charming little cottage in Bournemouth, on a bluff overlooking the sea. And by the time Louisa was thirteen, she'd come to the realization that those "maiden" aunts had once practiced the oldest profession in the world—as a team, no less. The elderly women would spy on the gentlemen's bathing section—where the bathing suit was one's own skin and nothing else—with a field glass, and cackle gleefully between themselves. Their reminiscences, when they believed Louisa otherwise occupied, had taught her a great many things that Mrs. Cantwell would have considered grossly indelicate.

The existence of unnatural acts in the bedroom, for example. And the fact that a woman could outlast such acts with her good humor perfectly intact.

So should Louisa's future husband find out that she had far less chest than he'd been led to believe, she could redeem herself by being lax in her standards in the bedroom—and not be particularly worse off, if her great-aunts' examples were anything to go by.

She had immediately set out to study every bust improver

in the house, speculating on just how much more they could be padded without making her look ludicrous. Unnatural acts she'd never thought of again—until now.

There was nothing openly lascivious in Lord Wrenworth's contemplation—Lady Balfour, glancing approvingly their way, clearly saw only an appropriate interest. But Louisa read in those same eyes a disastrous knowledge.

He had perceived that she was not as indifferent to him as she'd like to be—if only they hadn't run into each other outside the bookshop! But now, instead of regarding her as utterly beneath his notice, he enjoyed making her betray herself.

"Would you like me to introduce them to you?" he asked.

She could see both of his hands, exactly where they ought to be. Yet somehow it felt as if he had touched her, before all the other dinner guests.

"Introduce . . . whom to me?"

"The Marsden brothers, Lord Wyden's sons," he said, his manner kind and helpful. "Excellent gentlemen, one and all."

Then he smiled slightly, because she was so flustered that she forgot what they'd been talking about only seconds ago.

It was, she realized, going to be the longest dinner of her life.

$\mathscr{I}$t was, Felix realized, going to be the most riveting dinner of his life.

And possibly the most arousing.

He ought to be less pleased. As a rule, he was quite opaque, his true sentiments and opinions hidden behind a wall of amiability. But she must have read him accurately from the very beginning: Another young lady would be doing her utmost to impress him; she, on the other hand, only wanted him to go away, because she knew that he hadn't the least matrimonial intentions toward her.

But how could she expect him to go away when she was in such delectable ferment? Were she to rip apart her bodice, she could not be more conspicuous. Her sweet breasts rose and fell agitatedly, she had a death grip on her knife and fork, and from time to time she exhaled audibly, unsteadily, as if she'd been holding her breath for far too long.

It dawned on him that she was rather pretty after all, her skin fine and luminous, her chin a delightful shape and angle. And her eyes . . .

She was trying her best not to look at him. But he forced her hand here, pausing in the middle of his sentences, making it plain that he expected due attention, giving her no choice but to meet his eyes.

Every time their gaze held, he could sense the shock in her, as if he had reached under her skirts. Then a shadow of resentment deep in her irises, that he had this effect on her, that he could manipulate her reaction with nothing more than a desire to do so.

And he would experience a frisson unlike anything he'd ever known, a jolt of pleasure and of power.

Everything he did in life—with the exception of his astronomical interests, perhaps—was in the pursuit of power. Personal power, the ability to hold others in his thrall while he himself remained serenely unaffected.

And they had come willingly, surrendering their approval without a second thought, allowing him to retain the position of superiority in just about every friendship or affair.

He'd never known anyone who actively resisted. Or rather, who was torn about him.

Miss Cantwell was single-handedly introducing him to power of a different flavor altogether, as she struggled between her visceral need to escape him and her equally visceral attraction toward him.

So much so that after the ladies withdrew, he, who usually

enjoyed his after-dinner port and cigar with the gentlemen, chomped at the bit to be finished. When the gentlemen rejoined the ladies in the drawing room, he did not go to her—that would be far too obvious. But he did let her know that he was watching her.

And with relish.

It was another overcast, starless night.

Felix stood before his window, gazing out. He had returned home in an exuberant mood, feeling more alive than he had in a long time. But now that headlong rush of euphoria was beginning to wear off; the street below seemed deserted as the sky above. His bedroom, as he turned around and walk across to the bath, practically echoed.

He wanted something, something he could not quite grasp or name.

He turned on the light in the bath and came face-to-face with a framed piece of the late marchioness's needlework. Such pieces were scattered throughout both his town house and his country house—what devoted son would seek to remove such beautiful mementos left behind by his beloved mother?

He recalled many of the pieces from his daily allotment of time beside her, watching her embroider. In the beginning, they had served as reminders that he should be ever vigilant, lest he again taste the bitterness of love thrown back into his face. But it had been years now since he last paid attention to any of them; they had melted into the background and were no more likely to catch his eye than the pattern on the wallpaper.

But now he examined the tiny, meticulous stitches before him, a wine-red dahlia in bloom. One of his mother's later efforts. He remembered walking by her, a cigarette in hand, feeling sophisticated and grown-up because he could irritate her with a habit she despised.

Feeling well beyond the heartache and yearnings of his childhood.

Only to learn at her deathbed not a year later how deluded he had been. How little removed from the heartache and yearnings he thought he'd left far behind.

Was this the universe sending him a signal, telling him that he ought to be as wary of Miss Cantwell as she was of him? That perhaps there was something suspect about the delights he derived from her company?

He turned and walked out of the bath.

He knew what love was. What Miss Cantwell inspired in him was no more love than a random clump of clay was Venus de Milo. Love gave; he wanted only to take. Love ennobled— or at least it should; he was fairly certain his desire for Miss Cantwell was about to make him a far worse man than he had ever been.

She would cause him no discomfort or anxiety. He would not give her up to avoid some imaginary future disaster. It remained to be seen only how he would go about gratifying himself, where she was concerned.

Of course he would not marry her. He was a man who respected tradition. and what was a good, solid, traditional marriage without a certain amount of hypocrisy? He would be The Ideal Gentleman in his marriage, but with Miss Cantwell . . .

He hoped she already thought very, very ill of him, or she would have quite a shock coming.

CHAPTER 3

$\mathcal{T}$he ballroom at Fielding House boasted of bold crimson curtains, a deep blue ceiling, and a smooth marble floor, brilliant under three chandeliers afire with nine hundred candles. Moody, gilt-framed canvases by Flemish masters crowded the walls. A trickle of dark-clad gentlemen and pastel-hued ladies descended the staircase, flanked on either side by symmetrically arranged tubs of fronds.

It was yet early, the bulk of the invited still at the opera or various late dinner engagements. The orchestra played softly behind a Japanese silk screen, conserving its strength for the small hours of the night. But Lady Balfour always left her box after the first act of *La Traviata*. Therefore, Louisa found herself at Fielding House at a relatively unfashionable hour.

Sitting next to a window that rose twenty-five feet to the ceiling, her hands folded demurely on the apple-green skirt of her borrowed ball gown, she reviewed her plan of attack for the evening.

It had been a week since Lady Tenwhestle's dinner. Mr. Pitt

had returned to town and would be in attendance. Lord Firth was also expected. But what to do about his sister, Miss Edwards? After all Louisa's effort at pleasantry and flattery, Miss Edwards seemed to hold her in only greater dislike.

Beside Louisa, Lady Balfour reminisced with one of her dowager friends on the fashions of their youth. Wasn't a woman's outline much more elegant in the days of the crinoline, when a slender waist was superbly complemented by a flounced bell of a skirt? The bustles of the current decade made a lady much too bouffant to the rear, and one could never count on these treacherous devices to hold their shape after one sat down to dinner, or even a fifteen-minute call.

But the crinoline did have its drawbacks, they concurred. Preceding a gentleman up a staircase presented all sorts of dangers. And who could forget that dinner party during which Lady Neville's skirts caught fire without her even being aware of it?

"His lordship the Marquess of Wrenworth," bellowed Lady Fielding's most stentorian manservant.

Louisa started.

"Why, it's that dear boy!" Lady Balfour exclaimed with pleasure. "A bit early, isn't he?"

Several nights this past week Louisa had been victim to a recurring nightmare. In the nightmares, she and Lord Wrenworth would come across each other at a public venue, a park or a thickly attended party. She would be getting along just fine, but the very moment she saw him, she would realize, to her horror, that she was stark naked. No one else would notice it, but he always did—and would proceed to approach and touch her in unspeakable ways.

As he walked down the steps, serene and elegant, heat and dread alike buffeted Louisa. She would like to blame her dreams entirely on some dark sorcery on his part, but she could scarcely deny that she was the one who could not stop imagining, as she lay in bed, that he was somewhere in the shadows of her room, watching her, his gaze half desire, half malice, and all power.

He took his time, making a leisurely round of the periphery of the ballroom, before coming to a stop next to Lady Balfour and her friend, delighting them with compliments on their complexion and toilette. Louisa tensed, the way one held one's breath and abdomen to brace for a too-abrupt stop of the carriage.

"Oh, enough," Lady Balfour scolded happily. "Don't waste your charms on us old crows. Give your attention to my dear young cousin here. Surely you have not forgotten her?"

Louisa's marriage might have begun as a charity project. But her sponsor would be damned, now that she had taken Louisa in hand, if the girl didn't make a properly spectacular match.

"Yes, of course, Miss Cantwell." He scantly cast a glance her way, his attentive smile solely for Lady Balfour. "Your charge is the most charming dinner companion anyone could ask for."

"Good," said Lady Balfour. "That means you owe her a waltz, young man."

And that was how Louisa found herself in Lord Wrenworth's arms, spinning about the ballroom. It was sobering how adroitly he had manipulated her to the dance floor—and temporary privacy.

It didn't help that she had only the most circumstantial evidence and her intuition to support her belief that it *had* been a manipulation. After all, he did dance, from time to time, with unmarried ladies from well-connected families— at just the exact frequency to give cause for excitement, but not feverish hopes.

She wished she knew what he wanted from her. And why.

"That is a very pretty dress on you, Miss Cantwell," he said.

"Thank you," she murmured, all too aware of the gentle pressure his hand exerted on her back.

"Prettier than I remembered, when Lady Tenwhestle wore it a few Seasons ago."

A true gentleman would have kept that observation to himself. But she already knew he was no gentleman—he must have sold his soul to the devil for everyone else to continue to think of him as the epitome of gentlemanliness.

"Lady Tenwhestle has been very generous in the loan of this dress—and others," she answered defiantly.

He swung her into several consecutive 360-degree turns, giving her no choice but to hold on to him tight. The strength in the man's shoulders . . .

In her dreams he had pushed her naked person against a pillar and held her there with one hand.

"It's a pleasure to dance with you, my dear Miss Cantwell," he said softly. "I have been looking forward to it for days."

She shivered. Did he dream of her, as she dreamed of him?

"Have you, sir?" She prayed she sounded modest, rather than hopeful.

"But you aren't only pretty and light on your feet, are you, Miss Cantwell?" he went on. "You are also exceedingly clever."

She was forcefully reminded that the man was a minefield—why was he suddenly remarking on her cleverness?—and she could not allow herself a moment of distraction. "I'm sure I don't deserve such extravagant compliments from your lordship."

"I assure you, Miss Cantwell, you have earned any and all praise on my part. Few debutantes travel along their path to matrimony with as much purpose and design as you do, while appearing as guileless. You have been preparing for years, haven't you?"

It was all she could do not to trip. "My goodness, sir, do you really think me so scheming?"

He gazed at her, his eyes as clear and as hypnotic as ever. "I do, and I admire a woman of energy and initiative, Miss Cantwell. But I do wish you had consulted me ahead of time. For you see, your tactics are quite sound, but you have been less than thorough in the reconnaissance of your strategic targets."

Why did she feel as if he were contemplating kissing her? And why did she want him to, this man who did not have her best interests at heart? "I'm sure I don't know what you mean, sir."

"I will gladly explain. Take Mr. Pitt, for example. On the surface, his family estate seems to be the rare example that has successfully weathered the depression in agricultural prices. The farmland they own is excellent and the methods they have employed are modern and efficient. Moreover his father, Baron Sunderley, is keenly aware that he cannot afford to have all his eggs in one basket and has been carefully investing elsewhere.

"Alas, I have it on good authority that two of Lord Sunderley's most substantial investments have recently failed. Mr. Pitt's absence from London, in fact, was a direct result of these failures. It had always been his parents' desire that Mr. Pitt marry an agreeable girl who should either bring some profitable urban properties or a sizable dowry; now it has become imperative that he does so.

"Mr. Pitt, of course, is nowhere as well prepared or as resolute as you, Miss Cantwell. So I imagine he will still linger at your side for as long as he can. But you must realize that biddable nature that would make him such an admirable spouse also means that he would not find the wherewithal to contradict his parents' express wishes."

Louisa's hand tightened on the fine-twilled cashmere of Lord Wrenworth's evening jacket. If what he said was true, it would constitute a heavy blow to her chances at a successful marriage.

"Lord Firth, on the other hand," continued Lord Wren-worth.

Louisa faltered a step. She could see how he might have deduced her interest in Mr. Pitt. But how did he know about Lord Firth?

Lord Wrenworth pulled her back into the flow of the dance. "Lord Firth, now, there is an outstanding English gentleman, loyal to the Crown and his foxhounds. Did I mention that he also sleeps with his half sister?"

Louisa could not speak. She was not a naive girl who had never come into contact with the facts of life. But to hear something like this brought up in the context of people she actually knew—she was shocked to the core.

Lord Firth, upright, old-fashioned, *incestuous* Lord Firth? Was Lord Wrenworth telling the truth? But if not, why bother with such outrageous lies?

"But of course I would never have breathed a word of it, were I not concerned for your limited stay in London. I would hate for you to have wasted your time on gentlemen who are not worthy of your time, let alone your attention."

Her head reeled. "Thank you for your kind concern, sir. But perhaps you should never have said a word even so."

"You are correct. There are reputations at stake. But how could I remain silent, knowing it would lead to your severe disappointment at the end of the Season, my dear Miss Cantwell, when in your case there is just as much, if not more, at stake?"

The music should have come to a complete halt at that point, but Herr Strauss's waltz played on, as blithe and cheery as ever. And Louisa had no choice but to continue to turn about the dance floor with Lord Wrenworth.

For no good reason under the sun, her dismay seemed to magnify the physical pleasure of the dance. The warmth of his hand at her waist, the rain-cool scent of his person, the swiftness and surety of their spins—their bodies braced in a perfect equilibrium between tension and cohesion.

When they finally pulled apart at the end of the dance, he offered her his arm to walk her back to Lady Balfour. His manner was impeccable as always, but somehow she knew that he was enjoying himself to an indecent extent.

"Do you delight in my misfortunes, my lord?" she asked, too unhappy to be diplomatic.

"Never," he declared, a devilish light in his eyes.

"You, sir, are about as believable as a lordling who promises a milkmaid that his heart will never stray," she said, her tone more vehement than it should have been.

He only smiled.

When Mr. Pitt arrived later that evening, he came immediately to pay his respects to Louisa. But any relief she felt quickly dissipated as she noticed, for the first time, how frequently Mr. Pitt glanced toward one particular Miss Lovett. Miss Lovett was an heiress whose dowry was said to include large tracts of properties in Bath and Bristol; the way Mr. Pitt looked at Miss Lovett was obviously the expression of someone who knew he was not doing his duty and was fearful of the consequences.

When Lord Firth appeared with his sister, Miss Edwards, she gave Louisa her usual look of loathing. Louisa had always attributed it to sisterly possessiveness, which would diminish or perhaps disappear altogether when Miss Edwards finally had her own heart set on someone. But now plain to view was the way Miss Edwards wantonly pressed her much-exposed bosom into her half brother's upper arm, and the way she liked to speak, loverlike, lips to skin, directly into his ear.

Not only a jealous sister, but a jealous mistress as well.

And of course—of course—whose eye should she catch

at that moment of horrific realization? From across the ball-room, Lord Wrenworth lifted a brow, as if to say, *What did I tell you?*

She retired early from the festivities that night, beset by not only a persistent headache, but also a sense of inchoate nausea. Lady Balfour, blissfully ignorant of everything that had taken place, thought Louisa had done quite well. "A dance with Wrenworth, why, that's always reason for cheer."

If Lord Wrenworth had spoken the truth, Louisa supposed she should be grateful to him. But she could not, for he had not been out to help, but to injure.

She spent a sleepless night. The next morning she rose, determined to regroup. But wife and family were expensive propositions. There were more eligible females than males. And many gentlemen chose to remain bachelors. All of which made good proposals difficult to come by.

She danced; she chatted; she assessed each man who passed her way for his potential. Most men looked for heiresses themselves, or at least a wife who had *some* dowry. And those few for whom dowries were secondary concerns wanted a more exalted pedigree in their brides, or at least no whiff of scandal attached to the family name.

At night she lay awake, planning for a bleak future. Mrs. Cantwell held on fiercely to her status as a lady. The idea of her daughters working for remuneration was anathema to her: She was a lady only if her daughters, too, were ladies.

But Mrs. Cantwell could afford to make a fuss about being a lady; she was the one with the annuity that would last for as long as she lived. Her daughters had no such luxuries.

If Louisa were to fail in London, she must immediately find work. Mrs. Cantwell could tell everyone that she had gone to live with a distant cousin, if that would help her feel better. But if Louisa were not home, who would keep an eye on the budget? Cecilia and Julia both enjoyed buying things as much as Mrs. Cantwell did. Would the money Louisa would be able to set aside from working make up for the difference?

After Mrs. Cantwell passed away, everyone would need to work, of course, even Julia, who would hate to either instruct small children or fetch tea for old ladies. But Julia could fend for herself. Who would look after Matilda? Matilda needed someone to be with her at all times, to make sure she didn't fall down staircases or drown in a bathtub.

If Frederica stayed with Matilda, they would still require a place to live and enough money for essentials. Would Louisa, Cecilia, and Julia, working at positions that didn't pay very much, be able to support them?

And if not, what would happen to Matilda?

They had spoken of this only once, she and Matilda, not long after Matilda realized what would happen upon Mrs. Cantwell's death. Louisa had told Matilda then that she would never let Matilda be taken to the poorhouse.

I will take care of you, do you understand? Now don't worry anymore. Everything will be fine. You'll see.

Would that turn out to be an empty promise, after all?

CHAPTER 4

Felix left London for a week. The day of his return, he went to the Reading Room of the British Museum. After two hours with stacks of books before him, he stepped out from underneath the Reading Room's famous blue-and-gold dome to find himself a cup of tea.

Sitting in a corner of the nondescript refreshment room, a plate of wafer-thin cucumber sandwiches before her, was none other than Miss Louisa Cantwell, in the same green velvet walking dress from the time they had run into each other at the bookshop.

He blinked, not sure he hadn't somehow conjured her. He'd gone to Huntington, his country seat, because he had not wanted to waste the night skies of an unusually sunny week in the middle of a very wet summer. But one could argue that he had left to prove to himself that he would be quite fine were he to stay away from her.

He was fine, busying himself with his astronomical observations. He thought of her a great deal, but that was only to be expected, given that he had plots in place concerning her. Besides, those thoughts were quite pleasurable and gave him not a moment of distress or angst.

Ignoring her sandwiches, Miss Cantwell played with her napkin—something she would never do at a proper dining table—rolling it into a tight tube, then shaking it loose and folding it into a smaller and smaller triangle. He found her prettier like this, distracted, unsmiling, and without the air of utter agreeableness that she wore like a layer of theatrical makeup.

The next moment, something in her aspect changed. Her fingers, which had treated the napkin as only a napkin, now lingered over the linen, caressing it, then seizing a handful of the cloth as if in agitation—as if the fabric were that of the sheet upon which she awaited her lover.

He felt his own breath quickening. A little disconcerting to realize that she could arouse him even when she was not reacting to his presence.

She glanced up. The expression on her face when she saw him—as if he were a swaying cobra and she a hapless would-be victim, desperate to flee but mesmerized against her will. He wished he could distill and bottle the sensation. One drop of such an essence would turn a eunuch as virile as Hercules himself.

He approached her table. "Miss Cantwell, an unexpected . . . pleasure."

The way he lingered over the syllables of that last word—he might as well seduce virgins from good families twice a week.

He was saved from ridiculousness only by her even more disproportionate response. Her pupils dilated. A pulse throbbed visibly at the base of her throat. And she flushed everywhere—or at least all the way to her earlobes.

She cleared her throat. "Lord Wrenworth, we thought you still at your estate."

"I cannot long forsake the delights of London during the Season. May I join you?" He sat down before she could answer one way or the other and gave his order to the server who had sprung forward to inquire after his needs. "What brought you here to the Reading Room?"

He hadn't pegged her as the bookish sort. But this particular refreshment room served only to those holding readers' tickets—the public refreshment room was by the statue of Mercury, in the Gallery of Antiquities.

"Oh, idle curiosity."

Too bad books and manuscripts could not be taken out of the Reading Room—that would have made it easier for him to discover what she had come for.

She was no longer looking at him—or rather, no longer looking him in the eye. But he could feel her gaze elsewhere on his person, a heat that lingered for a moment at the top of his collar, then journeyed across the width of one shoulder and down the length of that arm, intensifying every inch farther south.

It would be alarming, the degree to which she stirred and tantalized him, fully dressed and sitting a respectable distance away, if he didn't feel himself completely in control of the situation.

Still, he brought up a sobering subject—sobering for her, at least. "And how goes your quest for a bridegroom, Miss Cantwell?"

Her resentment returned. And he, budding pervert that he was, found her sullen, suspicious glare terribly stimulating— the seemingly even-keeled lady in fact possessed quite a temper.

"You know very well, my lord, how difficult it is for a young woman of unexceptional birth, unexceptional looks, and no fortune at all to win the hand of a man in prosperous circumstances."

"Come, Miss Cantwell, London all but overflows with gentlemen this time of the year. Surely the loss of a mere pair of candidates should not detract from your chances of a successful match."

"You think so because you have no need to fret about *your* budget, sir, but everywhere else gentlemen are hurting in the family coffer."

"I am well aware of my good fortune in that regard. But I also know that I am not the only one so blessed."

"Indeed not, but the Duke of Lexington is still at university, as is the youngest Mr. Marsden."

She had done her homework. Not many people realized that the great fortune of the youngest Mr. Marsden's godfather would pass to the godson.

"What about the Marquess of Vere? He is not at university."

Miss Cantwell raised a brow. His question was designed to test the depth and breadth of her desperation and she well knew it: Lord Vere was known far and wide as an arrant idiot. "Yes, I would gladly marry Lord Vere. He is easy on the eyes and certainly rich enough. But Lord Vere prefers his debutantes both beautiful and propertied, and he has not come near me, except once, to spill some lemonade on my dress."

"And Mr. de Grey? He pays no court to heiresses, from what I have observed."

"I'm surprised you have not noticed the way he looks at his sister-in-law. He will not propose to anyone, not until he overcomes that obsession. And that would be far too late for me."

"Well, there is always Sir Roger Wells. He is desperate for a legitimate heir. And if you would but look kindly his way, he would offer his hand to you."

She leveled him with a nasty look—he relished her displays

of testiness; they made him feel supremely accomplished. "Now you are just toying with me, my lord. But I will tell you this: I do not want to be Sir Roger's wife, not because of that unspeakable disease of his, but because several reliable sources have assured me that he has squandered his fortune and is now deep in debt."

"So would you have married him if his fortune had remained intact?"

"No."

"No?"

"He is a despicable man even without that dread disease. I have come to London to help my family, not to martyr myself."

"But what if you have no choice at the end of the Season? What if Sir Roger becomes your only viable alternative?"

"My family is not so destitute as that, sir. We are not going to be turned out of our house at the end of the Season. My mother is in good health and can be reasonably expected to live many more years."

"But not forever. And when she passes on, what will happen to your sister, the one who is epileptic?"

She blinked, as if wondering how he could know so much about her family when she'd never brought up the subject before him. "We will take care of her, of course."

"How? If you were to find a position as a governess or lady's companion, you would not be permitted to bring her with you. Someone has to be with her all the time, I understand. Which means you need two people in that position, so that she is never left unwatched. How do you propose to finance that?"

A shadow crossed her face, but her words were relentlessly optimistic. "When God closes a door, He opens a window. I have other marriageable sisters. Not to mention Matilda herself is both lovely and sweet—some lucky gentleman just might win her hand and ensure himself a very felicitous domestic union."

He leaned in slightly. "Do you believe that?"

She had been looking either to the left or the right of him, but now she met his gaze squarely. "Perhaps not. But while I will marry a man I do not love, I will not take a husband I cannot stand."

Her eyes were large and wide-set, but, rather unusually, slanted slightly downward toward the outer corners, giving an impression of tremendous transparency, of being unguarded and trusting. He began to understand why most people considered her a darling innocent.

And why Mr. Pitt and Lord Firth both found her so appealing.

But she was, if not a shark, then at least a dolphin: smiling and sweet-faced, yet ferociously intelligent and undeniably a predator.

An interesting woman even when she wasn't quivering in unfulfilled lust for him.

"So . . . what *are* you willing to do?" he murmured.

Her lips parted, as if she found it difficult to breathe. And suddenly she and he were once again braced in that erotic tension that was infinitely addictive to him.

But before she could answer, someone called his name. "Wren!"

Startled, Felix looked up into the smiling face of John Baxter. Baxter by himself was more than harmless, but he happened to be the nephew by marriage of one Lady Avery, noted gossip.

He rose, shook hands with Baxter, and introduced him to Miss Cantwell. "It was quite a surprise when I saw Miss Cantwell here—not often do our most popular young ladies frequent the dusty environs of the Reading Room."

It would not do to give the impression of a prearranged meeting—not when it was the farthest thing from the truth. And certainly not when he had plans that depended on his *not* being seen as an admirer of hers.

Baxter took his leave quickly to get his sandwich. Felix did so immediately afterward, making sure Baxter witnessed his departure. "I'm afraid I must also give up the pleasure of your company. The books I have selected do not read themselves."

"Send Lord Vere my way, will you, sir?" she said by way of good-bye. "I do believe I shall be very happy with him."

He nodded pleasantly. "I will see what I can do."

Felix saw Miss Cantwell at the opera two days later. Lady Balfour's box was well visited during intermission, including stops by Mr. Pitt and Lord Firth, the latter of whom Felix considered his biggest obstacle. But the tête-à-tête at the Fielding ball had its desired effect: Miss Cantwell was quite cool toward Lord Firth and he did not stay long. Otherwise she listened, talked, and laughed, her manner all vivacity and animation.

He spied her again at the races and spent more time studying her than he did the horses—even his own. She looked quite fetching, which ensured a steady stream of gentlemen paying their respects.

Such was the fate of a pretty but penniless young lady—gentlemen still liked to look at her and even spend time with her. But they lacked the courage to marry her, not when a better-dowered wife could put lobsters on the menu and ensure that they need never descend a rung or two from their accustomed place in the world.

Felix was quite confident that Miss Cantwell would prove the rule and not the exception. Still, every time a likely gentleman was introduced to her, he grew uncharacteristically tense. Two men in particular, a Mr. Peterson and a Mr. Featherington, preoccupied him for days.

Mr. Peterson was a scion of industry, with pockets deep enough for a dozen epileptic sisters-in-law. It took Felix the better part of a week to find out that Mr. Peterson must marry the daughter of at least an earl and preferably a duke, or risk having his allowance cut off.

Mr. Featherington, a country squire with an income of eight thousand pounds, caused Felix to lose actual sleep. Until it became apparent that Mr. Featherington was leveraging Miss Cantwell's warm reception to gain the hand of a different lady.

The almost dizzying relief Felix experienced, as he read of Mr. Featherington's engagement in the papers, gave him pause. But he dismissed his responses as perfectly natural for a man no longer accustomed to failure, or even the possibility of it.

Of course he would be tense: He had a plan in place and he was invested in the plan's outcome.

He decided to adjust the plan, which had been made with a specific date in mind—late July, three days before he left London. But now he was convinced it would not be wise to wait that long. There was too much uncertainty involved. And the possibility of a knight in shining armor, however remote, was nowhere near enough to nil for his liking.

The time had come to preempt her decision, if possible.

For the venue, Felix chose a picnic organized by Lady Tenwhestle, at which Miss Cantwell was certain to be present. The picnic fell on a rare beautiful day, the sky clean and blue after the previous day's thunderstorm, the clouds as white and fat as newly fluffed pillows.

Clad in a cream muslin dress, Miss Cantwell played a game of croquet with the ladies. It was clear that she was unfamiliar with the rules of the game and had had very little actual experience with a mallet. Yet throughout the match, she managed to stand or walk in such a way as to always present her figure to its best advantage.

One truly must admire her discipline and dedication.

He waited, participating in a few overs of cricket, then sitting down on a picnic blanket with several members of his usual coterie. After their stomachs had been filled, the young people present decided on a game of blindman's buff.

She was not one of the participants—which gave him the opening he was looking for. He encouraged his friends to take part. Once they had departed, he eased into a stroll.

Predictably, though he did not venture near Lady Balfour's picnic blanket, she beckoned him with her fan. As it would be rude otherwise, he answered her summons.

"Lady Balfour, Miss Cantwell, how do you do?"

Miss Cantwell, her cream lace parasol over her shoulder, reached for a cluster of grapes, all the while looking down at the tartan blanket, presenting the very image of becoming demureness.

He, however, noticed that she swallowed even before she inserted a grape into her mouth.

The distance he had kept from her, it would seem, had not diminished his effect on her. The thrill this produced in him was out of all proportion to the observation's relative lack of significance. Of course nothing had changed in that regard. He hadn't even worried about it, had he?

Lady Balfour harrumphed. "We were getting on exceedingly well, until I realized you have not complimented Miss Cantwell on her toilette."

He was becoming rather fond of the old woman—certainly a ferocious champion for her charge. "How unforgivable of me," he answered lightly. "Miss Cantwell, may I be so forward as to mention how exquisite you look today?"

She glanced up, a soft blush upon her cheeks, and a bright, bright light in her eyes.

Which he realized the next moment was less arousal than a reflection of the panic simmering inside her. So she did feel it, the prospect of a good marriage slipping farther from her grasp with each passing day.

To his surprise, he experienced a twinge of guilt. Perhaps even a stab of it. But nothing strong enough to lead him to apologize. Or reconsider his plans.

"You are too kind, sir," she murmured.

"Now, now, Louisa," Lady Balfour objected. "Don't be so grateful. Lord Wrenworth has committed not a kindness, but a faux pas. And he must now make up for it by escorting you for a round in the park."

Had he paid Lady Balfour in advance, she could not have better performed her function.

Miss Cantwell objected modestly. "I'm sure Lord Wrenworth has no such—"

"I am determined to commit a multitude of faux pas in the future, if my penances all prove to be so sweet. Miss Cantwell, may I have the pleasure of your company for a short walk?"

"Yes, you may," Lady Balfour answered for her. "Now, off you go to speak of what young people speak of these days."

You should not give her such hope," said Miss Cantwell, as they left Lady Balfour's earshot.

She really did have a pretty walk, as if she were gliding, with just enough sway to her hips to give interest to her movement.

"I can truthfully avow I have never done anything to give her hope," Felix answered her charge, a tiniest bit of smugness to his tone.

She heard it. "I have noticed. At the end of the Season,

when she looks back and wonders why there is no proposal from you, she will see that every time we have been thrust together, it has been as a favor either to Lady Tenwhestle or herself—and that you have never sought me out on your own."

"I hope you would approve—that a man in my position does what he can to avoid marrying by accident."

Her parasol twirled. "I have no doubt you will be ultimately held blameless, but you cannot convince me that you are not aware of the hope you are sowing in Lady Balfour's heart."

"I will hold myself forgivable as long as I am not sowing those hopes in your heart," he answered glibly. And then, in a moment of genuine curiosity, "Am I?"

"I do not pretend to understand what drives your interest in me, save to know that it is not the kind that leads to a church."

Clever, clever girl. He beamed at her. "Then I need have no fear."

They passed the cluster of young men and women playing blindman's buff. Mr. Pitt was among them, standing next to Miss Lovett. He cast a glance of unhappy longing toward Miss Cantwell.

"Any—" Felix began.

"No," Miss Cantwell said simply.

"A pity. When Parliament repealed the Corn Laws, I'm sure all the eminent gentlemen who voted in favor never thought their decision would have such repercussions on your marital aspirations."

"You forgot to mention the gentlemen who made rail and steam transportation ever faster and cheaper, as well as those who modernized agricultural machinery," she replied glumly. "They, too, were not thinking of the future impoverishment of all the English squires who would have otherwise made wonderful husbands for me."

"The entire course of recent history seems to have been conspiring against you."

"At this point, I would not be surprised." She was silent for a few breaths. "And why, exactly, are you, sir, interested in my progression—or lack thereof—toward matrimony? You do not wish to marry me yourself, so that cannot be a reason. Despite our unusually frank discussions on the topic, you are no friend of mine, so that also cannot be a reason. Try as I do, I cannot think of anything else."

At last, an open salvo. They were reaching quite another level of intimacy, he and Miss Cantwell. "Do you spend a great deal of time pondering my motives?"

The handle of her parasol turned faster. "Sometimes. Does that gratify you?"

Yes. And how. "Sometimes."

"And my misfortunes—my inability to attract a suitable proposal—does that also gratify you?"

She had lobbed similar charges at him before. It tickled him that The Ideal Gentleman was accused of such a rampant case of schadenfreude. "It would make me a terrible sort of man, Miss Cantwell."

"But I am correct, am I not?" she asked, staring straight ahead. "Does it amuse you to see me founder like this?"

He lifted a low-hanging branch for her to pass. "It does not *amuse* me, per se. But I cannot deny it opens an opportunity for me to exploit."

She cast him a wary glance. "I do not see how you can possibly benefit from my inability to marry."

"I have been doing some calculations concerning your future circumstances, should you return home at the end of the Season without having secured an engagement."

"And did those calculations arouse compassion on your part, or scorn?"

"I did note that the sums required to keep all your sisters

and yourself in a state of reasonable comfort—a state of minor luxury, one might even say—consist of an amount that is negligible to my ledgers."

"My, how did I already know that a day's income for you, sir, would feed, house, and clothe my family for an entire year? It is too bad that rich men do not become—or remain—rich men by rescuing genteelly destitute ladies."

She could be quite scathing, this girl. He enjoyed that.

"Indeed, rich men do not finance poor ladies out of the goodness of their hearts. However, I could see myself offering a similar sum to you, for a fair return."

She stared at him.

He had to refrain from smiling. "Keep walking, Miss Cantwell. I see your mind has already gone down one particular direction."

She resumed putting one foot before the other, though she stumbled a little. "How many directions are there for such things?"

"True, not many. So let me be blunt: I will give you a house, not far from your family's current residence and superior in every way. It will be yours to do with as you wish, though I recommend putting it up for let, so that it will generate an income in addition to the annuity I will settle on you for the remainder of your life, one thousand pounds a year."

He had to remind her again to keep walking.

"For . . . sleeping with you?"

"For the pleasure of your company."

She looked as if she were barely holding back from whacking him with her parasol. "No."

Of course she would reject his proposition immediately. Of course she would be offended and outraged. His aim for the day, however, was not instant success, but the planting of the seed of possibility in her mind.

"Why not?" he asked, as if she had turned down not a

particularly salacious sale of her person, but merely a chance for a game of lawn tennis.

His question took her aback. When she answered, it was almost a sputter. "I will not sacrifice my reputation. Or disgrace my entire family."

"Who said anything about loss of reputation? Surely you do not think I aim to make a fallen woman out of a respectable young lady in broad daylight."

"Then how?"

He had anticipated few moral objections from her. Still, it was heartening how quickly they were moving on to the practical aspects. "Very easily, in fact. I host two house parties a year at my country seat, each one lasting from ten days to two weeks. I will invite you and a chaperone for you—then proceed to keep your chaperone busy."

She blinked at his facile answer. "What you propose is madness. There is a reason self-respecting young ladies do not consort with gentlemen in such a manner. There are consequences. What if I should become"—she flushed—"with child?"

"Who said anything about acts that would lead to procreation?"

She looked stumped for a moment, then flushed even more furiously. "So we are to engage in unnatural acts, then?"

He laughed softly. "Is that what you call amorous activities that do not result in a self-respecting young lady being in the family way?"

She took a deep breath. Both of her hands gripped the handle of her parasol. "I did not have a high opinion of you before, sir, but even so I could not have expected anything so obscene on your part."

Her rebuke stroked him pleasantly. "It isn't pretty, what I propose, no flowers or valentines. But it *will* prevent Miss Matilda from ending up in a poorhouse, when the rest of your sisters must scramble to keep a roof over their heads."

"She will *not* go anywhere near a poorhouse," Miss Cantwell replied vehemently. "She is a wonderful girl, and we have relatives who will gladly take her in."

"And which relative is that? Lady Balfour might not outlive your mother. And even if one of her daughters is willing to take in an invalid who must be looked after around the clock, do you think her husband would not object? Do you really want to count on their kindness when you can instead count on a fortune in pounds sterling and a house built to last?"

A horrible thought struck Louisa. "You've done this before, haven't you? Lured otherwise respectable young women in difficult circumstances into prostituting themselves."

He looked genuinely shocked at her accusation. "Of course not."

"Why me, then?"

He looked directly into her eyes. "Because I've never been wanted so much by a woman who dislikes me so. And I would like to experience that fully."

God damn his beautiful eyes. And the good Lord really ought to answer for why He so often chose to bestow comeliness upon the most corrupt souls.

"What is wrong with you?" she huffed.

"An aristocrat with degenerate tastes—how shocking," he murmured, not at all chastened.

She was rendered momentarily speechless by his gleeful embrace of his own wickedness. The Ideal Gentleman, her *arse*.

"You are possibly *the* most rational and pragmatic young woman I have ever met," he went on. "Think about what I have offered—and I do not mean merely security for Miss

Matilda. You will not have to endure marriage to a man you do not love. For eleven months out of the year, there will be no man around to disrupt the peace and quiet of your existence. You can travel, if you wish. You can choose to never step out of your house. Or you can spend all your waking hours in the Reading Room of the British Museum.

"What husband will give you freedom of such quality and quantity? What husband will be more generous with the pin money he offers? And what husband will, even if he is perfect otherwise, let you be your calculating and not so truly agreeable self?"

The man spoke with the devil's own sweet, forked tongue.

"No," Louisa said again, but with more difficulty this time.

He raised a brow. "Not even for dear Matilda?"

"Dear Matilda would never want me to subject myself to such degradation, especially not for her."

"You are so sure of her love?"

"I am. And if it should be the case that she does not love me enough, then why should I martyr myself for her?"

He smiled again. "Well said."

She felt a warmth that had nothing to do with the utter impropriety of the subject of their discussion, but everything to do with his approval of what the world might consider selfishness on her part.

She kept it hidden, that consideration for herself. Even her mother and her sisters did not quite understand it—they all thought her the good, self-effacing daughter who would be glad to do anything for her family.

But he liked her that way. In fact, he seemed to like her far more for her flaws than for any virtues she might possess.

"Then let me speak more to you of your own gains to be had. The house I will settle on you currently fetches rent in excess of five hundred pounds a year. Think of everything you can do with such sums. Or, knowing you, think of the pleasures to be had in watching your bank account grow fatter by the month."

She would like that, wouldn't she? She would eagerly compute the month's various revenues—rents and interests and perhaps dividends from prudent investments—a pleasure she'd never had in all her years of being impoverished. Then she would calculate how much her income exceeded her expenditures and giggle to herself at the cushion of comfort and security she was accumulating.

This time she had to struggle to speak with prim objection. "My lord, the only way a man will sleep with me is by marrying me first. And you are no exception."

"Tempting, but alas, I have no plans for marriage," he answered firmly. "However, are you sure I cannot entice you with a core collection to start your own library?"

The merest of trifles, yet she felt as if she had been struck by lightning: All of a sudden she understood the game in a way she hadn't before. To start, it *was* a game to him. He asked from her everything that was worth anything, but he had put up nothing more than—how had he phrased it earlier?—an amount that was negligible to his ledgers.

Two, he would not consider her response today to be her final answer. He had, in fact, given himself several weeks before the end of the Season for gradually wearing down her resistance, a process he would enjoy the way the master of Château Lafite Rothschild savored his own best vintage.

Three, there must be a way for *her* to play this game. Except she did not yet know how. She had heard his initial offer. Could she bargain for two houses? Or two thousand pounds a year?

And more importantly, did she want to? He asked for only four weeks a year, but she was not so naive as to believe that should they become lovers, thoughts of him would not dominate her waking hours the rest of the year. Was a house and a thousand-pound annuity—or even double that—enough compensation for being in thrall to him for as far as she could see into the future?

Don't forget the jealousy that is certain to come, added a voice inside her head. *You don't suppose he would remain celibate the other eleven months, do you? He will enjoy affairs upon affairs. Not to mention, one of these days he will marry.*

At the thought of the future Lady Wrenworth, a strange numbness spread in her chest. She could so easily imagine an accidental meeting of the three of them, which would of course take place well after he had tired of her. With an amused smile he would present his former plaything to his lady wife, who would be young, fresh, and beautiful, while Louisa would be approaching middle age, the very picture of dowdiness.

"And have I mentioned that I am a competent and considerate lover?" said the present-day Lord Wrenworth, dangling yet another lure before her.

"I do not doubt that," she answered. "In fact . . ."

Her voice trailed off.

"In fact what?" he prompted her.

She had very nearly mentioned those erotic thoughts that besieged her nightly. Under normal circumstances, it would have been a huge blunder. But were there such things as normal circumstances left, when Lord Wrenworth was involved?

"In fact"—she pushed on before she could stop herself again—"I lie awake at night, imagining you watching me in the darkness. And when I finally fall asleep, I dream that I am naked before you, unable to stop you from . . . many liberties."

This time it was he who stopped in his tracks, though he did not need any reminder from her to resume moving. "Miss Cantwell, are you trying to arouse me?"

Her heart had been beating fast for a while, but now blood roared in her ears. "I only speak the truth. I quite despise myself for these desires that run amok. But run amok they do. I daresay for the rest of my life I will dream of being fondled by you."

His eyes darkened; his hand tightened on the top of his walking stick. Her innards shook. With nerves, yes, but also with something that was almost exhilaration.

This was how she played the game.

"What do you have against making your dreams come true?"

"My entire upbringing, needless to say. But there is also something else, something that you, with your vast wealth, cannot possibly understand."

"Do please shed some light on the matter."

"We are poor, you see. Not indigent, as my mother still employs a cookmaid and has one-third share of a gardener— so we get by. But getting by means not buying much of anything beyond food, tea, and coal.

"There is a shop in Cirencester that had a telescope in its shop window. Every month for ten years, I stopped before the window to admire the telescope. I wanted that telescope more than I had ever wanted anything else in my life—I dreamed of it by night and I schemed for it by day.

"The telescope had been put there on consignment. The shopkeeper secretly revealed to me the lowest price he was allowed to accept for the instrument. But I couldn't afford it—any spare penny we had went into an emergency cache for Matilda. Then one day the telescope was gone. It had been bought by a gentleman for his ten-year-old son, for the original owner's full asking price."

Belatedly she noticed that they had both come to a stop. He watched her, his gaze unwavering.

"And?" he prompted.

"And nothing. I carried on. I was so accustomed to *not* having it that my life changed not at all. And so it will be with you. No matter how much I might want you, I will manage to endure it. And I will carry on as if nothing is the matter."

Melodramatic. But it was good melodrama, if she said so herself. *He* certainly seemed riveted.

She began walking again—they were beginning to attract attention from the blindman's buffers, standing there like that. A few steps later, he caught up with her.

"Why did you want the telescope?"

It was not the comment she had been expecting—not that she knew anymore what to expect from him. "That is of no relevance to the discussion at hand."

"I'd like to know."

"I will tell you when we are in bed together, but not before." She flushed with the image that brought to mind.

"And we will be in bed together only after I have pledged my name and protection before a man of God."

"Precisely."

"You are a devious woman, Miss Cantwell," he said.

She felt the warmth of his tone all the way to the pit of her stomach, as if he had licked her. "Only by necessity," she answered, feigning modesty.

"You would have been wasted on Mr. Pitt. And even more so on Lord Firth—that man would ask for a divorce were he to realize who you truly are."

"I would have made sure he didn't."

"And is that any way to be married?"

"It is how *you* will be married, with your lady wife never knowing who you truly are," she pointed out, to another surprised look from him. "So please don't say what you consider an excellent idea for yourself isn't good enough for me."

"Touché," he admitted.

He said nothing else. The silence was at once nerve-racking and electrifying. Had she been convincing? Or had she been *too* convincing? Had she further piqued his interest or merely managed to give him second thoughts?

Lady Balfour was all smiles upon their return. "I could see that it was an intense and intensely interesting conversation between the two of you."

"Miss Cantwell was fascinated by the house parties I give," Lord Wrenworth said smoothly. "She didn't realize gentlemen without wives or sisters entertained, both grandly and respectably."

Lady Balfour pounced. "Well, then, it behooves you to issue an invitation to Miss Cantwell. You cannot dangle such a lure before a young lady and then deny her the experience."

Louisa sighed inwardly as Lord Wrenworth said, with much innocence, "Oh, I do not intend to deprive Miss Cantwell of the experience at all. But she has declared that she intends to head back home at the end of the Season and recuperate for a good long while, without setting foot beyond her front door."

"Bosh, Louisa. I know you miss your family, but one should never pass upon a chance to enjoy the master of Huntington's hospitality, if one at all could."

"Indeed. My hospitality is the stuff of legends," said Lord Wrenworth with a seemingly guileless glance Louisa's way. "But the end of the Season is still far away and there is plenty of time for Miss Cantwell to change her mind."

"And change her mind she will," Lady Balfour said gruffly.

"I am sure you will prove prescient, my lady." He bowed. "Good day, Lady Balfour. And good day, Miss Cantwell."

It was not until Louisa was back in her room at Lady Balfour's town house, flipping uselessly through her notebook, that the enormity of what Lord Wrenworth had proposed fully struck her.

The man was playing with dynamite. And should things go awry, he had just as much to lose as she did. No, more.

He was the one with income in excess of two hundred thousand pounds a year. He was the one with the pristine, lofty reputation. And he was the one who had skillfully avoided the entanglement of eligible young ladies all these years.

If they were discovered, he would have no choice but to marry her.

The very idea of it emptied the air from her lungs. For a man who was neither impulsive nor stupid, this kind of recklessness was nothing short of stunning.

And stunningly telling.

Until this moment, she'd had no idea what he felt toward her, besides an inclination to toy with her for his own amusement. But now she could safely assume that he not only wanted her, but wanted her with an intensity that matched the fervidness of what she felt for him.

It was . . .

She rose from the desk and walked about aimlessly in her room, until she found herself at the edge of her bed. She sat down again, holding on to the bedpost.

It was . . . reassuring.

Of course, it was also immoral, depraved, egregious, abhorrent, appalling—and all the other synonyms one could find for absolutely dreadful.

But at least she knew now the madness that had descended on her had not spared him.

Not entirely, in any case.

CHAPTER 5

*F*elix felt exposed.

The strange sensation crept upon him almost as soon as he left the picnic. With every passing hour it intensified, growing stronger and more undismissable. By bedtime he was literally uncomfortable in his own skin.

The nearest parallel in his experience had been as a child, after having offered a carefully prepared present to one or both of his parents, waiting those terrible minutes to see whether his father would pick it up and whether his mother would, this once, after all her theatrical cooing, take it with her to her room or again leave it behind in the tea parlor, to be cleared away the next time the maids came through.

But the comparison was ridiculous. He had not offered Miss Cantwell a gift. His proposition was a monstrosity, an affront to decency, an incendiary missile catapulted inside the very walls of her castle.

How could he, then, the one on the offensive, fall prey to feelings of vulnerability?

Because you have not been so much yourself in a long time. Because you have let her see more of you than anyone else. Because if she were to reject this offer—

He told the voice inside to shut up. If she were to eventually reject his offer, it would have little to do with him, personally. Everything in her upbringing stood in the way. As did their entire social structure, predicated on the purity of the female body.

He would think no more on his secret discomfort. Instead, he would concentrate on those confessions of hers, of being naked and subject to his will.

For good measure, he took himself to his estate for another week, so as not to seek her out and appear impatient. Even after his return, for several days he chose the masculine refuge of his club over garden parties and *soirées musicales*.

He did, however, bestir himself to attend Lady Tremaine's ball, as otherwise the latter would have sent him a scathing note—they had been lovers at one point and had since settled into a solidly comfortable friendship.

At the ball, he danced with a half dozen young ladies, played a few hands of faro at the card tables, and spent some time by Lady Tremaine's side, inquiring after her doings.

"I can tell you have been to one of your factories today," he told her.

"Why? Do I still have machine grease on my face?" Lady Tremaine laughed. She was a glamorous and confident woman, entirely unashamed of her delight in manufactory and in the making of money.

"You radiate that sense of satisfaction that comes of either a spectacular lover or a spectacular income statement. And since I know you haven't taken anyone to bed lately . . ."

"Perhaps your intelligence is faulty."

"Never. Did you just find out that you are even richer than you were yesterday?"

She laughed again. "Yes. And by a good margin."

He scanned the crowd below, looking for a now-familiar head of shining dark hair—even though he knew Miss Cantwell would not be in attendance. "Congratulations. How do you plan to celebrate?"

"A Swedish lover, perhaps," said Lady Tremaine mischievously, "since I have already scheduled a tour of Scandinavia."

He returned his attention to her. "When?"

"I leave day after tomorrow." She shrugged. "I'm bored with London. Bored with the Season."

"In that case, make the most of your trip. Try a Norwegian lover, too. And is Finland on the itinerary?"

"Not this time, but Denmark is."

He drew back a little. "Lord Tremaine's sister is married to a Dane, is she not?"

"Yes. In fact, I plan to call on her when I pass through Copenhagen—I have always kept on very good terms with my in-laws," she answered, her tone defiant.

"Of course you have," he said soothingly. "I shall expect a full account of your Scandinavian experience when you return."

"That you will have." She sounded relieved to move away from the topic of her in-laws—from any topic that might extrapolate to her husband. "And you, any interesting plans of your own?"

"No, I shall simply have to endure the tedium that is London without you. And then the dreariness of throwing the same old house party."

"Ha. You are the last person to find Society a bore. You are too busy enjoying having your boots licked from one end of Mayfair to the other."

"If the world wishes to admire me, who am I to stand in its way?"

He gave her a slight squeeze of the hand, let her tend to

her other guests, and took himself to the music room for a little respite from the crowd. He did enjoy the adulation of the masses, but a man needed to breathe, too, and there was nothing like a crush of people at the height of summer to make a house as stuffy as one of the queen's mourning gowns.

The music room was dominated by a beautiful Érard piano, which Felix had always thought must have some interesting story behind it: Lady Tremaine, not at all musical, was not the sort to invest in such a fine instrument for herself. Nor was it ever used—she had another piano, a much more ordinary one, in the drawing room, for when her friends wished to have a song or two after dinner.

He suspected that the piano had something to do with the husband she rarely mentioned, the one who lived an ocean away in New York City and never visited. The perfect marriage, it had been labeled by Society—civility, distance, and freedom, unencumbered by tiresome emotions.

The truth was probably something else altogether. But he had never inquired. Their friendship rested on a firm respect of boundaries: Neither questioned whether the other was truly what he or she seemed.

Lady Tremaine was happy to be thought of as completely satisfied with her marital situation. And he was happy to be thought of as a man without actual flaws, when he was about as perfect—and possibly as empty—as her marriage.

The door opened, and in stepped the woman whose refusal to give in to his salacious demands was the very reason for his moment of introspection.

She wore a massive confection the color of cooked shrimp, indiscriminately garnished with deep lace flounces, garlands of velvet rose leaves, and puffs of crystal-spangled tulle. On anyone else, the gown would have been heinous. But with her seemingly transparent face, she turned it to her advantage— of course a young woman as sweet and unsullied as she should come to a ball in twenty yards of pink silk weighed down with every variety of trimming known to couture.

She leaned back against the door, as if she couldn't quite withstand the impact of seeing him again.

He had thought often of what she'd said about the telescope she desperately wanted, about the simple fact of carrying on without it. There had been a dignity to her thwarted desire. There never had been any dignity to his once hopeless needs, but only wretchedness.

He became conscious that an entire minute had passed and they'd exchanged not even a word of greeting.

"You are aware, Miss Cantwell, that we have already lost the princess royale's father-in-law this year and are likely to lose her husband, too, any day now?" he said, his tone more severe than he had intended. "Your frock might be considered inappropriately cheerful in some quarters."

"I am aware of that. But there is no color like raspberry sherbet for a country girl's complexion," she said softly.

And no color like raspberry sherbet for the craving that made her eyes feverishly luminous.

Standing there, the skin of her throat and shoulders gleaming under the bright lights of the music room, her chest rising and falling rapidly, her fingers splayed against the door, as if trying to hold on to something, anything—he would have propositioned her all over again, even knowing how exposed he would feel afterward.

"It's still a ridiculous dress—but as a piece of costume I will admit it has its merits." He braced a hand on the piano. "How did you know I was here?"

"We learned while we were at Mrs. Cornish's ball—guests were leaving to come here and they said you would be in attendance. So Lady Balfour decided to do the same. We didn't even have invitations, but Lady Balfour told me to hold my head high and simply march in."

"And you succeeded admirably, of course."

"I wanted to see you," she said simply. "And when I came out of the powder room, whom should I spy but you, slipping in here."

"Have you missed me?"

He didn't ask such questions. Or at least, he didn't ask such questions when the answers mattered.

Her left hand closed into a fist. "Of course I have missed you."

The floor stopped wobbling. He breathed again.

"Every day I wondered whether I hadn't made the biggest mistake in my life, declining to be your mistress. And every night . . ." She exhaled shakily. "Let's just say I had no idea of the range and ferocity of my own imagination."

"Tell me."

He wanted to know. He needed to know. That she was fiercely drawn to him was what made his sense of vulnerability bearable.

Her fingers worried a crystal bead at her hip; her gaze was somewhere in the vicinity of his feet. "You said that you would bring me to your estate. Well, Lady Balfour happens to have a guidebook to the great manors of the land, with three pages devoted to describing Huntington's every aspect. So now I know all about the cloistered garden, the lavender house, and the Greek folly across the lake from the manor.

"I can almost see it—the manor ablaze with light at night, the lake shimmering with reflection. I stand by one of the columns of the folly, and you come up behind me."

He felt strangely light-headed. "You do know that when I entertain, torches are lit near the folly, so that it is visible from the house at night?"

Her fingers dug into the fabric of her skirts. "Of course, you *would* do something like that, wouldn't you? Now I will be awake all night, thinking of how frightened I would be, even if I'm hidden behind a column. And I will wonder why, since it is an imaginary scenario, I don't simply stop you. Why I don't ask to be taken someplace less dangerously exposed— but let you continue to do everything you want."

Objectively, he had heard far better love banter, steamy words accompanied by a great deal of nakedness and no inhibitions at all. Miss Cantwell, with her reluctance and her inability to go into greater details than "let you continue to do everything you want," should have struck him as awkward and amateurish. But her inexperience, contrasted against her immediate embrace of being made love to in a semipublic place . . .

He could see it, too, now. Except he saw it even more perversely. His guests would not be in the house, but on the grounds for the bonfire party that always marked the last night of his summertime hospitality. Most would remain near the manor, but some would venture farther afield and almost stumble upon them, hidden in the shadows, still fully clothed, but with her skirts pushed up above her waist, and him hilt-deep inside her.

Her eyes met his. She swallowed: She had understood the direction of his thoughts.

"Would I have to keep a hand over your mouth to keep you quiet?" he asked, surprised to hear a slight hoarseness to his voice.

She swallowed again. "Probably."

He approached her slowly. "And I'm sure you understand that would only be the beginning of the night. You will need to come back to my apartment and remain there until dawn."

She gripped the doorjamb. "How many more times do you plan to make love to me that night?"

Her question was barely audible.

Until you beg me to keep you at Huntington all year round.
He stopped only when his lapels brushed the bodice of her

gown. Her eyes were nearly black, with their dilated pupils. The heat rising from her skin was palpable. Her lips parted wider, as if she expected all the air in the room to be taken away shortly—as if she expected him to lean in and kiss her.

He leaned in, his lips almost grazing hers. This close, her eyes were all willingness and surrender. It took every ounce of his control to cant his head a few degrees and whisper into her ear, "You have come to say yes, haven't you?"

She only panted.

"If the thought of exposure arouses you, there is another folly at Huntington, in the style of a Roman temple, with a belvedere on the upper level. The whole structure sits on top of a hill and commands quite a view of the surrounding countryside."

She breathed even more erratically.

"Do you know what would make it even more exciting than the Greek folly? We will do this one in daylight—perhaps not broad daylight, but at sunrise, let's say. And because you are a woman of perverse tastes, making love in public might not stimulate you as much as it ought to when the locale is too isolated to present immediate and tangible danger. So I will disrobe you. And for miles around, if anyone should think to point a good field glass toward the belvedere . . ."

Her hand came up to her throat.

"Say something," he ordered. "Or I might decide to take your silence as assent."

She blinked several times—he noticed for the first time that she had the most perfectly arched eyebrows. She pressed her gloved fingers against his lips, soft, warm kidskin that smelled faintly of cedar.

His heart stopped. He could already feel the sensation of her body against his, the paroxysms of pleasure that would rack her, just as the literal fireworks of the bonfire night set off into the sky.

"I'd better go now," she dropped her hand and mumbled. "Or Lady Balfour will wonder where I've been."

Now he was the one touching her, his gloved hand on her jaw to keep her gaze raised to his, when she would have looked away. "When will you admit you've changed your mind?"

Her eyes said she would toss and turn for hours when she reached home, that perhaps she would even be driven to touch herself. But she only replied, "Good night, Lord Wrenworth."

And escaped from his clutch.

Leaving him to slowly recover from his disorientation.

And to realize, well after she was gone, that the music room was actually quite dimly lit, and that his earlier impression of the brilliance of its illumination was only that: an impression.

It sounded as if someone on an upper story was dragging a table across the floor.

Louisa looked up at the ceiling of the bookshop for a moment, before she turned her attention back to the books. She always volunteered to pick up Lady Balfour's book orders. It was rare that she could afford a volume for herself, but she never passed up a chance to walk between walls of groaning shelves, running her gloved fingertips over rows upon rows of clothbound spines. An enjoyment that was more like an ache: an aesthetic appreciation butting up against a perennially unsatisfied craving for ownership.

Why not say yes to Lord Wrenworth? That would keep you knee-deep in books for the rest of your life, if nothing else.

Indeed, why *not* say yes to Lord Wrenworth?

When he had dropped out of sight for so many days after his initial proposition, she had grown increasingly certain, a sensation like a hole in her stomach, that she had woefully misread the situation. That what she had thought were but opening volleys actually constituted the entire transaction: offer tendered, offer refused, offer nullified.

That what she had thought to be real and sustained interest on his part was but a soap bubble under the sun, gone with the next blink of the eye.

Lady Balfour hadn't needed to encourage her to pretend as if she belonged at Lady Tremaine's ball. Had any servant tried to stop her from getting in, she would have gladly handed over her mother's pearl brooch as a bribe—so badly did she need to see him.

It was to her credit that she had kept her clothes on—there was something about the man, about the way he looked at her, that made her want to disrobe on the spot. Not languidly, deliberately, but as if her corset and petticoats were on fire and must be yanked off without a second's delay.

And when he had asked whether she had come to say yes, when he had renewed his offer and her hope, beneath her skirts her legs had trembled.

He would never know how close she had come to giving him the answer he wanted.

Yet for all her shaking relief that he was still interested—still committed to this lunacy of his—she had turned around and left.

Some part of her had recognized that the game was still very much on, and had not wanted to concede it. But how much longer could she play the game, when she had no idea how, or whether it was even possible, to win? Was she just playing to keep from losing, then? And what exactly did losing entail, in this particular instance?

Thunder like a field gun being fired right next to her ear

made her jump. Rain unleashed as if a dam had burst in the clouds. She realized that what she had thought of as table legs scraping the floor overhead had actually been the low rumble of thunder, which had been going on for a good while.

She would have to remain in the bookshop until the storm eased, not a terrible hardship. And since she was—or at least represented—a loyal customer of long standing, Mr. Richards, the owner, would not complain about her prolonged browsing.

"I'm looking for the young lady who came to pick up Lady Balfour's order."

Louisa blinked. Lord Tenwhestle—what was he doing here?

"My lord Tenwhestle." She came out from the stacks. "I'm here."

"Of course you are, my dear cousin." He nodded at Mr. Richards, came toward her, and instead of walking her to the door, led her deeper into the shop.

When they were out of Mr. Richards's hearing range, Lord Tenwhestle asked, with a mischievous smile on his face, "Have you ever read *Pride and Prejudice*, Miss Cantwell?"

His question baffled her. "Yes, years ago."

Mrs. Cantwell had been disappointed that no modern-day Mr. Darcy or Mr. Bingley had ever whisked one of her beautiful elder daughters into a grand manor. Louisa found it strange that her mother had nursed such hopes at all. Even Miss Austen herself had not found a real-life Mr. Darcy. Why should he materialize almost a century later, after his creator had turned into bone and dust?

"Do you remember the part where Mrs. Bennet dispatches her eldest daughter to Netherfield Park on horseback, knowing it would rain and force Jane to stay overnight?"

Louisa bit the inside of her cheek; she saw where this was going.

"My mother-in-law has contrived something similar,"

continued Lord Tenwhestle, confirming Louisa's suspicions. "She sent me to my club on foot, even though it was certain to pour, with the instruction that I must ensure that you arrived home warm and dry in case of rain."

What would Lady Balfour think if she only knew that while she planned her innocent tricks, Louisa was playing far more reckless games? "And since it is impossible to locate a hackney in this weather . . ."

"Precisely." Lord Tenwhestle winked conspiratorially. "When I groaned about my problem, a very fine gentleman stepped forward to put his carriage at my disposal."

One with more than one folly on his estate? Louisa almost asked.

They were speaking in low voices, but now she dropped hers to a whisper. "Do you not think, sir, that perhaps Lady Balfour is overly optimistic about my prospects? I'd hate for her to be disappointed, but if the gentleman is who I think it is, I have no reason to believe any offers of marriage will be forthcoming from that quarter."

Lord Tenwhestle gave her a gentle pat on the elbow. "You needn't worry, dear cousin. We are all grown-ups here. Besides, I have known the gentleman in question for years, and perfect though he may be, he is also quite wily at dodging scheming mamas and equally scheming misses. I will allow that once could be a coincidence—the time he came to dinner at my house because Mr. Pitt happened to be our missing fourteenth guest—but I do not think Lord Wrenworth accidentally offers his help twice to the same kin of the same debutante."

No, not accidentally. But whatever Lord Wrenworth did, it was for his own purpose: to have her standing naked on that belvedere at the break of dawn, while he had his way with her.

She felt a sharp pinch in her chest. Would this scenario only ever exist in her imagination?

"If you say so, sir," she said weakly.

A pair of footmen waited outside the bookshop, holding umbrellas. Lord Wrenworth stood by his sleek, splendid town coach under one such umbrella, looking as if he had stepped out from a fairy tale, the beautiful trickster prince—a fairy tale that must be bowdlerized before it could be safely read to children.

He greeted her with utmost propriety. His hold on her hand, as he helped her into the carriage, was light and decorous. And when he came into the carriage, his trousers did not even remotely brush the edge of her skirts.

All the same, it took only one swift, unsmiling look from him for heat to sweep over her. She clutched Lady Balfour's packet of books in her lap.

Lord Tenwhestle climbed in. The door closed behind him. Smoothly, the coach rolled away from the curb.

"I was just telling Miss Cantwell how grateful I was that you came to my rescue," said Lord Tenwhestle to the man who had proposed to Louisa, except not marriage. "And how thrilled I was not to have to seek a hackney in this downpour."

Louisa's lover—the appellation shocked her, but how else was she to refer to him?—inclined his head graciously. "My privilege to be of assistance."

My lover, she repeated the words to herself. They had not made love, but that was an insignificant detail, given that he had probed her mind, both erotically and otherwise. And she, though she had yet to be unclothed before him, had certainly laid bare a great many of her naked desires.

Traffic moved slowly. Lord Tenwhestle shouldered most of the small talk, some amusing incident of being lost in a similar downpour in the middle of Rome, while he was on his Grand Tour with his brother.

All of a sudden he exclaimed, "Goodness, I very nearly forgot! I am to meet my brother at his house in ten minutes—

some business with the solicitor about a useless plot of land we've been trying to get rid of for ages."

"If I'm not mistaken, Mr. Northmount lives on the next street?" asked Lord Wrenworth.

"That is correct. If I wasn't just telling a story about us, I wouldn't have remembered."

Lord Wrenworth relayed new directions to his coachman. Minutes later, Lord Tenwhestle was inside his brother's house and Lord Wrenworth and Louisa were headed toward Lady Balfour's.

Louisa felt strangely self-conscious, not because she was alone with her unconsummated lover, but because the ploy on the part of her kin had been so ludicrously transparent. She was both immensely grateful for Lord Tenwhestle's and Lady Balfour's sincere and kindhearted efforts—and immensely embarrassed.

Especially since she had more or less confirmed to Lord Wrenworth that she was nothing of the sweet, innocent girl that a self-respecting man would take for a bride; she was in fact a nymphomaniac who did not mind being taken in public, if only he would take her at all.

She removed the books from her lap, set them beside her, and traced her thumb along the twine that had been used to wrap the package.

"Tell me about the telescope," he said.

She looked up. "I thought I'd made it clear that is not something I will discuss."

"Not something you will discuss unless you are already in bed with me," he corrected her. "But that was for the reason you wanted the telescope. What I request is a description of the telescope itself."

"Why?"

"Because it interests me."

All at once she understood why she had not said yes two

nights before. Why she continued to play this dangerous game.

She was afraid of losing him.

Once she became his mistress, once he was free to satisfy himself on her, it would be the beginning of the end. But as long as she resisted, as long as his lust simmered unfulfilled, there was a chance he would remain part of her life.

Perhaps he would write her risqué letters on a typewriter, unsigned so that they could not be traced back to him. Perhaps he would find a reason to buy a property near where she lived—and call on her once every two years or so, when he came by to inspect the property in person. Perhaps he would—

"What is the size of the aperture?" he asked.

She hesitated. Her carnal infatuation she could not hide, but could she bear to expose more of herself, to be even more naked before him?

"Six inches?" he continued his questioning.

"Nine and a half," she heard herself responding.

"Focal length?"

"Twelve feet, four inches."

He tented his hands. "No wonder you were unable to afford it. Earlier I thought you wanted one of those five-guinea telescopes. But you, Miss Cantwell, are ambitious."

"For some things," she admitted.

"When you fancy a telescope, you want one that can show you each party of a double star. When you fancy a man, you want The Ideal Gentleman." With one finger atop his walking stick, he tipped it from side to side. "What else do you fancy?"

She should not tell him anything else. She should never have mentioned the telescope in the first place, never given him a glimpse into her private self.

"All I ever wanted was to be an independent spinster."

She winced inside. What possessed her to keep laying

herself bare before him? Granted, it was terribly lonely to be in love, and granted, his continued interest was—

Her thought process halted abruptly, as if it were a ship encountering a hidden sandbar. She stopped fiddling with the twine bow. What had just happened?

She had been so careful. Infatuation, besottment, madness—she'd used every word in the thesaurus to describe her state of mind.

Every word except *love*.

Because love wasn't a state of mind liable to change from hour to hour, day to day. Love was like smallpox: Even the survivors did not escape unscathed.

She looked at him as if seeing him for the first time, the beauty, the poise, the wickedness. She was in love with a man no woman in her right mind would approach, let alone want.

He tapped his tented fingertips against one another. "I can give you that, an independent spinsterhood. And a bigger telescope than the one you hungered after."

"You are as persuasive as the serpent in the Garden of Eden."

"And you are far cleverer and warier than poor Eve ever was."

He lifted his straight rod of a walking stick and, holding it near the base, set its handle on her lap, a frightfully intimate, invasive gesture that made flame leap through her.

The terrible thing was, the more he revealed himself to be dangerous and warped, the more she fell under his spell. And the more she fell under his spell, the freer he felt to reveal even more of his true nature.

His eyes met hers again. "Let me give you everything you've ever dreamed of."

But he couldn't. Or at least, he wouldn't.

For she could no longer be satisfied with an expensive

telescope, an exemplary spinsterhood, or his sure-to-be-magnificent body—or even all three together.

She was a woman in love and she wanted nothing less than his unscrupulous and very possibly unprincipled heart, proffered to her in slavish devotion.

She set her fingers on the handle of the walking stick, still warm with the heat of his hand. At first she thought it was but a knob made of heavy, smooth-grained ebony, but as she traced its curve with her hand, she looked down and realized that the handle was actually in the shape of the head of a black jaguar.

"Very fine specimen you have here," she said, a little shocked at both her words and her action.

She was *caressing* the part of him that he had chosen to extend to her person, her fingertips exploring every nook and cranny of the handle. His gaze, intense and heavy lidded, traveled from her face to her uninhibited hand and back again.

"You like it?"

He was as deliberate and self-mastered a man as she had ever met. Whenever she thought of him with access to her body, she'd always imagined a manipulative lover with infinite patience and control, making her pant and writhe, and then perhaps tormenting her a little—or a great deal—by withholding what she desperately needed.

But there was an undercurrent to *this* particular question that made her think of him pushing her up against a wall, or perhaps the column of a Greek folly, and taking her hard, all his patience and control gone.

Her voice shook slightly. "Yes."

"I have far better specimens I can show you."

"I'm sure you do. But this will always be my first."

The town coach seemed to have been built of glass, with large windows on every side. None of the shades were drawn, and they were hardly the only vehicle on the road.

Nonetheless, she raised the handle of his walking stick, leaned forward, and kissed it on the tip.

"You make me do such unspeakable things," she murmured, looking at the jaguar's head.

Slowly, he pulled the walking stick from her grasp. He examined the handle closely, then glanced back at her, his gaze heated yet inscrutable.

Rain drummed against the top of the coach. Thunder cracked. The wheels of the carriage splashed through the small river running down the street. Yet all she heard was the arrhythmic thumping of her heart, a staccato of hot, unfulfilled yearning.

The silence made her squirm. She was not someone who must speak to fill a silence, yet *his* silence seemed to turn a spigot in her, and words spilled from her into the space between them.

"Why don't you let me touch it again, the head of the jaguar? I quite like its heft in my hand."

He cast a look down and played, rather absently—or so it seemed—with the ebony knob. Except whatever he did made her breath catch and her face grow even hotter.

"Are you sure it is I who make you do unspeakable things?" he asked softly, his gaze pinning her against the back of the seat. "Or are you just naturally fond of gentlemen's . . . walking sticks?"

She shifted on the seat.

Felix would like to do the same: adjust certain parts so he was slightly more comfortable. But he also knew it would be no use: Nothing would take off the edge of his arousal—nothing except the possession of her.

He thought of her constantly: on her back, on her knees, on her feet, sometimes naked, sometimes not, but always with him inside her, and always with her eyes wide open, looking at him with that expression particular to her: lust, apprehension, covetousness, suspicion, and just a sprinkle of worship.

Even now he thought of it: using the handle of his walking stick to lift her skirts and push her knees apart, so that she would be exposed before him.

"I will find out, won't I, when I marry the butcher?" she answered at last.

His fingers clenched over the handle of his walking stick. He hadn't meant to react so obviously, but he hadn't been able to help himself. What did she mean, the butcher? "Does he have a walking stick you have been admiring?"

She twisted her fingers. "I'm sure I don't know about his walking stick—I have only seen him in his shop. He is a good man and not unpleasant in appearance. Rumor is that he fancies me, but Mother has let it be known, though perhaps not in so many words, that she would never allow any of her daughters to stoop to marrying butchers, greengrocers, and the like.

"But that's because her father was a gentleman. *My* father was a fortune hunter, and I am far less fastidious about which sort of man is good enough to be my husband. A butcher's money is just as good as a lord's. If he will take Matilda in, then I will marry him."

He did not want to believe her. But this was what truth felt like: a tight, hard knot somewhere in his chest. "*Will* he take in Miss Matilda?"

She shrugged. "That might depend on how well I convince him of my fondness for his walking stick."

The handle of the walking stick was suddenly pressed into her chest, between her breasts. He had no idea how it happened. He had no idea he was capable of such recklessness—or volatility.

She looked at him with astonishment—and made no move to touch the walking stick again.

"Sleep with me and I will provide you access to the best private telescope in England, something your butcher would never be able to do."

Her heart beat violently—each throb transmitting across the length of the walking stick to reverberate against his palm. "I thought I had made it very clear that I am not that sort of woman."

The thought of another man touching her . . . of her, with that agreeableness she did so well, encouraging this man . . . of himself, with only his memories for consolation . . .

His fortune privileged him over most other men in London, but how did he compete with all the "butchers, greengrocers, and the like"?

Slowly he retracted the walking stick. "You will certainly eat well, if nothing else."

He'd meant to project a certain levity, but he sounded caustic.

"One must look to the silver linings," she said quietly.

"I am sure you will manage very well."

"Yes," she said, with a grave solemnity. "I will always manage, somehow."

The carriage door opening startled them both. He had not realized that they had arrived before Lady Balfour's house. Suddenly Miss Cantwell was smiling sweetly and thanking him for his kindness in seeing her home. He, too, became all courtesy and gallantry, assuring her that he would have moved far greater mountains to ensure her ease and comfort.

As his coach pulled away once more from the curb, however, it was not their naughtier interaction that dominated his thoughts, but the determination—and melancholy—with which she assured him that she would survive marriage to just about any able-bodied man.

His entire plan had depended upon her failure to secure a man of her social station. But he had not counted on her willingness to marry beneath her. A butcher was an upstanding member of any community, but by becoming the wife of one, she could count on never again calling on Lady Balfour or the Tenwhestles.

Or friends she had made during her time in London. Or just about anyone else she knew from home. It was cruel, but until the world changed, the gentry would always hold themselves apart from butchers, greengrocers, and the like.

He imagined her in this new life, always making sure she appeared extra cheerful, because she never wanted her husband, her epileptic sister, or her new friends and in-laws to think her less than content. He imagined her coming occasionally across an old acquaintance and the awkward conversation that would ensue, especially if she happened to be accompanied by her husband. He imagined her reaching for a sheet of stationery, the beginning of a letter on her mind, and then hesitating, and finally giving up the idea altogether— she would not want to agonize the recipient with the decision whether to respond; nor would she want to anticipate a reply and then finally have to admit to herself one was never coming.

Not to mention the stars. The girl who wanted a telescope of that particular description wasn't content merely to view the craters of the moon or the rings of Saturn. She wanted to see the mountains of Mars. The very outer reaches of the solar system.

Why would she deprive herself of everything that mattered to her, when she could easily—

He stopped his thoughts from going any further in that direction.

Instead, he hurled his walking stick onto the seat she had vacated and cursed her obduracy and stupidity.

CHAPTER 6

Louisa had not told Lord Wrenworth everything about Mr. Charles, the butcher who fancied her.

Mr. Charles was indeed a good man and an excellent butcher, but he had a brother who drank and gambled and often came to him with one hand outstretched. He also had a widowed sister who depended heavily upon him to support her and her two young children. So even if he were desperate to marry Louisa, he would have to think twice—thrice—about taking on an invalid sister-in-law who needed looking after round the clock.

And suppose Mr. Charles somehow overcame his own qualms—could Louisa really marry him? There was an enormous difference between marrying a man one did not love wildly and marrying a man while wildly in love with someone else.

Who'd have thought, at the beginning of the year, that she had such a capacity for trouble? Everyone, herself included, had believed her the most placid, most levelheaded girl on earth, or at least in their part of the Cotswold. Had anyone told her that she would be brought low by romantic love, she'd have snickered. Had that sage prophet warned her about sexual infatuation, she'd have laughed hard enough to crack a rib.

And yet here she was . . .

"Louisa, won't you do us the honor?" asked Lady Balfour.

"Yes, of course, ma'am." Louisa rose from her corner and poured tea for the latest batch of callers.

Wednesday was Lady Balfour's at-home day. This afternoon, callers were particularly numerous due to the large dinner Lady Balfour gave two days ago. The women in their fine afternoon dresses stayed precisely a quarter of an hour, barely sipped their tea, and rose to pay their respects at the next house.

Louisa's embroidery needle moved slowly, absently. Five days had passed since the carriage ride with Lord Wrenworth. It was now the second week of July, and words like *Cowes* and *Scotland* were being thrown like grains of rice at a wedding.

People were making plans for the end of the Season, for where to go next to amuse themselves.

The end of the Season.

She ought to worry about the future, but like a lovesick girl half her age, she thought of Lord Wrenworth instead. Would she ever see him again after she left London? Ten years, five years, or even twelve months down the road, would he remember her with a pang of regret or a mere shrug?

Whether anyone else noticed her distress she could not say. In the middle of June, Lady Balfour had confidently predicted proposals by the first week of July. That particular week had come and gone with no matrimonial commitment from anyone; Lady Balfour, however, remained as ebullient as ever about Louisa's eventual success.

"Have I told you our story from last week?" she smugly asked her guests. "No, of course I haven't—I've been saving it for today."

It was past four o'clock. Those now occupying the drawing room were Balfour intimates whose long-standing friendship with the hostess gave them license to stay a bit longer than the allotted fifteen minutes.

"Recall, if you will, the torrential downpour of a few days ago," Lady Balfour continued.

"Quite ruined the hemline of my walking dress, it did," said Lady Archer, who had known Lady Balfour since before the queen was on the throne.

"Precisely. That afternoon, my dear Tenwhestle needed to bring Miss Cantwell home from the bookshop. But rain came all of a sudden. He was stranded at his club without a conveyance, there were no hackneys to be had, and of course, in a cloudburst of that magnitude, he couldn't simply pitch an umbrella and walk."

"Indeed not," concurred Mrs. Constable, who had gone to finishing school with Lady Balfour.

"Tenwhestle fretted. You know how seriously that man takes his obligations. But no sooner had he spoken aloud Miss Cantwell's name than a knight in shining armor stepped forth—or perhaps I should say, a knight in a shining town coach."

Mrs. Tytherley, Mrs. Constable's sister, exclaimed softly, "My goodness, do you mean to tell us that it was Lord Wrenworth again?"

Lady Balfour preened. "I do indeed."

A small crescendo of "oohs" and "ahhs" rose.

"We all know that boy protects himself beautifully from adventurous misses. Yet your Miss Cantwell had him for a dinner, a dance, a long walk at a picnic, a drive home on a rainy day—am I missing anything?" asked Mrs. Constable.

"No, ma'am," Louisa hurriedly said.

"Oh, but I must differ," said Mrs. Tytherley.

Louisa's head snapped up.

"I ran into Lady Avery at the modiste's this morning. And she told me that her nephew, Mr. Baxter, had seen Miss Cantwell and Lord Wrenworth seated together in a refreshments room at the British Museum a while ago. Though Mr. Baxter, being a man, had not bothered to mention it to her until very recently."

"Louisa!" exclaimed Lady Balfour, almost making Louisa prick her finger. "Mr. Baxter didn't know any better, but why have you not brought it up either?"

"It was the merest coincidence!" Louisa protested; at least this time she wasn't lying. "I certainly never thought to see him there, and I daresay the same for Lord Wrenworth."

"The meeting might have been a coincidence, but Lord Wrenworth could have simply nodded and moved on. That he sat down at your table was indisputably a conscious choice."

"I cannot agree more," said Mrs. Tytherley. "Furthermore, taken as a whole, I feel quite strongly that so many occasions cannot possibly all be coincidences. There must be some design to it—on Lord Wrenworth's part."

"I say whether it is design or coincidence, you are one lucky young lady, Miss Cantwell," opined Lady Archer. "In fact, you might prove to be the luckiest lady in London, if this current course holds."

"I do not mean to disagree with you, Lady Archer, but I—"

The rest of Louisa's argument never saw the light of the day, as the drawing room door opened, and Lady Balfour's footman announced, "His lordship the Marquess of Wrenworth."

The four older women in the room, with identical expressions of surprise—eyes wide, jaws slack—swung to face Louisa. Who stared back at them, similarly agape.

Lord Wrenworth strolled in, looking relaxed and stylish in a dove-grey Newmarket coat. Louisa closed her mouth and bent her face to her embroidery frame, trying not to stab herself as she pushed the needle through the velvet silk.

Afternoon courtesy calls were those threads in the fabric of society woven almost exclusively by women. Given that Lady Balfour ran no salon and belonged to no "fast" set, the presence of a man at this feminine place and hour—when he should be snoozing off his postluncheon stupor at his club— was extraordinary.

What did he want?

A theatrical rendition of normalcy was put on: Lord Wrenworth was offered a seat, fresh tea was called for, and comments on the weather—a bright afternoon, for once—were exchanged all around.

Some of the ladies were better actresses than others: Lady Archer was a natural, chatting about her meteorological apparatuses at home, her husband being very particular about the measurement of rainfall and of atmospheric pressure. But none of them were as good as Lord Wrenworth, who made it seem as if he took tea with ladies of his mother's generation every Wednesday during the Season.

He asked after Lady Archer's son, currently on a tour of the Continent. He inquired into a fence of Lady Tytherley's, which had apparently been giving all sorts of offense since the previous autumn. And he brought up the subject of Lady Constable's hybrid roses, which quite surprised and flattered the latter—even Louisa had no idea that she experimented with new varietals.

Was it possible that he had come on a whim? Perhaps he missed her a bit. Perhaps he missed her more than a bit. And perhaps he happened to be nearby and decided that he would rather cause brows to rise than go another day without seeing her.

She grimaced at her dangerously self-indulgent thoughts. More evidence of her besottedness, that: The old her would never have woven an entire tapestry of starry-eyed *amour* out of spools of a man's sexual curiosity.

The clock struck half past four. He had been in Lady Balfour's drawing room for ten minutes—five minutes left before etiquette dictated that he take his leave.

She wished she could understand what went on behind those hypnotic eyes of his. The man would not cause rampant speculation without a good reason. But if that good reason existed, she could not fish it out of the chaos in her head.

"And they are truly excellent on an arbor," Mrs. Constable said with a flutter of her hands, imitating the motion of a climbing rose. "In a few years you will have a profusion of blooms, exceptionally lovely in early summer."

"I will be sure to pass on the knowledge to my head gardener," replied Lord Wrenworth, looking for all the world as if he had nothing in mind except summer roses.

"I can have mine send the design for the arbor, too, if you like," offered Mrs. Constable, a little breathlessly.

"It will be most sincerely appreciated, my dear Mrs. Constable."

He smiled at the older woman and Louisa could feel her own heart pitter-patter. Now Lord Wrenworth reached for his tea—poured by none other than Lady Balfour herself—and took a sip.

A small silence descended. And extended, as Lord Wrenworth unhurriedly ate a piece of Madeira cake, seemingly unaware of the breathless anticipation building in the drawing room. Louisa doggedly wielded her needle—push, pull, push, pull—while her heart thumped like a war drum in the middle of a battle.

Finally, Lady Balfour could stand it no more. "Now, would

you care to divulge what brought you here today, Lord Wrenworth? It can't be just to sample my Madeira cake."

Lord Wrenworth set aside his plate. "Had I known how excellent your Madeira cake is, Lady Balfour, I would have presented myself at every one of your at-home days this Season. But you are right. I did come with a different purpose in mind."

Lady Balfour's voice rose perceptibly. "And that is?"

Another small silence. Louisa, her eyes fixed firmly to her embroidery frame, imagined him turning toward her, studying her with that sometimes inscrutable look of his.

"With your permission," he said, "I would like to speak privately with Miss Cantwell."

She neither dropped her embroidery frame nor poked herself with the needle. Such clumsiness would have required the ability to *move*. She only stared straight ahead, unable to believe what she was hearing.

"Louisa, Lord Wrenworth wishes for a word with you." Lady Balfour's voice boomed in her ears. "Show him to the morning parlor, won't you?"

And then, to Lord Wrenworth, "We expect her restored to us in ten minutes, sir."

Louisa carefully set aside the embroidery frame and rose. Looking only at the floor before her—a proper display of modesty, she was sure, except she did not feel bashful, only flabbergasted—she preceded Lord Wrenworth to the morning parlor.

The moment he closed the door, she spun around. "Have you lost your mind? What do you think you are doing? Those women in the drawing room are expecting a proposal. Of *marriage*. What am I to tell them when you leave? 'No, ladies, his lordship does not wish to take me for a wife. He merely wanted to hear me recount another one of my unseemly dreams.'"

He drew close—she noticed for the first time the understated swagger of his gait, that of a man who'd always had everything he wanted.

"Have you been having more of those dreams?" he asked, speaking into her ear.

She shivered as his breath brushed her skin. And the woods-after-a-thunderstorm scent of him—she wanted to bury her face in his neck and inhale for all she was worth. "Of course I have. But that is not the point. The point is that—"

"Narrate one of your unseemly dreams."

Was that the pad of his thumb tracing the line of her collar? She could barely feel it for the electricity racing along her nerve endings. "Now?"

"We still have a good few minutes. Why not?"

"*Why not?* I will tell you why . . ." Her voice trailed off as he undid the top button of her blouse. She gawked at him, her throat closing with both fright and thrill. "*What* are you doing?"

"What does it look like I'm doing? Do as I say or I'll keep opening your blouse."

She blinked, not sure whether she wanted him to stop.

He laughed softly. "My God, don't tell me you want me to go on."

"When have I ever given you the idea that I *wouldn't* want you to go on?"

He shook his head. "You give me no choice. Fine. I'll ask nicely. Please tell me one of your dreams, my dear Miss Cantwell."

She swallowed. "That isn't nice enough. You have to say 'my dear Louisa.'"

He looked at her strangely for a moment. "Won't you please, my dear, dear Louisa?"

Her name on his lips was pure music. She wanted to hear it again and again.

My dear, dear Louisa.

"For the past three nights I have dreamed that we are riding in a carriage together, a town coach not unlike yours, except it is made entirely of glass, even the floor. And . . . and I'm naked."

His eyes were a deep, dark green, almost wintry—like a pine forest in December—yet his gaze was all volcanic heat. "Go on."

"I . . . I fret about my nakedness. So you fashion a blindfold from your necktie and tell me that if I cannot see out, then I will not worry about those who might be peering in."

"Impeccable logic, that. What happens next?"

"Once I'm blindfolded, you touch me with something. You say it's your walking stick, but I'm not sure I believe you."

"Why the doubt?"

"Because . . . it is hot." Her face scalded. "And please don't ask me what happens next. There is no next."

In her dreams, she simply carried on in that state of horrified arousal.

He smiled slightly. "Do you like it when I touch you with my not–walking stick?"

She could see her hand reaching up, but she could not quite believe what she was doing, even when she had a lock of his hair between her fingers. "In my dreams, there is nothing you do that I do not like."

"It's worth abducting you from Lady Balfour's drawing room, before a full crowd of onlookers, just to hear that."

Dear God, Lady Balfour and all her friends. "Please tell me that wasn't what you came for."

"Of course not. I came to tell you that I have decided to rescind my offer. The idea has run its course—and expired."

The contents of her skull imploded. She couldn't think. She couldn't see. She couldn't breathe.

He wasn't a good man and she hadn't cared. She was willing to overlook any number of staggering faults, as long as he felt at least something of what she felt for him.

When he had been toying with her all along.

As if from a great distance away, she heard herself say, "You might as well, I suppose. I never would have cheapened myself by accepting that particular offer."

It was a lie. She would have hated to become his mistress—because it would mark the beginning of the end—but she had never, at any point, eliminated the choice from consideration.

"You don't look as righteously vindicated as you ought to," he pointed out, his voice insidiously soft, insidiously close.

"Rest assured my immortal soul is pleased. It's only my vanity that is crushed."

And her pathetic heart.

"My poor, darling Louisa," he murmured, the evil, evil man.

"It is still very ill done of you to come here and single me out, just to tell me you've thought better of your nefarious plans. What am I supposed to tell Lady Balfour in"—she glanced at the clock—"precisely forty-five seconds?"

And once those forty-five seconds flew by, once he walked out Lady Balfour's door, she might not ever see him again. Who else would like her for her scheming ways? Who else would applaud her for thinking of herself? And who else would ask her about the telescope she had loved and lost?

He touched her face—but to her horror, she realized he was only wiping away her tears.

"You may tell Lady Balfour that in exactly three weeks, you will be married."

She stared at him through the blur of her tears. "To whom?"

He only looked at her as if she were a very slow child who couldn't grasp that one plus one equaled two.

"I don't understand," she said, though understanding was beginning to penetrate her woolly brain.

"What is there to understand? I have made you an offer of marriage. Will you take it, or must I rescind that offer, too?"

Suddenly she felt as if she'd drunk an entire gallon of coffee. Her fingertips shook. "Of course I will take it—I came to London to marry the largest fortune I could find, and there is none available larger than yours. But why would you marry *me*?"

"Because young ladies who confess to pornographic reveries ought to be rewarded with riches beyond their dreams?"

But that made no sense at all. "I don't—"

"Our ten minutes are up," he said, buttoning her blouse and wiping away the rest of her tears, his fingers sure and warm. "I will not allow any eclipsed second to besmirch my sterling reputation. Time for us to return to the drawing room, Louisa."

He was already turning away when she gripped his hand.

Kiss me. Shouldn't you at least kiss me when you propose to me?

But when she opened her mouth, out came, "I still want my house and my thousand pounds a year—for the duration of my natural life. And I want those conditions written into the marriage settlement."

He tilted his head. She could not tell whether he was vexed or amused. "You do?"

She gathered her courage. "If something seems too good to be true, then it probably is. For all I know, you are secretly readying your solicitors for an annulment as soon as you've tired of me."

"*Such* a cynic."

"Better be unromantic than thoroughly used and still poor."

He took her chin in hand. "And if I refuse?"

"Then I will tell Lady Balfour that I turned down your proposal."

She could scarcely believe it, but she was extorting the most eligible bachelor in London.

"I will give you a house and five hundred a year," he countered.

Her heart was in her throat. "I won't marry you for a penny less than eight hundred. And it had better be a house with at least twenty rooms."

His fingers cupped her cheek. The pad of his thumb rubbed against her lips. His gaze was cool and severe, and she was suddenly in a panic.

No, no, it's quite all right. I will marry you for five hundred a year and a hovel. In fact, take my mother's pearl brooch. Take my great-aunt Imogene's jet pin. And you can also have the emergency money I've hidden away at home, all eleven pounds and eight shillings of it.

He smiled. "You will pay for this. You know that, right?"

The way he looked at her, so much wickedness, delight, and *camaraderie*. If she hadn't been born with the constitution of a horse, she would have fainted from both relief and a tsunamic surge of sheer happiness.

"Yes," she whispered. "Yes."

A thousand yeses.

CHAPTER 7

*L*ouisa's life changed from the moment Lord Wrenworth declared to a roomful of breathless ladies that Miss Cantwell had consented to become his wife.

Within the crisp, freshly ironed pages of the next day's *Times*, she found the engagement announced with all due pride and gravity. An hour later, an enormous bouquet of pink-tinged white orchids arrived at the house, courtesy of her husband-to-be. At noon, more evidence of his regard, a magnificent diamond ring, made its dramatic appearance, sending Lady Balfour into a swoon of ecstasy.

"What did I tell you, Louisa? *What did I tell you?*"

Notes of congratulations snowed upon the house, along with invitations to every event taking place from then to the end of the Season. Louisa spent two entire days answering the well-wishers. When she went on calls with Lady Balfour, amidst many an envious and sometimes incredulous look, much fuss was made of her.

The luckiest lady in London.

Louisa herself was no less staggered than any of her well-wishers. She giggled when she was alone. She gaped at her ring whenever she caught sight of it. Sometimes, as she lay in bed at night, she pummeled her mattress with both hands and feet, as gleeful and irrepressible as a child about to go on her first holiday.

But other times, her dumbfoundedness took a more sober turn. Clearly his proposal took place, but with each passing day it made less sense. A mistress was a temporary feature in a man's life, a passing fancy to be discarded or replaced anytime he so chose. A wife, on the other hand, was a permanent installation, almost as irrevocable as a mother.

What could possibly have induced him to make such a decision? She had a healthy regard for herself, but even if she esteemed herself ten times as much, she still couldn't comprehend what it was about her that had proved irresistible to a man who could have had any woman.

The tentative explanation she cobbled together was a discomfiting one. He enjoyed wielding power over her—almost from the very beginning, he had intentionally set out to disrupt and destabilize. She'd had to fight back for every inch of footing she could command, so that she was not entirely at his mercy.

It was possible that even with her resistance, he'd come to the conclusion that he would never hold greater sway over a woman. Or perhaps it was precisely her resistance that he relished, that in spite of it he could still prevail over her as much as he did.

She often thought back to the moment their engagement first became reality, that flash of euphoric happiness that he liked and wanted her enough to pledge his name and all the privilege that came with it. But the fact remained that she could trust him no more now that he was her fiancé than when he had been merely a devious and amoral would-be lover.

When they were married, she would not try to deny his dominance in the bridal bower—in that particular arena he would probably always render her breathless and helpless. But that was the only weakness she would ever admit, lust of the body. Her mind would remain her own. And her demented and slightly shameful love she would carry as a secret to her grave.

It was the only path through the dangerous and, someday, very possibly heartbreaking terrain of her marriage.

*L*ouisa's epic success brought her family to London. Their departure from home was delayed two days by Frederica's continued refusal to leave her room. Frantic telegrams arrived for Louisa, who cabled back, *Tell Frederica Lord Wrenworth has the means and the connections to make her skin marble smooth again.*

Whether anything in the world could accomplish what she promised was immaterial. At twenty-seven Frederica was still a head-turningly beautiful woman—her problem had far less to do with dermatology than with perception.

"Your task, when they arrive, is to make her feel as lovely as the first star in the sky," she told Lord Wrenworth.

It was the first time they had seen each other since the day of their engagement—she'd been quite buried by the work that came with mounting a wedding, in three weeks, of the magnitude and splendor required by his station in life.

"What?" he mock-exclaimed. "I am out a twenty-room house plus eight hundred pounds a year. *And* I have to play the swain to the sister-in-law, too?"

He looked both commanding and delicious standing by the window of Lady Balfour's drawing room, bathed in the light of the afternoon. She was proud one moment, covetous the next, and then fearful the moment after that. It would always be like this, wouldn't it, being the wife of a man she loved but couldn't trust, whose true motives were as murky as the bottom of the sea?

"It will save you—well, me, actually—money on milk baths and exotic emollients later."

"And why would I want to save you money?" He rounded to the side of her padded chair and looked down at her. "Wouldn't I prefer it if you had to spend it all and come begging for more?"

She stared at his lips. He had not kissed her, ever. She would like him to, but she refused to ask. She even held back from reaching out and touching the hand he braced on the back of the chair. It was one thing to try to undermine his mastery of the situation with unwholesome speech and action, quite another to betray heartfelt desires that only further strengthened his hand.

"I couldn't spend eight hundred pounds a year if I tried."

"Don't let anyone hear you speak like that. My reputation will never recover if it is known that I married a woman who can make do with eight hundred pounds a year. Besides, what will I have to complain about at my club if my wife isn't suitably spendthrift?"

My wife. A wife could be the object of unabashed adoration or simply another nuisance in a man's life. Where would she fall along that continuum? And would his, if not black, then at least darkish grey heart ever be hers?

She folded her hands together primly. "Does no one complain about their wives being too insatiable in bed?"

His gaze swept her entire person. Her skin tingled. He wanted to do wicked things to her—it was the reaction she had hoped to provoke—but he touched her nowhere, not even the fabric of her enormous sleeves.

He took a seat opposite hers, his long legs taking up most

of the space between them. "Are you planning on being an overly enthusiastic wife?"

The way he studied her both absorbed and unsettled her. "Would you like me to be?"

"I am much more interested in the wife you cannot help being," he said, the firm last word on the subject.

He wanted to strip her bare in every way. Her naked body was only the beginning. From there, her undisguised thoughts. At last, her unhidden heart.

She took a sip of her tea, her fingers tight around the handle of the cup. "So . . . will you promise to shamelessly flatter Frederica?"

*T*wo days later, as Lord Wrenworth strolled into Lady Balfour's drawing room to meet Louisa's family, there was a reverent collective intake of breath, as if the Cantwell women were a group of mortals who had accidentally stumbled into the presence of Apollo himself.

Louisa, too, felt as if she were seeing him again for the very first time, her eyes blurring with the potency of his physical perfection.

You, sir, are a scoundrel.

As if he'd heard her thought, he glanced her way. Their gazes held, a pair of miscreants recognizing each other in a roomful of upstanding people.

It lasted only a moment, but the sweetness of that secret communion lingered: a joy that was also an ache in her heart. They were two of a kind—she wished she wouldn't need to always guard herself from him.

"May I present his lordship the Marquess of Wrenworth?" said Lady Balfour, still giddy from having pulled off the most spectacular match—or mismatch, as Louisa sometimes thought of it—in years. "Sir, my dear cousin Mrs. Cantwell, Miss Julia, Miss Matilda, Miss Cecilia, and Miss Cantwell."

Frederica, addressed as Miss Cantwell, as she was the eldest, kept her head lowered.

Lord Wrenworth approached her chair. She still sat with her head down.

Much to the surprise of everyone present, he lowered himself to one knee, so as to be level with her. Flustered, she turned her entire body to one side. He studied the angle she presented him, then calmly rounded to her other side.

Lady Balfour and Mrs. Cantwell both glanced toward Louisa, who could only shake her head to show that she had no idea what he was doing.

He straightened. "I understand you have been mourning the loss of your beauty for years, Miss Cantwell. What I do not understand is why your family has allowed such an act of rampant narcissism."

Frederica looked up in shock.

"The only imperfections I see are a few shallow pockmarks on your right cheek. I would never have permitted any sister of mine to brood over such minor blemishes for the better part of a decade.

"Had you come for a London Season, you would not have dislodged Mrs. Townsend from her perch as the most beautiful woman in London. You might not even have disturbed Miss Bessler's place third on that list. But make no mistake, you would have been mentioned in the same breath as those women. Instead, you have wasted your youth grieving for a gross misfortune that never took place: You are perhaps five percent less lovely than you would have been without the pockmarks, not fifty percent.

"Miss Louisa asked me to compliment you, but I shall not, not when you can go out and garner hundreds of them on your own with minimum effort. And if you will not, then there is nothing anyone can do for you—the matter is not with your face, but your head."

Without waiting for a response, he moved on. "My dear Miss Matilda, did you have a pleasant trip?"

*I*f anything, Louisa had expected a charm offensive—and a charm offensive this was not. He acted as if he'd never encountered such a ridiculous thing as Frederica considering her looks ruined.

It *was* ridiculous, except Frederica refused to believe her family when they tried to convince her otherwise, certain that her mother and sisters were lying out of love—or pity. But Lord Wrenworth's simple, almost brusque repudiation of the truth she'd long held to be self-evident had a far more dramatic effect on her. By the time he was saying his good-byes, Louisa caught Frederica looking surreptitiously at herself in the mirror hanging over the fireplace—when she'd studiously avoided any reflective surfaces for years upon years.

She was not the only one who noticed.

"Did you see that?" asked Cecilia, as soon as Frederica and Lord Wrenworth were both out of earshot.

"I saw that!" Mrs. Cantwell exclaimed. "Think of the wonderful match she can still make for herself, if only she would go out and let herself be seen. There is bound to be a rich widower somewhere who would be thrilled to marry her."

"Now, why didn't we talk to Frederica like that earlier?" said Cecilia.

"We did," Matilda pointed out. "We talked ourselves blue in the face. We said everything Lord Wrenworth said—we just didn't say it the way he did."

Lady Balfour nodded authoritatively. "And the way he said it made all the difference."

Mrs. Cantwell turned toward Louisa. "I hear they call you

the luckiest lady in London, my dear. I think you must be the luckiest lady in all of Britain."

That same general sentiment prevailed. Matilda, with whom Louisa shared a room at home, was the only one to say, before they went to sleep that night, "I know everyone else is saying how lucky you are, Louisa, but I think he is the lucky one. Just think how much Mr. Charles will envy him in having you for a wife."

Louisa reached over and hugged this most beloved sister. "Thank you, my dear."

"I hope you aren't only marrying him because we need the money," said Matilda. "You do like him, don't you?"

Louisa had never asked herself that question before. Fortunately—or unfortunately, depending how one looked at it—the answer was all too obvious. She did like him, his villainous ways included. In fact, his villainous ways might be the very reason she liked him so much, this darkly gleeful secret that he shared only with her.

"Not only do I like him," she answered, "I would have volunteered to be his mistress if I couldn't be his wife."

That sent Matilda into a fit of giggling. She hugged Louisa back. "I'm so glad to hear that. I am sure you will make him very happy, and I hope he will do the same for you."

Louisa had her doubts. She had no idea what made her fiancé happy or otherwise. Nor did she know how she would handle herself should the day come when he was no longer excited by the prospect of sleeping with her—when he would go on to bed the next woman who titillated him.

His heart in the palm of her hand might—*might*—act as insurance against this infelicitous eventuality. But where was the path to his heart? Did he have great trolls guarding it? Perhaps a fire-spewing dragon, chained before the castle gate?

Assuming, that was, The Ideal Gentleman had a heart at all.

* * *

I'm in your debt, sir," Louisa told Lord Wrenworth the next time she saw him.

A week had flown by since the day he was presented to her family. During that time, Frederica made a quick appearance at the afternoon tea party Lady Balfour had hosted to welcome the Cantwell ladies to London—*and* she'd gone to the dressmaker's in an open carriage, wearing only a veiled hat that didn't do much to hide her face at all.

"That is terrible. You will only ever be able to pay me with my own money," he said as he handed her up into his carriage. It was pouring again. Since they were now affianced, however, he was allowed to fetch her from the bookshop on his own. "But joking aside, do you mean to tell me that my words had some effect on your sister?"

"Yes. She now has a mirror permanently attached to her right hand and studies herself constantly."

"Sounds like symptoms of a mental disorder."

With his walking stick, he knocked on the ceiling of the carriage to signal the coachman that they were ready to go. Louisa had not seen him with that particular accessory since they were last in the town coach together, before his proposal. She couldn't stop herself from staring a moment at its ebony handle.

And he certainly didn't help matters by moving his thumb in a slow circle around that stylized jaguar head.

"Take your hand off it," she said.

He looked at her with a half smile that made everything inside her shift and drop, and set the walking stick aside. "Better?"

"No, not really. But what were you saying?"

He smiled again. "That your sister's new tendency to study herself constantly in a mirror sounds like an affliction."

"It does, but it is a much better affliction than the one she'd suffered for so long. We are all delighted. My mother especially—she is beginning to speak again of Frederica as the future spouse of a very wealthy man."

She looked at him sideways. "In fact, she thinks rather wistfully of you as that very wealthy man. I believe she is ever so slightly embarrassed that you will have me instead, when she has so much prettier daughters."

"Your mother actually thinks that any of her other daughters could possibly hold the slightest temptation for me?"

She ought not to, but she adored the dismissiveness of his tone.

"That is a very smug smile on your face, my dear, dear Louisa."

"That is a very smug sensation inside my heart, my dear, dear Lord Wrenworth."

The carriage turned a corner and his walking stick went sliding. They both reached out, but she caught it first.

"Maybe I ought to keep a better grip on it," he said.

She laid the walking stick across her lap. "There, I'll make sure it isn't up to mischief."

He glanced at the walking stick for a fraction of a second longer than completely appropriate, before he looked up into her eyes. "By the way, our marriage settlement is being drawn up as we speak. When you meet your solicitor again, he will tell you that you will have five thousand pounds a year in pin money."

She nearly dropped the walking stick. "Five thousand!"

"Don't be so loud, don't look so astonished, and don't, for goodness' sake, appear grateful. I would not be able to show my face in Society if it became known that my wife managed to squeeze only eight hundred pounds a year out of me."

"You offered me only five hundred," she said indignantly.

"And you were the worst negotiator ever, asking for only

a thousand from a man who has two hundred thousand a year. Shame on you."

Her face heated. "Well, you have always known that I am a country bumpkin."

"I thought you were ambitious. You were certainly more ambitious where telescopes were concerned."

"Your proposal caught me off guard."

"Excuses, excuses, Louisa. Were I less mindful of my reputation, you would have been robbed."

Hardly, when she would have given him the eleven pounds, eight shillings she'd studiously scraped together for emergencies, just so he didn't withdraw his offer.

Still, five thousand pounds a year, just for her. She wanted to laugh: She was now her own rich man.

Suddenly she remembered her deception. "Goodness gracious. There was something I was going to let you find out for yourself after the wedding. But at five thousand pounds a year, my conscience won't let me keep quiet anymore."

He cast her a sidelong look. "So your conscience was fine at eight hundred a year?"

"Did you really think my conscience was the sort that couldn't be told to keep quiet when only eight hundred a year was a stake?"

"True, morally upstanding you are not. So what dastardly secret am I going to find out now?"

Was that *fondness* in his voice? Why did she feel as if she were slowly melting? "I employ an array of bust improvers."

He shrugged, unperturbed. "So do at least half of the ladies in London. God does not make that many perfectly waspish figures."

"Well, my bust improver doesn't so much improve my bust as create one where none exists."

He glanced at her bosom. "So how much of that is actually yours?"

"Twenty-five percent. Thirty-five at most."

His eyes widened.

"I apologize!"

"Only sorry to be caught, I see."

"Well, I always did plan to make up for it."

"How?" Was that a barely suppressed smile in his voice? "Isn't it a bit late for you to develop a bigger pair?"

"I once heard Lady Balfour talk about her brother-in-law's mistress. She said the woman was completely flat-chested, but was willing to take part in all kinds of unnatural acts."

He made the sound of choked laughter. "Sorry, go on."

"So I thought . . ." She pulled at her collar. "I thought if I would consent to unnatural acts, then perhaps it would not be so difficult to achieve my husband's forgiveness in this matter. And, well, you are most certainly the sort to incline toward unnatural acts."

"Am I?"

"Are you not?" She couldn't tell whether she was asking out of hope or apprehension.

He didn't answer her. "Suppose you had become engaged to Mr. Pitt instead. Would you have just remained silent on the matter?"

"I would have started putting on progressively less exaggerated bust improvers and hoped that he didn't notice. But if he did, there were always the unnatural acts."

"He might never again believe anything you say the rest of your life."

She was hardly worried about Mr. Pitt. "What about *you*?"

"I have never trusted a word you said, since the very beginning."

"I do tell the truth *sometimes*," she pointed out, half pouting. "Besides, now that I have ensnared myself a rich lord and confessed my sins regarding my undergirding, I have no more lies to tell."

"Is that what you think marriage is, a hotbed of honesty and transparency?"

"Well, no . . ."

"Exactly. If I know you, you will go on lying, bust improvers or no."

"Then why did you propose to me?"

It always came back to this central mystery, this seemingly benign puzzle at the foundation of her current good fortune.

"Because you will never have headaches," he answered in apparent seriousness.

"I beg your pardon?"

His lips quivered. "Nothing. Just know that I am looking forward to being the most happily married man in the empire."

He smiled at her. And it was such a gorgeous smile that a few moments passed before she remembered that she, too, never trusted a word he said.

*W*hy *had* Felix proposed to her?

He had not answered her because he was coming to the realization that it was impossible to prevaricate when he couldn't pin down the truth.

Like affixing the position of stars in the sky—if one didn't know where one stood, the exercise became futile. An accurate knowledge of the truth was, for him at least, a necessary starting point for any well-crafted lie.

He, who could look people in the eye, smile, and spin a perfect yarn on the spot, was dodging her question because he had failed to find the real reason behind his action.

Was it merely because his conscience itched over what he'd said about Lord Firth? Because he pitied her? Because he'd always planned on marrying a country bumpkin anyway, and she was as good as any rosy-cheeked girl he could have in twenty years?

He was able to become The Ideal Gentleman because he knew every last one of his faults intimately—and therefore understood exactly how he ought to misdirect attention and create illusions.

But now he had based one of the most important decisions of his life on a shifting foundation.

Perhaps more alarmingly, he almost didn't care—not when there were bust improver–sized revelations to be had. The knowledge gave him a secret elation, an expansive pleasure, so that when they parted that day, he told her, "Go on wearing those bust improvers. In fact, have some bigger ones made."

Her expression of befuddlement and suspicion was also a thing of joy.

He further misdirected her attention by opening lines of credit at various establishments and gifting her mother a house that had thirty rooms. As if she weren't busy enough with a wedding breathing down her neck, she was now also required to inspect chairs, drapery, and side tables.

"If you are trying to make me drop dead from exhaustion, you are not far from succeeding," she accused him the last time they saw each other before the wedding.

No one else spoke to him as she did, with as much frankness and . . . could he call it affection? Yes, he decided, exasperated affection, but affection all the same. "Will you ever stop suspecting me of ulterior motives?"

"Yes, when you stop harboring as many of them as a Medici pope."

"Then whom will you suspect for fun?" he answered cheerfully. He usually enjoyed himself around people. Her company, however, he *adored*.

And tomorrow they would join in matrimony, for as long they both should live.

He had been trying not to think of the wedding night—no

need to torment himself lusting after what would soon be his. But sometimes he couldn't quite help the direction of his thoughts.

Dear, dear Louisa was in for a night to remember.

She cleared her throat. "You said you'd come to give me my wedding present."

So she'd caught him ogling her—forgivable for a man the day before his wedding. "Your wedding present is currently being set up in the conservatory at Huntington. After all your sisters and your mother each told me separately about the telescope, I had no choice but to buy one exactly like the one that slipped from your fingers."

Her eyes narrowed dramatically. "You mean you wouldn't have bought it for me on your own?"

"Of course not. I'd have bought you a much better one, but now you are stuck with your heart's desire."

Her scowl turned into a smile. "Well, I can live with that."

People smiled at him all the time, but when she did it, he felt . . . supremely accomplished.

The thought gave him pause. Wasn't that how he had felt earlier, when he'd made her testy?

He ignored that particular insight. "But it is hugely unsatisfying to be told that one's present is hundreds of miles away, so I brought you this." He took out a book from his pocket and handed it to her. "A telescope is useless unless you know what you are looking at."

The book was a first-edition copy of *Catalogue des Nébuleuses et des Amas d'Étoiles*, otherwise known as *Messier's Catalogue*.

She frowned. And suddenly he stood chest-deep in uncertainty, not knowing how his present would be received, fearing that it would be cast aside as soon as he left the room.

It wasn't even a real gift, just something he had taken from his study at Huntington on his way out to meet the train, after he was satisfied that the telescope had been correctly set up, because he thought it would please a girl who loved the stars.

"Don't worry if you can't read French." His tone was stilted and formal. "There are far more comprehensive catalogs and star maps published these days."

"I'm sure there are better works published these days, but this is the one I have always wanted to have," she said, her eyes downcast, her fingers rubbing against the binding of the catalog.

He wasn't sure he believed her. "Then why do you look so consternated?"

She turned the book around once in her hands. "Because it disconcerts me that you can so easily guess my heart's desire."

All the apprehension drained away, replaced by a startling buoyancy. How silly he'd been to be prey to such needless concerns. "I am to be your husband. I should be able to read your heart's desire."

She looked up, her gaze meeting his. "You are the sort of man who is just as likely to grant a woman her heart's desire as to torment her with it."

And she was the one woman who knew that he was the furthest thing from The Ideal Gentleman, yet still wept when she thought he would never have anything more to do with her. "May I remind you that you were willing to take me and my lady-tormenting ways for a measly eight hundred pounds a year."

That brought a reluctant smile to her face. "I haven't been able to make a single good decision since I fell in lust with you."

Her sexual infatuation with him had always gratified him immensely. Yet for some reason, this iteration of the fact didn't thrill him as much as it usually did. It was as if he wanted more.

What more, he couldn't say—if the girl was any more willing, they would be copulating in the streets. Perhaps he was simply impatient to at last pin her underneath him, and watch her face as her pleasure gathered.

"I will leave you to study your new book then."

As he turned to go, she took hold of his hand. They touched as infrequently as they ever did, and the sensation of her skin on his was almost numbing in its intensity.

"I do not mean to imply that I am not grateful," she said.

"But you are not," he pointed out.

"I am. I am just also wary, as any woman with half a brain ought to be, when it comes to you."

And with that, she kissed him on his cheek. "I will see you at the wedding."

CHAPTER 8

The wedding was a tremendous success, not that it was ever intended to be anything else. The bride's gown, the wedding breakfast, and the greenery that filled the interior of the cathedral—each aspect of the occasion was praised as sumptuous yet tasteful. Everything The Ideal Gentleman's wedding ought to be.

"I am pleased to have been accessory to one of the most perfectly orchestrated ceremonies of our time," said Felix's new wife, when they were at last alone in his private rail coach, speeding north toward Huntington.

It was her way of telling him that this entire ceremony had been all about him—his good name, his stature, his importance.

He smiled. "And thus concludes my reign as the most eligible young man of the realm. It is the end of an era."

She rolled her eyes.

He smiled more broadly. "The same could be said of you. When did you start preparing for your London Season?"

"Eight years ago."

"And now that, too, is behind you. What plans do you have for yourself?"

She straightened the sleeve of her new traveling dress, a stylish, yet understated piece in charcoal grey—a garment that did not draw attention to itself, yet upon close examination, proved to be of flawless construction and exemplary fit. He did not believe that it had come by this state of inconspicuous perfection by accident: She would have given quite a bit of thought to how she wished to appear as Lady Wrenworth and must have decided that she preferred to let him have the limelight, but also to present herself in such a way that no one should be able to find fault in his choice of wife.

"Between fittings for my gown and trousseau, shopping with my family, and answering all the questions from Lady Balfour and your secretary concerning the wedding," she said, straightening her other sleeve, "I haven't had a minute to think about the future."

"Liar. You'd stop breathing before you stop preparing for what's coming next. What is it you are scheming about now?"

Her eyes were wide and limpid as she answered, "I have a thirty-room house, five thousand pounds a year, and a good telescope, not to mention *Messier's Catalogue*. There is nothing left worthy of maneuvers."

He rested his head on his palm. "But you are ambitious. I'll bet you have tried to read astronomical journals, when you could get your hands on them. And I'll bet you found it difficult, because you have had a woeful education, particularly in the area of mathematics."

"I am not innumerate."

"Oh, I'm sure you can calculate a household budget and a man's wealth very well. But can you solve an equation?"

She looked as if he'd accused her of rampant honesty. "Of course I can solve an equation. I can solve paired equations."

"What about quadratic equations?"

She flattened her lips. "No."

"Do you know anything about trigonometry?"

"No."

"Non-Euclidean geometry?"

"No."

He set one hand beneath his chin and considered her.

"You make me nervous," she said quietly.

"Because now I know you would like to be fluent in calculus?"

She sighed. "Because you read me like an open book, when I know I am not. I am no more transparent than a slab of slate—or at least I shouldn't be."

With anyone else, he would simply smile and let that be the end of it. But it was his wedding day, he had vowed to cherish her, and he was feeling very charitable.

"Then let me tell you this. Everything I need to know about you, I already learned the first night we met. And yet after I've read you like an open book all this while, you still remain something of a conundrum."

This mollified her enough for the set of her shoulders to relax. "So . . . I don't trust you and you don't understand me."

He laughed despite himself. "No wonder we get along so well."

A beat of silence passed. She turned her face slightly to the side and glanced at him out of the corner of her eyes. "So what should we do now that we've established that our marriage is based on ignorance and general misgiving?"

He leaned forward. "Do you play cards, my dear Lady Wrenworth?"

* * *

*S*he not only played cards, but proved to be one of the best Felix had ever played against.

"Where did you learn to play like this?" he exclaimed after she had taken yet another round from him.

"At home. We've no books and no instruments—guess what we did to pass time."

"Do you count cards?"

"Of course," she answered, as if there were no other possible choice.

"And you are the best player at home, no doubt?"

"No. I can hold my own with Cecilia and Julia, but Matilda is a terror at the table."

That surprised him. "Really?"

"Had she been a man, we'd have sent her to Monte Carlo to win a fortune."

"So what did you use as stake when you played at home?"

"Stake? What sort of question is that?" She shot him a look full of scorn. "We played to *win*. Now will you please let me concentrate?"

He wished it had been possible to capture her expression of contempt. For a poor fortune hunter's daughter, she could rival a dowager duchess in haughtiness, when she was in the mood. "Certainly, Lady Wrenworth."

She had already lowered her gaze to her cards, but now she slowly looked up. "You won't stop calling me Louisa, will you?"

Little things like this made her the conundrum she was: that she would tell him openly that she did not trust him, and then in the next breath demand this intimacy from him.

"There is a time and a place for it," he told her.

She gestured at the private rail coach, empty except for the two of them. "We are already in private."

He only repeated, "There is a time and a place for it."

Her cheeks colored—neither the time nor the place was too far away now.

"Right." She cleared her throat. "Your turn, sir."

*I*t was rather difficult to concentrate after that, but since Louisa wasn't the only one distracted, she still defeated her husband soundly.

"Good thing you only play to win," he teased her. "Remind me to never put any money on the table."

"As long as you say nothing to your friends. I am not averse to taking *their* money."

"I'd like to see you go up against Lady Tremaine. She is quite the player."

She made a face. "Your former paramour Lady Tremaine?"

"My current good friend Lady Tremaine. I lost five hundred pounds to her once. You will be my vengeance and seize the sum from her—with high, compounding interest, of course."

"Are you sure I am a better player than she?"

"Her advantage over most men is that she has a noteworthy chest, which she displays shamelessly when she sits down to a card table. You, however, will not be distracted by a pair of breasts."

Louisa suddenly had the image of him with his hands on Lady Tremaine's noteworthy chest—and it made her feel spectacularly underendowed. "Is she invited to your house party?"

"She is always invited to my house party. But she is out of the country this month, sampling the male species all over Scandinavia."

"But if she comes, you will be distracted by her breasts?"

"It's nothing to do with her. I sometimes find myself staring at sculptures of bare-breasted women around Huntington—speaking of which . . ."

They drove past the gate of the estate.

"Welcome to your new home," he said softly. "I hope you like it."

She had, of course, thoroughly studied the passage concerning Huntington in Lady Balfour's book on the great manors of the realm. But dry, matter-of-fact descriptions could not possibly capture the charm and tranquillity of the place, all rolling hills and green glens.

Then the land opened and there stood the manor, grandly and dramatically illuminated by the rich, golden light of sunset. It was a Tudor house that had, during the course of its long life, acquired a lavish, baroque flair. The once plain stone front now boasted an elaborate cupola and twelve pilasters that rose three stories high from a gorgeous terrace accessed by double-returned flights of steps. Twenty-seven windows, nine to each bay, shone down upon the circular reflection pool in the center of the formal French garden.

"It's almost unfair," she told him. "The master of this place should look like the Hunchback of Notre Dame."

"Sometimes he does," said her husband, pulling on his gloves. "When you visit the family gallery, you will see that my ancestors are not the most prepossessing lot."

There was no time for her to ponder his statement. The carriage had come to a stop before the manor, and it was time for her to meet the staff.

Afterward, she was led upstairs to her apartment, which had a private bath with walls and floor of blue and white marble, and a sunken bath with hot and cold running water.

She made sure to betray little of her marvel as her new maid ran her bath and showed her how to use the faucets. But when she was alone, she covered her mouth and screamed a little.

It was too much, her good fortune.

She stepped into this decadent bath, lowered herself into the perfumed water, tilted her head back, and felt . . . impatient. She smiled to herself. At least in this respect, there was nothing improper about her marriage. She would have married him as long as he had enough money to support Matilda. And if he hadn't, they would have found a way somehow.

Schemers and schemers alike, the two of them.

And tonight they were headed to a place where she would have complete confidence in him: the marriage bed.

She finished her bath humming.

*I*t was becoming more and more difficult for Felix to be objective about his new wife.

If his first impression was correct, then she was just a passably pretty woman who was very skillful at presenting herself to her best advantage. But as she entered the drawing room tonight, glowing, he could not remember a thing about her artifice.

She was stunning.

"You are a vision, Lady Wrenworth," he whispered in her ear as they walked arm in arm toward the dining room.

"And you would have fortune-hunted most successfully if you'd had to do it, what with your charm, your wiles, and your sweet, Apollonian face."

He felt an unfamiliar flutter in his stomach. "That's the best compliment I've ever had before dinner."

"I hope to also compliment you a great deal after dinner. Will dinner be long?"

He laughed softly. "No, dinner will not be long. The kitchen has been instructed to not overtire you with too many courses, as you've had a long day and would naturally prefer to retire early."

"Naturally," she answered as he pulled out her chair himself.

He would have never considered himself the sort of man who touched his wife while there were others present, but of their own volition, his fingers trailed across her nape, as if the softness of her skin had acted as a magnet.

She expelled a breath.

He walked to his seat with as much nonchalance as he could manage. "If you will look out of the windows, I believe you can see the Greek folly."

Especially illuminated tonight, for her pleasure.

Her eyes widened. "Dear me, those are some very slender columns. They conceal nothing, do they?"

"They are not quite as slender as that," he reassured her. "The folly appears closer at night than it actually is."

"When will your friends be here?" she asked.

"Day after tomorrow."

There had been no question that they would honeymoon at Huntington and that his summer house party would proceed as usual. How else was he to make her erotic dreams come true?

She sucked in a breath. "It is a *fascinating* pavilion."

And she was a fascinating woman. He could not imagine now what he had been thinking when he'd believed he'd marry a girl twenty years his junior with a tremendous pair of breasts and nothing upstairs.

"I have a Roman folly, too, you know," he informed her grandly.

And much to the befuddlement of his footmen, they both burst into laughter.

CHAPTER 9

They reached the end of dinner in forty minutes, a record at Huntington. She rose and withdrew with a significant look his way. *Don't make me wait.*

But he did make her wait—she ought to know better than anyone else that he was that sort of bastard. He enjoyed his glass of Armagnac with a smile—and perhaps a leer—on his face, thinking of her willingly spread thighs. He walked up to his apartment imagining the moans of her helpless pleasure. And as he slowly prepared himself for bed, in his head he could already hear her pleading for more.

And more. And even more.

He barely managed to duck a flying hairbrush as he opened the connecting door.

She stood at her vanity table, still in her evening gown, her hair loose, her face screwed in displeasure. "I told you not to make me wait."

"My goodness." He laughed. "I didn't marry just a liar, but also a virago."

She turned her head away with great, hair-tossing drama. "I am not in an amorous mood anymore."

"What a thing to tell a man who's come to make love to you," he said, stalking toward her. "And why, pray tell, if you were in such an amorous mood, did you keep on your dinner gown?"

"I dismissed my maid before I left for dinner. I was planning to use you for a variety of menial tasks tonight—including brushing my hair, by the way, which I had to do myself, because you were probably out in the gardens staring at big-busted statues."

He pinned her between himself and the vanity table. "Quite wrong. I was picturing *your* bust and hoping it would be spectacularly diminutive."

He gathered her hair to one side so he could press a kiss to her nape. She expelled a whimperlike breath. "Why would you want me to be *that* flat-chested?"

He kissed her earlobe, delighting in the tremor beneath her skin. "Because I like secrets, the bigger the better—and the size of this secret is inversely proportional to the size of your breasts, my dear, dear Louisa."

The buttons on the back of her dinner gown presented very little challenge. She watched him in the mirror as he undid every last one of them, her lips parted, her gaze heavy lidded. He extricated her from the gown and started on her corset.

"Where is this mythical bust improver of yours? I'm most anxious to make its acquaintance."

"This one is built into the corset."

He had now loosened the corset enough to slip it over her head—and examine its amply augmented interior. "Well done."

"Thank you—I suppose."

"Now, if you will allow me to help you out of these petticoats, we will be able to tackle your combination and see just how much you've exaggerated."

"Can't you see that I am practically concave on top?"

The petticoats slid to the floor. He turned her around. "Promises, promises."

She bit a corner of her lower lip. "I wish I could tell my mother your enthusiasm concerning my hollow chest. She was quite apprehensive during our 'talk.' I do believe she barely restrained herself from suggesting Frederica, who needs no help filling bodices, as a substitute bride."

He rubbed a finger along the neckline of her combination. "Your mother is proving herself an exceptionally silly woman. Did she manage to tell you anything useful?"

"No. I believe you taught me more about the male anatomy with your walking stick."

They tittered, she winking conspiratorially at him. He was still smiling when he began to toy with the topmost button on her combination. She was so very pretty with her hair tumbled all about her in fat, bouncy curls, her limpid eyes fixed on him, her gaze on his hand one moment, on his eyes the next.

He, on the other hand, watched only her face. The size of her breasts was quite irrelevant—what excited him was the transparency of her desire, the depth of her hunger, and the thoroughness of her infatuation.

Her skin, however, *was* rather exceptionally fine-grained and smooth beneath his fingers. And the expectancy in her eyes, that tinge of nervousness, was most gratifying—she wanted to please him with her body.

With almost a sense of noblesse oblige, he glanced down.

Somewhere in the back of his mind was an almost inaudible voice, reminding him that he had lost his objectivity where she was concerned, and therefore ought to temper his reaction with a healthy dose of skepticism.

But he wasn't listening. All he heard was the sudden roar of blood in his veins. And all he saw was perfection, sheer, absolute perfection.

Small breasts, yes, but high, firm, and marvelously shaped, with the most beautiful nipples he had ever seen, rosy and most eagerly erect. His mouth went dry. His hand reached out and caught one nipple, so firm, yet so incredibly soft and satiny.

His heart pounded. His breaths turn ragged. And he became so hard, so fast, he was light-headed with this southward rush of blood.

He looked back at her face. Did he used to plan, step-by-step, a watertight seduction of this miraculous creature? He must have. He vaguely recalled things he meant to do to her, words he meant to whisper in her ears.

But the rawness that had overtaken him made him incapable of such finesse. His hand behind her nape, he yanked her to him and kissed her. Ravaged her. Somewhere inside he knew that such pure devouring was all wrong for a first kiss. But she didn't seem to mind. Her hands dug into his scalp; her lips fastened upon his as if she were trapped underwater and he the reed that brought her precious air.

Without breaking the kiss, he lifted and carried her to bed. Still without breaking the kiss, he rid her of the combination altogether. Greedily he touched her, incapable of strategy, or even tactics. All he wanted was more. More of her heart-stoppingly smooth skin, more of her intoxicatingly sweet mouth, more of her unbearably supple bottom.

His fingers slipped between her thighs—and the grunt of helpless lust he heard was his own: She was as ready as if he had been preparing her for hours. Days.

The entire Season had been one excruciatingly drawn-out loveplay.

His lips never leaving hers, he touched her in that secret place. She moaned; she writhed; she kissed him with a desperate fervor. Then suddenly she was crying out, her body tensing.

A heartbeat later he was deep inside her, filling her with

his essence, convulsing with a pleasure that turned him inside out.

The tremors of his paroxysm lasted and lasted, draining him to the last drop—or so it seemed. Yet he found himself still rock hard, still beside himself with the need to possess the delicious woman beneath him.

He kissed her cheek, her lips, her chin. He did not neglect her throat or her shoulders. And at last he tasted her delicate nipples. The moans he drew from her made him thrust into her with the force of a battering ram.

She gasped.

He forced his lower body to hold utterly still. His unsteady hand caressed her hair; his lips pressed into the tenderness just beneath her jawline. She smelled faintly of flowers, of fresh, dew-covered petals.

"Tell me to stop and I will." His voice was hoarse, nothing like how he usually sounded.

And his eyes were tightly shut. Dimly he remembered that he'd meant to look his fill of her as he brought her to one trembling peak after another. But the sensations of her person were all he could handle; the sight of it would undo him altogether.

"I never want you to stop," she whispered, kissing his ear as she spoke, jolting him with another surge of lust. "Never."

Her hands gripped his arms. Her thighs parted wider beneath him. And dear God, she lifted her hips, as if trying to draw him deeper.

The pleasure of her—he was mindless with it. He invaded her again and again, her whimpers of pleasure a fire in his blood. Her name escaped his throat; he could not stop telling her how exquisite she was and how much he craved her.

When her body tightened voluptuously around his cock, he lost any and all control he might have still possessed. And gave himself up to the most explosive pleasure he had ever known.

* * *

*T*he night was nothing of what Louisa had anticipated—
and everything she could have hoped for.

Knowing him, she had prepared herself to be the willing
but hapless mouse in a cat-and-mouse game. He would tease
and torment her to the limit of her arousal—and probably
make her beg for everything along the way: kisses, touches,
any kind of satisfaction.

But this unbridled lover who came out of nowhere was so
much more gratifying for her vanity.

And the things he said to her. Some of the words she had
never heard in her life—and none of them she had expected
to pass his urbane lips. So raunchy, dirty, and, well, *raw*.

So she *could* drive him out of his mind—and with her
puny chest, no less.

She smiled.

She might have giggled a little.

When he pulled away from her, she turned onto her side
to snuggle close to him.

"Did I hurt you?" he asked, his arm over his eyes.

"You can't make an omelet without breaking eggs," she
told him cheerfully.

It had stung at first, and she was still rather sore, but it
was nothing she couldn't handle. Especially not when there
were mind-boggling pleasures to be had, such as when
he rolled her nipple on his tongue, touched that place between
her legs with his finger, *and* drove into her all at the same
time.

She kissed his shoulder. "So . . . we will do this all night
long, right?"

Unless she was very much mistaken, when they'd discussed the Greek folly—the Greek folly public copulation,
as she termed it—he had told her that it would be only the

beginning of the night. That afterward he was taking her to bed and keeping her there until dawn.

She could see no reason for them not to pleasure each other until the small hours of their wedding tonight.

"Absolutely not. That would be execrably inconsiderate of me."

She removed his arm from his face. "Not if I want it."

He opened his eyes. She'd never seen him like this, tousled and slightly glazed, which she found enormously appealing. It made him seem more human, and less like a djinn whose intentions could veer from malice to mischief—and back—in the blink of the eye.

He reached out, slowly, almost reluctantly, to play with a strand of her hair. "Your body is not meant to be abused like that. Not tonight, in any case."

Pouting, she pushed away from him. But the distance was also meant to give him a far better look at her naked person. If it worked once . . .

He exhaled audibly.

She lifted her hair out of the way, so that it would not conceal her bosom. The motion drew her breasts high and taut. And as he stared, her nipples tightened.

As if in a trance, he slid a palm across one nipple. She whimpered. He placed it between two fingers and played with it. She moaned.

And now he did what she really wanted: took her nipple into his mouth. The man had a most talented tongue, and wrought unutterable pleasures.

She wrapped her legs around his waist. "You make me willing to do anything with you—and for you."

Her flattery did not go to waste. The next second he was inside her again, hot and huge. She pulled him in for a kiss, and did not let him go until her pleasure was winding tighter and tighter and she was struggling to breathe.

It was like the sky falling.

Beyond, the stars.

*F*elix couldn't stop touching his wife.

Not lasciviously, and not with the intention to arouse—at least, not at the moment. At the moment it was only for the pleasure of his hand on her skin. He also traced the sweep of a brow, the hollow of a cheek, and the outline of her bottom lip. She kissed him on the pad of his finger, her eyes smiling, but also beginning to close with drowsiness.

"It is not even midnight, Marchioness. Are you already in your dotage?"

"You, sir, obviously know nothing about weddings. I had to get up at the crack of dawn to look worthy of upholding The Ideal Gentleman's boutonniere, let alone his name."

"And here I thought you would demand to be made love to at least twice as many times."

"Who says I won't? This is just a nap to refresh myself," she retorted, though her words had become slow and mumbly.

He leaned forward and kissed her on her forehead, her cheek, and the tip of her nose. By the time he had kissed her on her chin, her eyes had closed completely—and his body was stirring anew.

He wanted to nibble every inch of her person, especially the nooks and crannies. He wanted to make her moan and writhe in her sleep. He wanted to repeat yet again the brain-melting pleasure of coming deep inside her.

Not that he would actually do any such thing—the poor girl clearly needed her rest. He restricted his hand to her hair, her arm, and her back, his mind on how he would wake her up at dawn, in a way she was certain to approve.

She shifted.

"Sorry," he murmured. His stiffly starched cuff might have scraped her slightly.

His stiffly starched cuff? He was still wearing his *shirt*?

He looked down at himself. He had come to her room in his shirtsleeves and his trousers, and he still had on both—the shirt buttoned, the trousers pushed below his hips, but no farther.

He didn't know which was more shocking, that he had been in such desperate haste that he hadn't disrobed, or that he had been in such a state of erotic intoxication that he hadn't realized.

His cock twitched, heavy with lust and straining toward her. A moment ago the sight would have amused him, and perhaps even made him smug—he hadn't been eighteen for ten years, but he was proving he could still get it up half a dozen times a night.

Now, however, the sight bothered him. He pulled up his trousers and shoved his member inside. The discomfort that caused only served to underscore the dismay that was beginning to coalesce in his head.

What had happened?

He'd always intended to fully enjoy every second of his wedding night—but with a certain serenity, as if at the same time he was making love to her, he were also observing the proceedings from a suitable distance.

He clearly recalled the nearly entire hour he'd deliberately whiled away after she'd left the dinner table—he had been cool, calm, and detached. Even after he'd entered her room, he'd retained complete mastery over himself, bantering with her, disrobing her at a most leisurely pace.

He got out of the bed. She made a sound at the loss of his warmth. He pulled the counterpane over her and tucked it snugly around her person.

A sight of her nipples, had that been all it had taken? Did that mean, if he averted his eyes from her bare breasts in the future, he would be safe from such a comprehensive loss of control?

As he looked down upon her, however, with the counterpane up to her chin and not an inch of skin below her face visible, he couldn't wait to touch her again. To kiss her. To hear her whisper, *You make me willing to do anything.*

He took a step back from the bed, then another. He could deal with an occasional loss of control. What he could not countenance, under any circumstances, was this kind of covetousness.

But how had he fallen into this kind of covetousness in the first place?

He gazed at her another moment and extinguished the lights. In his apartment, he pulled on a pair of shoes, shrugged into a jacket, and stepped out the door. The corridors of the manor were dark and silent. He walked without a hand candle, long accustomed to the shadows of his own house.

He meant to work for some time in his observatory, located inside the cupola he'd added to the manor. But all he did was pace back and forth on the roof, his fingers pressed to his temples, an occasional profanity leaving his lips.

He had been The Ideal Gentleman too long, and his success had annihilated his sense of caution. When he couldn't stop thinking about her after their first meeting, when he began accepting invitations with the specific goal of being in her vicinity, when he persuaded Mr. Pitt to leave town straightaway after receiving his parents' cable, so he could take the latter's place at the Tenwhestle dinner that evening— he could have stepped back at any point and seen his idiocy for what it was.

Even if none of those actions had struck him as outlandish and entirely unlike himself, he should have reined to a full stop when he began concocting the scheme of making her his mistress. It appalled him now to think he had formulated, let alone tendered, such a proposal. How had the sheer inanity of the idea not struck him like a bludgeon to the head?

Had he recognized it sooner . . .

He had. All along, the saner parts of himself had been issuing warnings that it was a terrible idea to fixate on this girl. And all along, doltishly preoccupied with her, he had ignored all the danger signals.

While telling himself that he was only after a bit of perverse fun, as if Captain Ahab had somehow come to the belief that he was only a recreational angler, even as he pursued his obsession all over the seven seas, a harpoon at the ready.

Obsession. He winced at the word, but there was no denying the truth: He had been obsessed for months.

He stopped midstride, horrified. To assuage his conscience and make sure that she was not forced to marry a man beneath her station, all he'd had to do was settle the thousand pounds a year and the house on her, but without the condition that she repay him in bed.

He would not have missed the outlay. She would not have suffered for knowing him. And he would have been free of her.

But the thought hadn't even occurred to him until now.

Of course not. There was no idiocy bigger than that committed by a man who believed himself the cleverest creature under the sun.

His head throbbed. He didn't want to stand here, flogging himself until the sun came up. He wanted to go back to his marriage bed and make love to her again, and let her sweet eagerness make everything better.

Dear God. At this juncture, he still wanted to be closer to her.

What was the distance between obsession and love? And

how near was he to that disastrous tipping point? Would he wake up tomorrow, look into her eyes, and simply accept his fate?

No.

Why not? asked an insensate part of him. *She adores you. The real you.*

She does not know the real me, you moron.

A man who wanted nothing had the world at his feet. A man who yearned for something—anything—was doomed to disappointment and heartache.

And he'd had more than enough disappointment and heartache for a lifetime.

He pressed his knuckles into his forehead. He wanted her much too much, but it was not the end of the world. Not yet, in any case. Given time and distance, sexual ardor would cool, both on his part and hers.

Until then, he would stay away from her.

CHAPTER 10

$\mathcal{L}$ouisa was vaguely aware of the thunderstorm that took place at some point in the night. She pulled the bedcover tighter around her person and let the percussion of the rain lull her into a deeper sleep.

She woke up to a sunlit morning. A few seconds of disorientation followed as she stared first at the unfamiliar canopy, and then around to the unfamiliar everything.

It was the morning after her wedding. And she had been most suitably ravished, if she did say so herself. She covered her mouth and giggled.

The man had such a nefarious influence on her. First he turned her into a nymphomaniac—that was the scientific term for a sexually insatiable young lady, wasn't it?—now he turned her into a giggler.

She had never been a giggler. She had always been the girl who looked to the consequences, the one who minded the budget and gave admonishments when Cecilia or Julia overspent their allowance. The boring one—according to Cecilia, at least—like the middle Bennet sister, except without the mediocre piano playing and the constant sermonizing.

She imagined saying to Cecilia, *At least I am really good in bed*, and giggled anew.

She stopped only when Betsey, her new maid, entered with a cup of hot cocoa on a tray. Then the two of them giggled together at the sight of all the clothes strewn about the room. Then yet again when she had to put on her dressing robe under the covers, so that she didn't emerge from her bed stark naked.

As she lowered herself into a hot bath, the place between her legs stung rather potently for a moment. But then she was quite all right.

Ready for more.

She was going to need two of him, she thought to herself, which, of course, led to even more giggling.

When she was properly coiffed and gowned, a footman respectfully showed her the way to the breakfast room. She envisioned her husband looking up over the top of his newspaper with a slight leer on his face. She would, of course, leer right back at him. And provided there was privacy, she would tell him her new theory that he would perhaps prove not quite man enough for her.

He was not there in the breakfast room.

The scoundrel. She would bet that it was intentional. It would be just like the man who'd waited an entire hour to come to her last night to tease her with his absence the next day.

But since this was her first day at Huntington, there was much to occupy her. She spent her morning doing her best to stop her jaw from dropping repeatedly: The estate was beyond anything she had known in scope. There were fifty indoor servants, forty gardeners, thirty men in the stables, and a gamekeeper's staff that took care of the pheasant population—which was somewhere in the vicinity of forty-five hundred, she was told.

It was a good thing she did not have to lead this army of servants directly, her only experience with staff being regularly pleading with Sally, the Cantwell cookmaid, to not abandon them, and taking on some of Sally's chores—behind Mrs. Cantwell's back, of course—to lighten the maid's load, since they couldn't afford to pay her more.

Here the much more detailed taxonomy of duties and positions gave rise to a pyramid of authorities. Situated at its very top, Louisa needed only to consult the housekeeper, Mrs. Pratt, the butler, Sturgess, and the chef, Monsieur Boulanger, all of whom seemed frightfully competent in their respective domains.

A tour of the domestic offices dazzled her; the belowstairs operation of a great country estate was a thing of military efficiency. The kitchen in itself was bigger than the house she had lived in with her mother and sisters. The laundry department consisted of a washhouse, a drying room, a mangling room, an ironing room, a folding room, and a laundry maids' room arranged in a smart sequence so that dirty clothes went in at one end and clean clothes came out at the other. Louisa blushed, realizing that her love-soiled sheets were about to make quite a public trip through the facilities.

Mrs. Pratt, after briskly showing off her storeroom, china closet, and stillroom, took Louisa to see the rest of the great mansion. Louisa had been forewarned that Huntington was open to the public, but still it was rather startling to see tourists craning their necks round and round to take in all the architectural details and fine furnishings of the immaculately kept state apartments, whose ornately draped beds had once received crowned heads. The room she had spent the night in, however, was shielded from curious eyes, being situated in the private family wing.

The long gallery was empty of tourists when she came to it. As she viewed the portraits of her husband's ancestors, she remembered what he'd said to her the evening before, that sometimes the master of Huntington did look like the Hunchback of Notre Dame.

The thirteen Marquesses of Wrenworth who had preceded him—and a number of viscounts before the family was elevated to a marquessate—were indeed a plain bunch.

The way Mrs. Pratt explained it, though not in exactly so many words, was that the men of the line had more often than not been pragmatic in marriage, and preferred to choose wives with great fortunes over those with beautiful eyes.

"But you can see, my lady, that was not the case with his lordship's father," said Mrs. Pratt, stopping before the late marchioness's portrait.

Louisa could see that indeed. Portraits, in her opinion, rarely did great beauties justice. Even so, one could see that her late mother-in-law must have been quite stunning. "My goodness. Did you ever see her in person, Mrs. Pratt?"

"No, ma'am. I came to Huntington in 1880 as an underhousekeeper, several years after her ladyship had passed away."

Louisa was surprised—for some reason she thought Mrs. Pratt had spent most of her life in the family's employ. Was not such more or less the case at the great houses, that the upper servants, with the sometime exception of the French cook, rose up the ranks?

"His lordship asked that I show you the library last, ma'am," said Mrs. Pratt.

Because he knows it would be my favorite?

But that was not the reason. She had been wondering where exactly was the conservatory, the fabled location of her new telescope. As it turned out, the conservatory was accessed via the library.

And there, the wedding present for which her entire family had begged—very prettily, no doubt. It was worth any amount of begging, standing serenely at a corner of the conservatory and gleaming with perfect craftsmanship.

"This particular panel can be swiveled open," said Mrs. Pratt, pointing at the sheet of glass directly before the telescope.

Louisa walked around the telescope, agog at its beauty and, at the same time, confused as to why he had chosen to have it placed in the conservatory. The telescope had an equatorial mount, which allowed the instrument to remain fixed on any celestial object that had a diurnal motion, by driving one axis at a constant speed. That lovely feature would be quite wasted at this particular location, given that once the telescope had turned a few degrees, it would be looking at the fronds of a palm tree.

Next to the telescope was a small bench. On the bench was an envelope marked, *To Lady Wrenworth*. She picked it up and turned it around—it had been sealed with her husband's signet ring. Inside, a piece of stationery that bore the same crest.

I hope you like what you see. W.

He certainly possessed much prettier penmanship than hers. And more cryptic intentions. What could she see from here?

She looked at the note again. It was dated three days ago. So he had been here, personally supervising the setup of the telescope, knowing full well it would be completely underutilized.

And the angle the telescope had been set at was also too low. What could she see, so close to the horizon, except perhaps Venus and a rising moon?

She removed the covers from the eyepiece and the lens and looked—and gasped.

The telescope pointed straight at the Roman folly. At first she thought there were two people on the belvedere, but they were only dress dummies, one covered in a large swath of pink fabric, the other in something that resembled a man's evening jacket—the way she and Lord Wrenworth had been dressed when they first discussed being naked and up to no good upon that particular belvedere.

She barely restrained herself from laughing aloud. The man's villainy was adorable.

She walked into the dining room hoping to thank him, only to learn that she would have to take luncheon by herself, too, as his lordship was out inspecting roofs that had been damaged by the storm during the night. She sighed. Adorable villainy and responsible stewardship—could a woman ask for any more in a husband?

After luncheon, she made a dent in the mountain of thank-you notes that she must write, approved menus for the next week, then spent an enjoyable hour in the library, where she discovered an entire dossier of older issues of *Astronomical Register: A Medium of Communication for Amateur Observers and All Others Interested in the Science of Astronomy.*

A most pleasant start to married life, she must admit.

Which would only become pleasanter as day turned into night.

*F*elix stared at the billiard table.

In his mind his wife was stretched out on the green baize, naked. *Take me*, she would murmur. *I have been waiting all day.*

He struck the cue ball with great violence, scattering the fifteen red balls on the table.

His tenants had been surprised to see him, a man only one day wed, away from his house and his new wife to see to their roofs. They congratulated him and tried to hide their puzzlement. He explained without being asked, in his best happy-rueful air, that the new missus had taken it into her head to get to the running of the household as soon as possible, without him around to provide distractions.

A lift of the brow that suggested he'd give plenty of distractions later satisfied those simple, deferential folks. They wanted him to be well shagged and happy. But he could not be both, at least not with her, now that he realized the sway he'd allowed her to hold over him.

"You can teach me how to play. Then you won't need to play alone."

He looked up sharply. The billiard room was a masculine refuge—that he was inside signaled he didn't wish to be disturbed by any woman.

She stood by the door in a very pretty pastel blue dress, the expression in her very pretty eyes essentially stating that she would be more than happy to lie down on the table, naked.

"I saw the belvedere from the conservatory, by the way. The dress dummies were a stroke of genius."

He should have known something was wrong with him when he had driven the dress dummies out to the foot of the hill and then carried them the rest of the way by himself. His excuse had been that he hadn't wanted to make such strange requests of his servants, but in truth he had enjoyed every step of his silly little gesture.

So much that he didn't even mind the repeated trips between the house and the belvedere, so that the dummies would appear at just the correct angle when she put her eye to the telescope.

"What do you say we pay them a visit tomorrow?" she went on, her voice husky.

He could see her standing on the belvedere, her elbows braced against the top of the half wall, looking over her shoulder at him. She would look perfectly respectable from the waist up, her blouse buttoned to the chin, her jacket similarly closed, her hair neat, her hat prim. But the lower half of her would be entirely naked, except for her walking boots and stockings, perhaps. And she would lean forward just a little, angling her round, pert bottom at him.

He was already hard.

"That would have to depend on the weather, don't you think? It might rain again," he said.

"Being coy, I see." She tilted her head. "Are you trying to draw out my anticipation for as long as you can?"

"What do you think?" he asked, his tone carefully noncommittal.

"And are you going to make me wait just as long tonight?"

"Longer." At least that was one promise he could make truthfully.

She wrinkled her nose. "What a way to endear yourself to your bride."

"I am full of just such winning manners and tactics."

"Ha. Two can play this game. For your insolence, I shall wear something particularly low-cut tonight—while employing one of my most robust bust improvers."

Her oblivious cheerfulness drove a stake of pain through his chest. "I shall look forward to an excellent view at dinner then, Lady Wrenworth."

She left, but the next moment, she was back. "By the way, Mrs. Pratt told me she had been in your employ only eight years. I thought she must have served some twenty, thirty years in this house."

"No, she hasn't."

"And Mr. Sturgess? How long has he been here?"

"Ten years, or thereabout."

"Monsieur Boulanger?"

"No more than five years."

"Is that not a little odd, that all your upper servants are so relatively new?"

"My father and my mother died within six months of each other. They both left generous bequests to longtime retainers, which led a majority of them to choose either to retire or to pursue other vocations of interest."

He did not mention that once he had come of age and gained control of his fortune, he had offered further financial lures for those older servants who still remained to leave service and enjoy a life of ease and security—he had not wanted anyone in his employ who could remember the time before he was The Ideal Gentleman.

"That must have been lovely for those retainers," she said, smiling at him.

She blew him a kiss before she left for good this time, her footsteps growing fainter and fainter.

*W*hen Louisa arrived in the dining room on her husband's arm, she found the table packed from one end to the other with epergnes and candelabras. When she sat down, she could barely see him with all the obstructions in place.

The sneaky rascal. But still dinner was enjoyable, their conversation centered largely on matters having to do with the estate.

It was only nine when she rose from the table. So she sat down in the drawing room and wrote a long letter to her family, extolling the beauty of her new home.

He did not join her in the drawing room, sneaky rascal indeed. But she could not deny it: His distance was having the desired effect. Her heart was beating fast as she returned to her bedroom and changed out of her dinner gown.

This time she would make sure to disrobe him. Slowly.

She'd seen so little of his body. She wanted to touch him, study him, and perhaps map out tiny imperfections on his person like constellations in the night sky.

She glanced at the clock: half past ten. He would come to her at eleven; she knew it. So she pulled out two pieces of stationery and wrote a letter each to Lady Balfour and Lady Tenwhestle.

It was two minutes to eleven when she was finished. She extinguished most of the lamps in the room and climbed in under the bedcover: She planned to emit some thunderous snoring noises when he opened the door.

She giggled to herself, imagining his response. They would probably burst out laughing in unison. And then she would grab him by the lapel and not let go until sunrise.

The connecting door, however, remained stubbornly closed. She listened, but couldn't hear any sounds. Vexed, she sat up in bed. The man was being insufferable. Yes, a certain amount of waiting whetted the appetite. But beyond that certain amount, appetite was replaced by irritation!

At half past eleven, she'd had enough. She left her bed, shrugged into her dressing robe, and yanked open the connecting door. His bedroom was unlit. Light meandered in from her room, enough to show that there was no one inside. She walked to various doors leading out from his bedroom—nothing. The entire apartment was empty.

She went back to her bedroom, lit a hand candle, and set out for the billiard room, hoping she remembered the way correctly. Her sense of direction served her just fine, but the billiard room was deserted. As were the smoking room, the library, and the conservatory, and all the other rooms she passed along the way.

Muttering under her breath, she checked his apartment again. Still dark and vacant. Where in the world could a man go at this time of the night? Surely he did not mean to compel her to search the house room by room?

She sat down on the edge of the bed and rubbed the back of her neck. This couldn't possibly still be a game, unless the point was to give offense and cause frustration. But if it wasn't a game . . .

If it wasn't a game, it would mean he'd had enough of her for the time being.

Impossible. The night before he had been so aroused he had not even taken the time to disrobe. He must want her still—and intensely, too.

Yet after an entire day away, instead of seeking her company, he had chosen his own.

She lay down on her bed, her mood glum. She wished she knew where he was. She wished she understood what drove his strange decisions. She wished she'd remembered never to lower her guard where he was concerned—she was to trust him only in bed and nowhere else, no matter how adorably he styled the dress dummies.

She fell asleep dreaming that he came through the connecting door, full of smiles and apologies.

CHAPTER 11

*L*ouisa would have preferred to hunt him down the next morning and demand an answer, but she woke up to a house preparing itself for battle. The first batch of guests for the house party was expected in the afternoon. And had she somehow come to the belief that she needed only to stand back and let the great machinery belowstairs rumble on by itself?

How wrong she had been. This was an army, and she its general. It didn't matter that she'd never been anywhere near a proper campaign; dozens and dozens of decisions now fell to her.

Some obviously mattered: Funds needed to be approved so that the extra help hired specifically for the occasion would have their coin at the end of each day. Some were of passionate importance to those directly involved: Mr. Sturgess could not stop agonizing about the combination of linen and fresh flowers at the table—should it be a white tablecloth to show off the vibrancy of the ranunculus, or should it be a dark tablecloth so that the late marchioness's blush roses could be displayed to their best advantage? And some made her feel like both a complete bumpkin and a wonderful sage for not caring one way or the other: Should the east lawn be trimmed to the correct height for croquet and the west lawn for tennis— or vice versa? She pretended to reflect on the difference, and then instructed the groundskeeper to seek the master of Huntington.

"Did Mr. Connelly find you?" she asked the master of Huntington when she finally saw him, an hour past luncheon, coming down the grand staircase in a light tweed suit, The Ideal Country Gentleman.

"Yes, he did." He addressed her with an affable familiarity, as if they'd been married years and a night missing from her bedchamber were nothing for anyone to be concerned about.

"And how did you answer him?"

"The west lawn for tennis and the east lawn for croquet— that way there will always be shade, as on hotter days tennis is usually played in the morning and croquet in the afternoon."

"A rich man's concern," she scoffed.

"A rich woman's too," he answered with a smile at her. "Don't forget what you have become, Lady Wrenworth."

It was only a half smile—or perhaps less, perhaps only a quarter. But all the same, it was as dazzling.

"If you will excuse me, I must go out and inspect the grouse we will soon be shooting," he said, leaning in so that his lips brushed her cheek.

She laid a hand against his heart, the tweed warm beneath her hand. "I missed you last night."

Maybe marriage was not a hotbed of transparency and honesty, but she had never lied when it came to her physical desire for him.

Now he no longer smiled. Now he looked at her as he had

in their bridal bower, with a ferocity that bordered on vehemence.

Only for a second. Then he took her hand in his, kissed her across the knuckles, and departed the front door without a backward glance.

Leaving her unsure whether she felt better—or even worse.

*L*ouisa's husband stepped into her room just as Betsey pronounced her toilette finished.

He dismissed Betsey and came to stand behind Louisa, inspecting her in the mirror, his hands behind his back. She had chosen an ornately embroidered dinner gown in a pale lilac brocade, a double strand of pearls—a wedding present from Lady Balfour—about her throat.

"Very nice," he said. "But not quite right yet."

"I would look better if I were more satisfied in bed," she retorted.

"Really?" He brushed one hand against her pearl necklace. "I would have said you looked quite ravishing when you'd gone twenty-four years without."

No doubt she would have come up with a witty and biting repartee, but he did something with her necklace, his warm touches upon her nape causing a cascade of sensations inside her.

And now he removed the necklace altogether, placing it on the vanity with a soft click.

She wanted him to keep touching her. When he did, she felt less adrift, less . . . cast aside.

He pulled a handful of something from his pocket, which, as he placed it around her throat, resolved itself to be a sensational diamond necklace, the gems brilliant with an icy flame. "From my mother's jewelry collection. All the pieces are yours to keep."

She could not care less about the necklace, or the other pieces—her attention was solely focused on his fingers. Did they linger as he worked the clasp? Did he display the slightest interest in her skin?

No, he was completely impersonal, needing no more than three seconds to fasten the necklace.

"Now you look perfect," he said, his words just as impersonal. "Shall we go?"

*I*t took Louisa the entire predinner chitchat and the first course after sitting down before she was able to shove herself back into the role that she'd played so often and so well during the Season.

There were adjustments to be made, of course. Now it was the ladies she must cultivate. For while her husband's wealth and stature gave her a certain cachet, that was not, by itself, quite enough to elevate her standing to the kind of stratospheric height he enjoyed.

And for five thousand pounds a year, she owed him a wife as popular and well-thought-of as he. To that end, she made sure she appeared amiable but also sure of herself—her public persona reflecting, at least in some measure, his cool sophistication.

After dinner, the gentlemen rejoined the ladies in the drawing room. From that moment until the ladies retired, he spoke to her only once, to ask what time she had arranged for coffee and biscuits to be brought in—an inattentiveness that was exactly as it ought to be, as the duty of the host and the hostess was to see to the guests, rather than to each other.

Yet she felt herself constantly under observation, a sensation not unlike what she'd experienced the night of their first meeting. He would be speaking to each of their sixteen guests in turn, or participating in a game of cards, or taking part in a duet, his singing voice remarkably pure and warm—and she would feel the tangible weight of his scrutiny.

No solid evidence of this observation, only her intuition. But even her intuition could not quite decipher the nature of his inspection. Did it mean anything at all, or was he merely making sure that her performance as his wife was satisfactory?

At ten o'clock coffee and biscuits were served. The ladies, herself included, retired shortly thereafter. She had told her maid not to wait up for her. That freedom of movement now allowed her to conceal herself in the darkness of the solarium, across from the billiard room.

A quarter of an hour later, the gentlemen arrived in a herd.

"A game, Wren?" asked someone. "I'll put down twenty quid."

"Tomorrow, maybe," answered Louisa's husband. "I will not be staying long enough tonight for an entire game—I am a married man now, with a married man's duties."

His friends chuckled. Some of them teased him good-naturedly. Louisa rubbed her finger on the heavy toile that covered the wall behind her. Did he mean it, or was he only acting the part?

Good for his word, he left the billiard room after only a few minutes. She slipped out of the solarium and followed him. At the stair landing, he stopped and turned around, his person only a silhouette. She caught up to him and together they ascended the steps.

"I am not following you around the house," she said, a little defensively, once they were out of earshot of those still in the billiard room. "I only wish for a minute of your time."

"And you are, of course, entitled to that," he said politely. "Shall we go to my sitting room?"

He was making her nervous, and not in a pleasurable way. Instead, she felt like the insolvent young woman she had been until very recently, attempting to persuade a shopkeeper to extend her more credit.

She preceded him into his apartment. A moment later a light came on, then another. She blinked, looking about, not sure what she was seeing.

The decor was not English, nor exactly what she thought of as the French style. His apartment was an ecstasy of pastels—white, gold, and sky blue. She almost could not imagine how exuberant it would appear during the day, with sunlight streaming in through the windows.

The plaster medallions on the wall, the fresco paintings of pastoral idylls, a ceiling that was the brightest, cleanest sky, with birds in flight and even a hot-air balloon.

What the inside of a fairy-tale castle looked like, more or less.

"It's beautiful. It's . . ."

"Rococo is the word you are looking for, I believe."

"Yes, I suppose." She had no idea what the word meant, except to know that it was the last thing she'd have extrapolated from his otherwise clean, spare style.

She liked this rococo interior. It was luminous and joyful. But instead of uplifting her mood, it only made her feel more apprehensive. What else didn't she know about him?

"I would ring for some tea, but the staff has already retired for the night," he said, quite formally.

"Thank you, but I don't need any tea."

"In that case, what can I do for you?"

She bit the inside of her lower lip. "Perhaps you can explain why you are no longer my lover."

"Am I not?"

"You haven't touched me in two days."

"And forty-eight hours is enough to disqualify me?"

"We are on our honeymoon. And you have given me every expectation that I may expect an attentive and *frequent* lover."

"You might be recalling things I'd said when I had you in mind as a mistress, whom I might see as little as twenty days out of the year. Marriage is something else altogether."

"Yet I am confident you said to me, on our wedding night, that you would—that you wanted to—fuck me every hour of every day."

The inside of her mouth felt as if it were on fire. The word was incredibly vulgar, yet strangely potent and muscular.

His eyes narrowed, as if he couldn't quite believe what he was hearing. Then he leaned forward a little, his manner almost conspiratorial. "Let me tell you something, my dear: You should never believe what a man says when he is fucking you."

Now it was the inside of her chest that burned. "If I cannot trust you even in bed, then where can I trust you?"

"I am disappointed. I thought you prudent enough to never trust me anywhere, at any time."

She was just as disappointed in herself, but there was a small part of her that still couldn't quite believe that all her worst suspicions were coming true. That the marriage she'd thought might prove to be ultimately heartbreaking was breaking her heart this moment.

"I should have had it written into the marriage settlement—how often I must be made love to," she said, trying to sound flippant.

He said nothing. She had the sense that he was already waiting for her to leave.

Her heart clenched. Was this it? Was her loss to be so abrupt and unceremonious? And would she accept this banishment so meekly, with barely a murmur of protest?

She took a step toward him. He regarded her with an impatient condescension, the grand aristocrat who found the country bumpkin a terrible bore. But she couldn't quite comprehend this new reality yet. When she looked at him, she still saw the man who had gone to great lengths with the dress dummies to make her laugh—and only that man.

So she took another step forward. And then another. And placed her hand over his heart.

His fast-beating heart.

She gazed into his eyes. For some reason she could see no contempt in them, only a barely leashed desire. Her hand moved to his jaw, followed by her lips. A chaste kiss, then a touch by the tip of her tongue.

He jerked away, but she only moved closer. This time she put her lips to the side of his neck, just above his starched collar. The rain-fresh scent of him made her light-headed with yearning. She grazed him with the moist inside of her lower lip.

And found herself picked up and pushed against a wall. They stared at each other. Her beautiful lover kept a tight grip on her shoulder, merciless enough to hurt, except she could feel only a desperate thrill.

"I seem to have married the horniest girl in all of England," he said softly, but with a sharp edge to his words.

"You knew it long before you married me."

His eyes were now on her lips. "Yes, I did, didn't I?" he murmured.

"Kiss me," she heard herself say. "Kiss me as you did the other night."

"But how will a kiss satisfy you? It is satisfaction you want, isn't it? Say yes, and I will give it to you."

She almost could not believe what she was hearing. "Yes," she said. "Yes. And yes again."

His hand moved lightly down her arm. For a brief moment, he encircled her wrist with his thumb and middle finger. But the next second he was dragging her skirts up, his motion swift and efficient.

His hand parted her legs, seeking her through the slit of her combination. She was caught off guard. She wanted him to touch her everywhere, of course, but the way he went about it seemed so . . . focused, as if there were no other pleasure to be had except through that one place.

But she could not quite deny that it was a quick and instant source of pleasure. She was glad now of his hand that still pinned her to the wall at her shoulder—without it, her knees just might not support her weight. His fingers, God, those clever fingers, gentle and forceful by turn, knowing just what to do.

Her eyes fluttered closed. The sound of herself panting filled the room. Then she was crying out, her pleasure peaking and cresting.

His lips were close to her ear. His breaths, too, were shallow and irregular. She opened her eyes and turned toward him, his forehead against the wall, his eyes tightly shut.

She put a hand on his arm. But before she could say a word, he pulled back. Just like that, dropping her skirts and walking away. Halfway across the room, he took out a handkerchief from his pocket and wiped his hand, as if he'd touched something dirty.

And then he tossed the handkerchief into a wastebasket.

She was suddenly shaking.

"I believe my work here is done," he said coolly.

She was too stunned to move—or to cry. She'd never once in her life considered herself unfortunate: She had a healthy, loving family; their roof might leak but it was still a good enough roof, and they'd always had money to buy food and enough left over to look respectable.

But not until this moment did she realize just *how* fortunate she had always been.

She had never before been dealt such deliberate cruelty. He had *meant* to humiliate her. He had *meant* to mock her desire for him. And he had *meant* to show, once and for all, how little he cared for her.

She pushed away from the wall and walked out without another word, or another look at him.

*F*elix stood in place for what seemed half the night.

He'd always known that he was every inch his mother's son. But still he was stunned by his own viciousness. Being The Ideal Gentleman meant that his cruelty was treated like a piece of ancient weaponry at a private museum, an *objet* kept inside a glass cabinet, sometimes studied in the abstract, but rarely handled and never actually wielded.

But he had such paltry defense against her. Keeping himself away and otherwise occupied had made him think about her more, not less. The entire time in the drawing room, as he saw to his guests, he was acutely aware of where she was and what she was doing—each time she laughed, it was as if she touched him.

And when she actually put her hand on him, he almost could not remember why he must keep away. All he wanted was to spend the foreseeable future in her arms—make love, make her laugh, then make love again.

Already he thought of how best to make amends. He could write her family for a list of her favorite things. He could show her all the features of her new telescope. He could teach her the mathematics she needed to calculate the orbits of comets and the gravitational pull of planets.

He grimaced. *This* was why he must never allow himself to love. He was all too capable of it, all too willing to give, and all too accustomed to keep giving, even when his gifts were rejected left and right.

When he finally took himself to his observatory, clouds had already rolled in. But there he remained until dawn, under a sky he could no longer see.

CHAPTER 12

*A*t the end of the first week of the house party, the guest head count at Huntington had climbed to forty. The house existed in a state of permanent bustle, its occupants consuming caviar by the stone and guzzling fifty-year-old claret as if it were so much lemonade.

Bread was brought in by the cartload from the village. Crates of crabs, sturgeon, and whitebait arrived packed in straw and ice. Hens, ducklings, and guinea fowls came in latticed cages, emerging from the kitchen only after having been roasted, stuffed, and stewed.

Temporary cookmaids and scullery maids chopped and washed alongside frantic sous chefs. Footmen were permanently out of breath. The laundry department operated six days a week, bravely attacking mountains of napkins and undershirts.

During the day, Louisa rarely had a moment to herself, and she was glad for it. Every servant who approached her with a question or a problem was a welcome distraction, each guest who wanted her attention likewise.

At night, well, it actually wasn't too difficult to fall asleep, given that she now woke up at four o'clock each morning to spend time with her telescope, which she'd had moved to the balcony outside the sitting room of her apartment.

She started with the much bombarded face of the moon, dear old friend to those lovers of astronomy who could observe only with the naked eye, or a pair of binoculars at best. Then she moved on to the planets. She still remembered her star map, memorized during long-ago childhood summers, so she needed only look for heavenly bodies that were out of place. Mars's moons, Jupiter's spot, Saturn's rings—celestial entities she'd never before seen with her own eyes bowed before the powerful magnification of her telescope.

Only once did she turn the telescope toward the hillock on which the Roman folly sat. The sun had just risen, the belvedere was bathed in a lovely, champagne-colored light, and the dress dummies were nowhere in sight. Vanished, like her husband's interest in her.

She joined other early risers on daily hikes across the breadth of the estate. Her husband never did, though he was always there to lead interested parties on grouse-terminating expeditions.

His friends were people of boundless energy. Groups of cycle enthusiasts regularly charged down country lanes, to the bemusement of nearby cattle. The gentlemen played cricket and association football. Ladies thwacked away on the tennis courts set up on the west lawn. And almost every afternoon, rowing parties and impromptu races took place on the lake.

And since one could not come by the appellation of The Ideal Gentleman without also being a superlative sportsman, Lord Wrenworth rarely idled, taking part in everything, as graceful and surefooted running across a grassy field as he was turning about a ballroom.

He was the best tennis player among the gentlemen, it was commonly acknowledged, and also the best shot. As for who was the fastest swimmer, that particular question was settled with a contest.

Louisa was on a different side of the house, ensconced among the half dozen or so guests who preferred painting, reading, and gossiping to the more vigorous pastimes. But at the news that at least a dozen gentlemen had waded out into the lake, these supposedly sedentary guests leaped up into a sprint, leaving Louisa no choice but to follow in their wake.

A crowd had already gathered at the edge of the water. She would have been glad to remain at the back of the spectators. But once her guests realized that she had come, they stepped aside and waved her through to the front.

A dense pack of men were in the waters off the far shore. She couldn't see their faces, but from the rapidly forming wagers, it became apparent that her husband was among the contestants.

Near the middle of the lake, the three or four strongest swimmers separated themselves from the pack.

"Mr. Dunlop is in the lead, Mr. Weston behind him, and Lord Wrenworth in third," a sharp-eyed matron beside Louisa reported.

A man snorted behind her. "Dunlop'll fade soon enough—fellow doesn't know how to pace himself. But that should be an interesting contest between Weston and Wrenworth. Weston's a bit heavy, but he swims like a fish."

As he predicted, Dunlop soon dropped out of the lead, and it came down to a spirited sprint between the two others. Louisa held her breath, not so much invested in the result of the race—what did it matter who came in first?—as unhappily gnawing over the prospect of being seen as riveted by his doings, when he couldn't bother to reciprocate that interest.

Lord Wrenworth won by a full body length. He and Mr. Weston came ashore, laughing, shaking hands, and congratulating each other in easy camaraderie.

They were both minimally clad. Her husband had stripped down to his shirtsleeves. And what garments still remained on him were plastered to his person, limning the strong, lithe form his more formal attires only hinted at. He rolled up his sleeves as he emerged from the lake, exposing long, sinewy arms to the afternoon sun and much avid feminine scrutiny.

"Oh, my!" murmured a lady to the right of Louisa. "What a sight."

"I had better send someone to collect all the clothes left on the other bank," Louisa said, very sensibly.

"Leave them," said another lady, entirely insensibly. "We have no need of them."

It would have seemed odd if she didn't join the ensuing tittering, brought on in large part by the collective admiration for her husband's fine physique, so she did, though all she wanted was to leave, to hide places where she could not possibly be exposed to his beauty and fitness.

That was when he saw her, her hand over her mouth, in a fit of silly giggling.

She kept on giggling, she was sure—the sound echoed in her head. But a scalding mortification filled her, as if he had just wiped the hand that had touched her on a handkerchief and discarded the latter as not worthy of ever being inside his pocket again.

He came to her and kissed her on her forehead. "Aren't you proud of me?" he murmured, just loud enough for those nearest to overhear.

He touched her like this from time to time, decorously, always before an audience, and always with just a hint of loverly familiarity: a hand on the small of her back, a nudge with his shoulder, and once, a playful tug on her hat ribbon as he passed her.

She knew why he made such gestures. Without ever consulting each other, they played a pair of secretly devoted lovers, as if they'd been colleagues in the same theatrical production for years upon years.

She peered at him from underneath her eyelashes, the pad of her index finger alighting upon a still-wet button on his shirt. "Maybe."

Their gazes held for a moment. Twin arrows of lust and pain pierced her person. It would be so much easier if he weren't such a good actor—if in one brief look he didn't make her feel as if he would give up his entire fortune for one night with her.

"My, my, Felix, what *delicious* dishabille!"

Startled, Louisa looked toward the speaker, a striking, raven-haired woman in a gown of burgundy and gold stripes.

Lady Tremaine. Back from her man-sampling up north.

She approached Lord Wrenworth, her gloved hands outstretched. "What is this, Felix? I go off for a few weeks and come back to find you *married*?"

Felix. Appalling intimacy, when everyone else, even his oldest friends, thought it quite adequate to adhere to his title or some variant thereof.

He did not seem to mind at all. "My dear," he said to Louisa, "allow me to present the Marchioness of Tremaine. Lady Tremaine, Lady Wrenworth."

The two women shook hands.

"We are so glad you could come, Lady Tremaine," said Louisa. "And did you find the . . . charms of Scandinavia as delightful as you had hoped?"

Something flickered in Lady Tremaine's eyes, as if she hadn't expected such a cheeky question from the country bumpkin her former lover had married. "The salmon was certainly of exceptional quality everywhere. And may I tender my congratulations on your marriage. I am sure Lord Wrenworth is an exceedingly fortunate man to have won your hand."

"He thanks his lucky stars every day," Louisa said sweetly. She turned to him. "My dear, best change before you catch a chill."

And then, to Lady Tremaine, "I'm sorry we didn't have advance notice of your visit. But shall we get you settled?"

*L*ater that afternoon, another guest arrived, an expected one this time, but one as unwelcome to Felix as Lady Tremaine must be to his wife.

Drummond.

The man had an uncanny nose for marital discord—and rarely hesitated to take advantage of a wife's displeasure with her husband to present himself as everything the poor sod wasn't. Such tendencies had scarcely mattered to Felix when he was a bachelor. And would have scarcely mattered to him as a married man, had he and his wife remained cocooned in erotic bliss.

But erotic bliss did not characterize the state of his marriage. And as Drummond monopolized Louisa after dinner, Felix felt as if he were an incarcerated convict who could only rattle the bars of his prison with impotent frustration as another man circled his wife, getting ready to exploit his absence.

"Well, tell me," said Lady Tremaine, pulling his attention back to her. "Why did this girl succeed whereas so many before her have failed?"

She had beckoned him to her earlier; they stood in a corner of the drawing room, half separated from the rest of the crowd by a Japanese screen.

He settled for a noncommittal reply. "Excellent timing?"

She appeared skeptical. "I thought you planned to marry the female equivalent of Lord Vere—tremendous looks and very little brain."

Would that he'd adhered to that laudable plan. "And you believed me?"

"I had no reason not to. Many men like that kind of woman."

"Obviously I decided against a dim-witted wife."

"She *is* rather sharp, your lady." She leaned forward an inch. "And how do you like married life, by the way, Felix?"

He had not thought much of Lady Tremaine's unexpected arrival—this was where she was accustomed to spending half of her August, so why should she not have availed herself of his hospitality, when she found herself back in England sooner than expected? He also had not thought much of her interest in his sudden marriage—it would have come as quite a surprise to her, since the last time they spoke he'd had no idea himself that his bachelor days were coming to an end.

But now he was beginning to be a little wary. There was something in the tone of her voice. Perhaps it had been there since she stepped into Huntington, but he'd been first too distracted by his wife's touch on his shirt button, and then even more distracted by the sight of her smiling at Drummond, her fan fluttering prettily.

"Married life is more or less as I'd expected," he answered, choosing his words carefully.

"What? No paean to marital felicity?"

"Since when do you believe in marital felicity?"

"You are right. What a vulgar concept—and quite beneath The Ideal Gentleman."

"I wouldn't go that far. My wife and I deal with each other very favorably, you will see. And I have every expectation we shall maintain great harmony in this house for decades to come."

"Well, then, my congratulations," said Lady Tremaine.

But he was already once again distracted. In the mirror above the mantel he could see his wife tapping on Drummond's arm with the tip of her now-closed fan, in an almost flirtatious manner.

He'd thought she could not stand the man.

"Thank you, my dear. Now, if you will please excuse me, I believe Drummond has something he wants to say to me."

Drummond, of course, didn't yet know that he wanted to say anything to Felix. But Felix planned to steer him into a conversation about horseflesh. And if there was anything Drummond could not resist, it was a discussion on the making of a prizewinning stallion.

He set his hand for a fraction of a second on Louisa's lower back, before placing an arm around Drummond's shoulders. "I know firsthand how irresistible Lady Wrenworth's company is, but I do believe Mallen was hoping to arrange a match between your Gibraltar and his Lady Burke."

"Oh my!" exclaimed Drummond. "Lady Burke has a fascinating bloodline, from what I've heard—a worthy match for Gibraltar."

"Forgive us," Felix said to his wife, as he maneuvered Drummond away from her.

She nodded, a thin smile on her face. "Of course you are forgiven for every trespass, my lord. Always."

For days, it had seemed that the house party would never end, that Louisa would always need to have her public demeanor firmly in place, sixteen hours a day. Then, abruptly, the last full day of the party was upon them.

The morning saw a vigorous tennis tournament. Louisa did not participate in the matches, but she was obliged to watch and applaud as her husband handed out one defeat after another.

For several days after the handkerchief incident, it had seemed as if she were made of cold ash, incapable of even the smallest embers of lust. She had thought that it would always be so, that his contempt had permanently smothered all her yearning.

Unfortunately that had not proved the case, especially at times like this, when she must keep her eyes on him to maintain her image of the devoted bride. So much athletic grace, so much stamina, so much cleverness and strategy—the angles of his shots were a thing of beauty—not to mention, from time to time, sheer physical dominance, when he simply overpowered an opponent with a muscular forehand.

It made her almost thankful for Mr. Drummond's presence at her side. He did not criticize Lord Wrenworth's technique or shot selection, but no one else escaped his criticism. And his constant faultfinding grated on her nerves just enough for her not to be prostrate with desire for the husband who did not reciprocate it.

Without that lust on his part, she was just a woman to whom he gave five thousand pounds a year, and who existed in the periphery of his life as a mobile ornament for the estate.

After luncheon, it began to rain. Many of those who had taken part in the tennis tournament were down for a nap, in order to be in top form for the bonfire party in the evening. Of those left awake, the ladies stayed in their rooms to write letters and the gentlemen made use of the billiard room. For once, Huntington was quiet and relaxed.

Louisa retreated to the window alcove in the library, to spend time with a volume on the care and proper operation of telescopes. It was a wonderful book, tailored to a novice, the explanations detailed yet clear—or at least she thought so. She could be reading a housekeeping manual, for all she knew.

Why had he married her at all?

And was that the limit of her womanly appeal, all exhausted in a single night?

He made her miss the man who had baldly schemed to make her his mistress. At least that man had wanted her enough to take risks and damn the consequences. Whereas this man . . .

A thousand times she had cautioned herself against trusting him. But stupidly, she had been anxious only that she should not translate the physical pleasures he would give her into cascading verses of love. That he would distance himself from her during the honeymoon itself—the thought had never even crossed her mind.

The door of the library opened. The alcove was hidden behind a bookshelf that could slide along on concealed rails. It offered wonderful privacy, but on the other hand, the bookshelf, its back entirely paneled, made it difficult for Louisa to see who had come into the library.

But the sound of the gait was nothing like her husband's. A woman, most probably. The woman made a round in the library and left after less than a minute.

A light fog had descended on the lake along with the rain, obscuring the opposite bank like a gauzy curtain. But now that curtain drew apart and Louisa found herself looking directly at the Greek folly.

A marble-columned pavilion stands by this lake.

A quick sentence in a matter-of-fact guidebook, yet in those days when he had tormented her with the possibility of becoming his mistress, she had concocted an entire three-act play around that setting. Act I: The girl, staring longingly at the great manor from across the lake, is ravished in the shadows of the pavilion. Act II: The girl, staring longingly at her evilly perfect lover, is ravished all across the grounds of his extensive estate. Act III: The girl, back home after a fortnight of ravishment, stumbling about like an empty shell of her former self, hears the doorbell ring at a most unusual hour.

A two-and-a-half-act play, rather: The clear-eyed realist that she was had never been able to picture opening the door of her house to *him*. The real Lord Wrenworth would not call, write, or send presents. She would just have to wait months upon months before staring longingly at him again.

Then he'd proposed, and her world had turned upside down in the most pleasurable way. And she had forgotten that around him she always needed her shield and her sword. Had walked into the dragon's lair naked and unarmed, with nothing but the foolish conviction that the dragon would never incinerate a girl he liked.

But looking back, ought she to have been surprised? He had deliberately made her simmer in a state of arousal at the dinner at Lady Tenwhestle's house. He had clearly enjoyed informing her that her preferred suitors were both deeply flawed. Not to mention he had never experienced the slightest qualm about enticing a respectably raised virgin to sell her body.

Why shouldn't such a man prove himself capricious and heartless?

The door of the library opened and closed again.

"There is no one here," said a woman. "I came through just a minute ago."

Lady Tremaine.

"And pray tell, why is the lack of a public so important?" That serene voice belonged to none other than Louisa's husband.

"Privacy is always nice, don't you agree?"

He chuckled but gave no reply.

They were coming closer. There was a rustling of fabric,

the sound of a woman sitting down and adjusting her skirts. "Care for a seat, Felix?"

Lady Tremaine sounded as if she were speaking directly into Louisa's ear.

"I will be able to better admire your toilette, Philippa, from my superior vantage point right here," he answered.

There was a smile in his voice, a cool smile.

Lady Tremaine laughed, a sultry sound. "Look all you want, Felix."

A long pause. Lurid images exploded in Louisa's head. Then Lady Tremaine spoke again. She did not sound as if there were a man pressed against her. "Congratulations on your stellar results in the tennis tournament."

"Thank you."

"You were very, very vigorous."

"I am a man of twenty-eight, rusticating in the country. If I didn't abound with energy, I'd need to consult my physician."

"You are also a man on your honeymoon. Shouldn't you have conserved a bit of stamina for pleasuring your wife?"

"Your concern is very kind. But I am sure I will somehow gather the wherewithal to see my wife to her satisfaction."

Liar.

"Maybe you can, but are you? For every day of my stay, I have seen you from my window at half past four in the morning, coming back into the house."

It was hardly news to Louisa. But that Lady Tremaine should know about it . . . She flushed with hot shame.

Lord Wrenworth did not address Lady Tremaine's point, but instead asked, "What were *you* doing up at half past four in the morning?"

"Having trouble sleeping, obviously."

The sound of rustling silk again, and of someone standing up. Footsteps. Louisa imagined Lady Tremaine circling Lord Wrenworth like a she-wolf about to pounce.

"I have been observing your wife. I do not believe she loves you. I do not even believe she likes you."

He was silent for a long time. Louisa hoped he was at least chagrined that anyone would toss such a thing in his face. It was almost enough to make her embrace Lady Tremaine in friendship.

"My wife does not like to make her sentiments public," he said at last. "What she feels, only she and I know."

Lady Tremaine snorted at his answer. "So I'm right, then. Don't worry; I won't demand to know the why and wherefore of her sentiments. Or yours. I am interested only in what you can do to help *me* sleep better."

Louisa found it difficult to remain quiet. She seemed to be able to take in air only in huge gulps. Even with her hands over her mouth, her trembling inhalations echoed in her hiding space.

"Since we are both awake in the middle of the night," continued Lady Tremaine, "come and make love to me instead. At least you know I like you. In fact, sometimes I adore you."

"Hmm, a tempting offer," he said.

"One that you'd regret declining."

"Would I?" His words were low and soft.

"You remember what it was like." Lady Tremaine's voice was all willful seduction. "We were magnificent together."

"I remember."

"Midnight, then."

"I haven't said I'd come."

"You'd be a fool not to, wouldn't you?"

And she departed on that triumphant note, walking out of the library. The closing of the door echoed in the silence.

Louisa gasped when the bookshelf was pushed aside.

"I thought you might be here," her husband said coolly, as if he hadn't just failed to turn down an invitation to adultery.

And what should she say in return? *Sleep with her and I will give you a concussion with my telescope stand?*

"Yes," she said, "it's a comfortable spot. Pretty view, too."

"I will leave you to your reading, then."

"Thank you," she said politely.

Then she bent her face to her book, indicating that she had nothing else to say to him.

A few seconds later, the bookshelf slid back into place, shutting her in.

*F*elix remained where he was.

He wanted to leave, but his feet were rooted in place, and his hands kept reaching out to push the bookshelf aside again. Madly enough, he didn't want to shove her against the wall and claim her with the force of an asteroid strike. In his mind, he sat down next to her and together they watched the clouds depart in the wake of the rain, revealing a clear, spotless afternoon sky.

He left only when he must, to supervise the preparation of the fire pit, with an emptiness in his heart that felt, unhappily, all too familiar.

Along with a strange anxiety.

He wasn't worried about what Lady Tremaine might or might not do. He knew her very well: If she wanted him, it was only as a distraction—something about her Scandinavian trip had upset her.

His wife, on the other hand . . .

On bonfire nights, no formal dinners were laid out. Instead, a buffet supper was served on the grand terrace, which had been lit with dozens of lanterns suspended from a pergola set up specifically for the occasion.

His sense of misgiving doubled when she appeared on the terrace clad in the same dinner gown she'd worn on their wedding night. Without looking left or right, she went directly to Drummond, who bowed and kissed her hand.

They stood by the balustrade and chatted, ignoring the buffet supper altogether. As they spoke, with only the barest nod at subtlety, Drummond inched toward her. She seemed perfectly conversant with the game. From time to time, she would rest the tip of her closed fan against his chest, to slow his inexorable progress. And once in a while, she would slide a foot to the left, to keep a respectable distance between them.

Then, all of a sudden, not only did she stop moving away, she leaned toward Drummond. And when he lowered his head to say something in her ear, she tilted her face and gave him a sideways smile.

A smile that spoke of a Greek folly lit by torches, of slender columns that could barely conceal a grown woman, and of hot, frantic coupling in the shadows, perhaps only a few yards from those who oohed and ahhed over the display of fireworks.

In the wake of the smile, she whispered to Drummond and pointed to the very pavilion across the water, the one Felix could not look at without an echoing sense of loss.

She left Drummond with a flirtatious caress of her fan down his arm, to mix with the other guests. Felix felt as if there were a hand at his throat, choking him. He had *not* agreed to an adulterous affair; surely she could recall that. He had not turned down Lady Tremaine flat because he had not wanted to interrogate her on why she was propositioning him out of the blue, knowing that they were not truly alone.

He found Lady Tremaine and led her down to the lawn, out of earshot of the others. "Regretting it yet?"

"I don't know what you mean."

"You do know what I mean. You were wondering whether to have a headache or pretend to be too drunk when I showed up at midnight."

She sighed. "Why must you know me so well?"

"I assume it's not anything your Scandinavian lovers said

or did." He doubted that she'd had any lovers at all; she was not the sort to sleep with a man on a short acquaintance.

She looked away. "Tremaine was in Copenhagen."

Her permanently absent husband. "At his sister's house?"

"No. I mean, I'm sure that's where he was staying, but we ran into each other quite accidentally." She exhaled. "And he had a woman with him."

"I'm sorry."

She shrugged. "It's just the shock of it. I will be all right in no time."

He touched her on her arm. "Come back at Christmas. I'll pack the house with handsome men and you can have your pick."

She laughed rather valiantly, her hand reaching up to adjust the scarf his valet had draped about his neck against the eventual chill of the night. "That's right—instead of the ugly men you usually host."

Her barely-beneath-the-surface pain reverberated inside his own chest. He was feeling too much these days—and no longer knew how to stop.

He squeezed her hand. "I will even get rid of the homelier footmen, just for you."

They both laughed rather valiantly at that. She kissed him on the cheek. "Thank you, Felix."

And of course his wife would choose that moment to look his way, her gaze hardening into daggers.

At ten minutes to midnight, Felix walked into the folly.

His wife was already there, her hand on a pillar, looking toward the bonfire on the opposite shore of the lake. He still couldn't quite believe it—that she had arranged a rendezvous with a man she actively disliked, just to spite him.

"Beautiful, isn't it, this house?" she said without glancing behind her. "I used to study a tiny picture of it, and imagine how it would look in person, lit up like this, impossibly majestic against the night."

He had come to tell her that he had already dispatched Drummond—by letting it be known that a man to whom Drummond owed a large gaming debt would be among those coming to watch the fireworks at midnight. Drummond had fled almost before Felix had stopped speaking, rather to Felix's disappointment. He would have preferred to enjoy the man's panic for a bit longer.

Her head tilted up. "And such stars. Have I ever told you of my interest in astronomy? I have always been intrigued by the night sky, ever since I was a child. To think that there is a vast universe out there, full of deep, marvelous unknowns."

She had never told him, directly, of her fascination with the stars. Never allowed him to share her sense of wonder.

"But you didn't come to hear me prattle on. Please proceed with what we've agreed upon."

He felt a burning in his throat. *What we've agreed upon.* What *had* they agreed upon?

He meant to speak, to let her know that Drummond had vacated the premises. Instead, he found himself standing directly behind her, his hands on her cool, bare arms.

She trembled. With disgust—or desire? How could she feel anything for that dunce, whom Felix tolerated only because he was nephew to Felix's former guardian?

He kissed her hair, the lobe of her ear, the side of her neck, his fingers spreading over her collarbone.

"Such a workmanlike approach, sir. No praise for my slender throat or my velvety skin?"

He bit her shoulder in response, not hard, just enough for her to emit a sob of arousal.

"Did you bring the blindfold?" she asked, her voice unsteady.

His hand tightened. That, too, was a fantasy that belonged to them. She couldn't have displayed a little originality and found something different for Drummond to do?

He took off his scarf and used it to blindfold her.

She turned around. A little hesitantly, her hand lifted and felt its way to his jaw. Could she not tell that it was him?

"I used to dream of riding in a glass carriage, naked and blindfolded. There was a man in the carriage with me. It doesn't matter who the man was. All that matters is that—"

He silenced her with a hard kiss. He could take no more of her cruel words; nor could he care anymore that he was giving in to his obsession.

She kissed him back almost as bruisingly, her hands gripping his hair. He pushed her against the pillar as she dragged his shirt up, her hands hungry for his skin.

He had no recollection of either shoving aside her skirts or freeing himself from the encumbrance of his trousers. The next thing he knew was a desperate upward plunge as he entered her—and the gasps that echoed between them.

The ferocity of her lips, the avarice of her hands, the sheer, agonizing scorch of her person. He didn't know how he remembered to clamp a palm over her mouth—perhaps only when he heard someone calling, from no more than fifteen feet away, "Quick. The fireworks are about to start."

Their own fireworks ignited first. He barely protested before surrendering to the demonic pleasures of her body clenching and shuddering about his.

She was heavenly. Her hair smelled of chamomile, her skin was paradise, her hips beneath his hands sweetly pliant.

But reality seeped back, winding a cord of dismay around his heart, softly, nearly imperceptibly. Then there came a sharp, cruel yank.

She'd let Drummond touch her. Invade her. Spill his seed inside her.

He stumbled back a step. Then another.

Her breaths were still erratic, but she calmly shook and rearranged her skirts. Just as calmly, she took off her blindfold.

The hour was late and the torches that lit the pavilion were guttering. But he could see her face clearly, and she must see his just as well. He waited for her shock and outrage. Neither came. She only cast him a look halfway between desire and loathing, turned, and walked away.

He reached out and grabbed her by the arm. "I was never going to sleep with Lady Tremaine."

She pried his hand from her person. "And I told Drummond to stay away from the pavilion, because of the wasps."

And then she was gone, marching to the explosion of fireworks overhead.

It was not long after Louisa lay down in bed that her husband joined her. He didn't speak, but only kissed and caressed her in the darkness, until she could no longer remain still and silent.

He spread her arms to the sides, linked their fingers together, and drove into her, wreaking havoc with every thrust.

She lost count of the number of times he brought her to pleasure. Enough to make tears roll down her face, when she was once again alone, sometime in the small hours of the night.

CHAPTER 13

*L*ate in the morning, as they waved good-bye to successions of their guests, Felix studied his wife.

He could not stay away from her—that much had become obvious. Everything else, however, was pure chaos. With so much injury inflicted and only a fortnight into their marriage, how would they carry on? How would *he* carry on, knowing that a part of him was now at her mercy?

Before he climbed into bed with her last night, he already knew he would have to make amends when the sun rose. A simple matter, he'd told himself: When a man behaved badly, he admitted to his mistake and tendered an apology. Nothing to it.

But now, in the light of day, with her demeanor cool and opaque, he could not completely suppress his inner agitation. It felt as if he would be seeking her approval—and he had always adamantly refused to seek anyone's approval.

When the house had at last emptied, he said to the woman who had not looked at him once the entire time they saw off their guests, "Well done, Lady Wrenworth. Word will spread now of your brilliance as a hostess."

"And of our general domestic felicity, no doubt," she countered, with that grande dame haughtiness she sometimes used with him.

He remembered how amusing he'd found it before, but now that capacity for sangfroid unsettled him.

Now she knew how to punish him.

"I have given the staff the rest of the day off, but there is a picnic basket that has been packed for us. Would you care to join me?"

"You are too kind," she said coldly. "Five thousand a year is all I require from you, sir, nothing more."

"Five thousand a year is the bare minimum of what I should do for you. I would be quite remiss as a husband if I left it at that." A phaeton, with the picnic basket already in the boot, arrived. "Now, shall we?"

She shot him a brief, hard look. She knew he was exploiting the fact that she guarded her public image carefully and would not turn her back on him before the coachman who had brought the carriage: Even his gesture of apology was not free of manipulation.

It made him feel less vulnerable to be up to his old tricks.

He dismissed the coachman and took the reins himself. They drove in near complete silence. Had he felt more in charge of the situation, he would have wheedled and cajoled her, until she laughed despite herself. But he was as hesitant as he had ever been in his adult life, an uncertainty that smothered any lighthearted words that might otherwise have emerged.

For the picnic, he had selected one of his favorite spots in the surrounding countryside, atop a high bluff overlooking a panorama of hills and valleys. She made no comment on the beauty of the place, though she did help him weigh down the corners of the picnic blanket on a patch of lush, soft grass.

"Thank you," he said, from the opposite corner of the blanket, down on one knee.

She made no reply, but rose to her feet and walked to the edge of the bluff to inspect the view, the hems of her skirts fluttering in the breeze.

He unloaded the contents of the picnic basket, setting out three salads, four meat pies, five bottles of beverages—and the basket was far from emptied.

"I said to pack what you like," he told her. "It would seem the kitchen staff put in everything for which you've ever expressed a preference. We've enough to last us in a siege."

She turned around and glanced at the laden picnic blanket. He was still extracting ever more foodstuff from the basket: a loaf of bread, a wedge of cheese, a bowl of fruit.

"If you want to bed me outdoors, you have but to say the word." Her tone was uninflected. "No need to go to so much trouble."

"When I wish to bed you outdoors, I *will* but say the word," he answered. "But now I'd like to feed you."

Her jaw worked. He could not tell whether she also blushed.

When she came and sat down at the edge of the picnic blanket, her features were quite composed. Ignoring all the prepared dishes, she reached instead for a cluster of grapes.

She'd done the same at a different picnic, the day he suggested that she become his mistress. An era of blissful ignorance, that, when he had no idea just how deeply he was already mired in his obsession.

"Did you and your family picnic?" he asked, uncorking a bottle of raspberry wine.

She studied him. He realized that she considered the picnic a Machiavellian game of power on his part, with every move intended to undermine her. He could not blame her for thinking so—he'd always enjoyed his upper hand in all their dealings.

His current motives, however, weren't quite so despicable. He wasn't callous enough to use her body when he needed to and ignore her the rest of the time, so he must make amends for his earlier cruelty. And he would like to do so while keeping his pride intact.

"Occasionally," she said at last, rolling a single grape between her fingers. "But we didn't have such fine foodstuff—for us it was tea and sandwiches."

He poured a glass of wine for her. "How are they getting on without you?"

She peeled the skin from the grape in small strips. "Matilda has taken to directing the big move and my other sisters complain she is more draconian than I ever was."

"She is the one who shared a room with you, is she not? She must have absorbed some of your generalship."

The grape was now naked. She looked down with a frown, as if vexed that she might actually have to eat something.

"Do you want to give that to me?"

She didn't. She put the grape in her mouth and wiped her hand with a napkin. As she was about to toss the napkin aside, her face changed.

Between them hung the moment he'd thrown his handkerchief into the wastebasket.

"I'd like to repair matters between us," he said impulsively.

She yanked another grape from the bunch. "Why, I did not know relations were strained."

Her words were full of condescending bite. He realized with more than a little startlement that she might be mimicking *him*, rather than some imaginary dowager duchess.

"I behaved abominably and for that I apologize."

She fixed him with a flat stare. "Why?"

"Why apologize?"

"Why did you behave abominably? You never do anything without a properly thought-out reason."

If only that were, in fact, the case. He had been going from one ill-thought-out reason to the next ever since he first laid eyes on her.

"I wanted to preserve our interest in each other. Since we are to be married a long time, God willing, it seemed prudent to not erode our delight in each other too soon."

An easy lie, since he knew precisely why he stayed away from her: to preserve the fortress that he had made of himself, the foundation of which was sliding into an unseen abyss even as he spoke.

She snorted. "I'm disappointed, sir. You can lie better than that."

He could not help smiling a little. "I love it when you take me to task."

She served herself some cucumber salad and rammed her fork rather forcefully into the mound on her plate. "So this is how you repair relations then, by feeding me more lies."

"No, this is what happens when you ask too many questions," he said. "You should let my action speak for itself."

Louisa set aside her plate. "What action?"

His hand, the one on which he wore the carnelian signet ring, toyed with his glass. She was reminded of the night she first saw him, of her—in hindsight, especially—utterly justified hesitation to lift her eyes to his face. As if her instincts had already sensed that he would prove to be the bane of her existence.

He rose with the grace of a big cat and came toward her. Quietly and efficiently, he removed her hat and maneuvered her onto her back.

"You've done this before and it doesn't prove anything," she said.

He gave no reply, except to push up her skirts.

"The crudeness of your method is excruciating," she went on, keeping her tone clipped.

The grass was cool and fragrant beneath her, the sun warm on her face and the exposed band of skin above her stockings. She ought to feel a certain mortified titillation from the fact that he was making a spectacle of her where anyone could chance upon them, but she only felt like a very small raft on a very turbulent sea, buffeted from every side by both need and fear.

He had a powerful, effortless hold on her and he knew it.

The only thing he didn't know was the exact strength of this sorcery he wielded.

He removed her drawers and parted her thighs. There had been a time when she would have gladly opened her legs to tantalize him, when the pleasure he brought her did not immediately touch off a cascade of pain in her heart. But now she had to bite down on her lower lip in order to not clamp her limbs together again.

"And the grapes were too tart," she said when he still didn't reply.

He pushed her legs farther apart, kissed her on the inside of her thigh, and made love to her with his lips and tongue. The wickedness of it shocked her, as well as the intimacy. The pleasure made her gasp and moan. His tongue was so clever, so demanding, and he knew exactly where to stroke with his fingers and when to apply the pressure of his teeth.

The peak he took her to was sharp and voluptuous. But he did not stop. As if that initial burst of pleasure were but a foundation on which to build ever bigger climaxes. And he created those ever bigger climaxes, until they came right on the heels of one another, until she was but one sustained vibration of extraordinary pleasure.

Afterward she kept her eyes shut, unable to face him. He rearranged her skirts so she was decent—if one didn't inquire too closely into the whereabouts of her drawers. And when the heaviness of her breaths no longer blocked out all the other sounds, she heard the soft pops of several grapes being detached from the bunch.

"You are right," he said half a minute later. "The grapes are too tart, especially compared to the sweetness of you."

Her face, already warm, turned hot.

"I will also concur that my method is crude. And if you still feel this proves nothing, let me know, and I will gladly repeat the experiment and see if we can't generate better results."

She forced herself to open her eyes and sit up—she had to face him at some point. He was on the far side of the picnic blanket, reclined with his weight on his elbows, studying her from beneath his eyelashes in just such a way as to make her heart thud. Reminding her that even when he seemed somewhat humbled, he was still every inch the predator.

"Can I serve you something?" he murmured solicitously. "You've scarcely touched any food—and of course the grapes must have been terribly unsatisfying."

She flushed again. "No, thank you. I'm not hungry."

He drank from his wineglass. "I am. For you, that is."

She swallowed. "Then you must exercise your husbandly prerogative."

He held her gaze. "Do you want me to? And do not answer as an obliging wife—I already know I have an obliging wife. Do *you* wish it?"

Yes. No. "I don't know."

"Hmm," he said. Then he beckoned her with one finger. "Come here."

She should remain exactly where she was, at a safe distance. But she was pulled in by the same undeniable force that had had her revolving around him from the very beginning, a once freewheeling asteroid caught in the gravitational pull of a ruthless planet.

There was no such thing as a safe distance from him.

She lay down next to him. He shifted his weight so he was on his side, his head in his palm. His other hand took hold of her chin, keeping her face turned toward him—as if she could look away.

"You have such pretty eyes," he murmured, "and such pretty skin."

His words invoked a black pain not unlike the one she'd experienced whenever she'd thought of his eventual wife. She was his wife now, but the anguish remained the same, that of being replaced and forgotten.

"If you were trying to preserve your interest in me earlier, it must mean now you are trying to weary of me sooner," she heard herself say.

He kissed her on the lips. "Do you believe I could ever weary of you, my dear Louisa?"

Of course she believed it—as much as she believed in the elliptical orbit of the Earth around the sun. It was the reason she could never trust him. The reason she would never tell him that she loved him.

"As long as we weary of each other at the same rate, I'll have no complaints."

His hand tightened on her jaw. A moment later he let go of her face altogether to trace a finger down the center of her bodice. "How you punish me, my dear."

He lifted aside her skirts and, still fully clothed, entered her, his eyes never leaving hers—a man who wanted to see his power over her reflected in her features.

She let him see it. Because they were in the middle of love-making, and she could justify her hunger as that of the body, and not that of the soul. Her hunger, her need, even her fear.

"Spread your thighs wider, darling," he told her, his voice only a little unsteady. "I want to be all the way inside you."

The things he made her feel . . . even the sanctity of holy

matrimony might not keep her out of the flames of hell. In desperation, because she did not want to be the only one so tremblingly affected, teetering so close to the edge despite the deliberate, leisurely pace he set, despite the peaks she had already experienced only minutes ago, she whispered, "I have wanted to spread my thighs for you ever since I first saw you."

He made an animal sound in the back of his throat, his gaze losing some of its focus.

"All my nights lying awake, all my naked dreams—that's what it was all about, wasn't it? Wanting you inside me."

He grimaced, baring his teeth. His body slammed into hers, shoving her back a few inches, pushing her so close to the precipice she could already feel the involuntary contraction of her muscles.

But she did not want to lose control alone—that path led directly back to the pit of despair. "Come in deeper. Are you in me as deep as you want to be?"

Now they were tumbling off the edge together; now his control was as shattered as hers. And now she finally closed her eyes and let herself be swept away by the surge of pleasure.

And by his harshly uttered words in her ear, as he gripped her close: "I can never be in you deep enough. Never."

When she had on her drawers again, and her skirts were decorously in place, she allowed Felix to sit her between his legs, his arms wrapped around her.

He was not sure what he had accomplished this day, or whether he had even truly resolved this lovers' quarrel between them. But it didn't seem to matter, not when he could bury his nose in her hair and inhale.

"It smells just like yours, my lord," she said, her tone arch, forestalling a compliment on his part, "since I'm fairly certain we have the same soap."

"Then my hair must smell divine. And you might as well call me Felix in private—we wouldn't want Lady Tremaine to be the only one enjoying that privilege."

"Huh," was her dismissive response.

But then she followed that with an offer of the coffee cream she was eating, her person half turned, her spoon held out toward him. "Do you want some? It's rather nice."

He ate from her spoon. The coffee cream was more than nice; it was delectable.

"Just to let you know," she continued, "I am still angry with you. I simply cannot express it very well when I am in direct physical contact with you."

"Then I must make sure we remain in constant direct physical contact. I like it when you cannot express your anger very well."

"Huh," she said again.

He leaned back against the tree behind him, so content he could melt. "Tell me about your childhood intrigue with the night sky."

"Must I?" She offered him another spoonful of the coffee cream.

"You mentioned it last night, when you knew it was me standing behind you. So yes, now you must."

She gave the next spoonful of the coffee cream to herself, looking up at the day sky. "One night, when I was three, my father woke up all his daughters and took us outside, promising a special treat."

Given that she was born in 1864, she must have seen the Leonid shower of 1867, which was not as grand as the meteor storm the year before, but still impressive.

"They tell me that for a week afterward, I would wake my father up every day after midnight and make him take me to see more shooting stars."

"Did he?"

"My mother said he did. She said that he would read until I came to fetch him and then stay out with me for as long as I wanted."

He kept his envy from his voice. "A doting father."

"He was. According to my mother, he was an expensive man to have around. But we all adored him. Too bad he didn't live long enough to see me carrying on the family legacy of fortune hunting so successfully. He would have been tickled about the bust improvers."

"I am honored to be tickled on his behalf."

Her head tilted forward. He moved his to the side, to see a slight smile on her lips. Impulsively he kissed her on her cheek.

"Don't be so pleased with yourself," she admonished. "I distrust you and will continue to do so."

"Your distrust is the spice that gives my life flavor," he said grandly. "Long may your suspicions simmer."

Little did he know how much he would come to regret that sentiment.

CHAPTER 14

*L*ouisa had never brushed her teeth or combed her hair at quarter to four in the morning. But her lover had said he would be coming to her room at four to see how she was getting on with her astronomical observation, so here she was, seeing to her toilette in the dead of the night for a man she couldn't trust.

It was always a problem when he put his hands on her. His touch diminished both her capacity to remember the past and her ability to plan for the future, so that she was liable to think only as far back as the previous time they had made love, and forward only to the next time they would make love.

Her common sense was further decimated, given that she'd spent at least an hour sitting between his legs, with his arms around her.

Had he never stopped coming to her bed, had he never shown her the kind of cruelty of which he was capable, she would have been deliriously happy by now.

She was still too pleased for her own good, but it was a happiness with thorns.

At exactly four o'clock, he walked in, kissed her on her hair, and led her out through her sitting room to the balcony where she'd stationed the telescope.

"Let me show you something."

He removed the tarp from the telescope and pushed it, on its wheeled base, out to the edge of the balcony—he was a pleasure to behold, in his shirt with two buttons open.

"Find Jupiter, will you?" he said.

She wrested her gaze away from him. Telescopes, marvelous as they were, magnified only a tiny patch of the sky. She had better know at which coordinates she ought to point the thing before she looked into the eyepiece.

Jupiter came into view, a slightly blurred cream-and-orange sphere. "It looks the same as usual."

"Let me see." He took her place at the eyepiece. "Hmm. This telescope should be able to achieve a greater resolution than this."

He maneuvered various knobs, a rather adorable scowl of concentration on his face. And those strong, shapely forearms, bared by his rolled-up sleeves—she couldn't stop looking at them.

Remember this, she thought to herself. *Remember this weakness in yourself. Remember that you do not know why he behaved abominably a fortnight ago, or why he is sweetness and sunshine now. It could all go away again in the blink of an eye, without warning, without explanations.*

"Aha!" He felt around the base of the telescope, opened a drawer she hadn't even known was there, and swapped in a different eyepiece. "Now come see."

When she looked this time, Jupiter was much smaller, barely the size of a farthing. The image, however, had become razor sharp. Not only could she see two of Jupiter's moons, but she could see the perfectly round shadow one of them cast on the giant planet's surface.

A solar eclipse on Jupiter. She sucked in a breath. "How did you know it was going to happen?"

"I didn't. I saw it myself only half an hour ago. So I thought I'd show it to you, too."

"Where is your telescope?" She knew he had to have one.

"Somewhere on the estate," he teased.

She would not beg him to show it to her. Well, not yet. Putting her eye to the eyepiece again, she asked, "So how did *you* become interested in the stars?"

"I used to have trouble sleeping as a child. So I would slip out, walk about, look at the sky, and, after a while, notice the wheeling of the stars."

"Was your health frail?" She couldn't quite imagine him as a sickly child.

"No, I was quite sturdy."

She glanced back at him. Perhaps it was his stillness, the darkness of the hour, or the soft light spilling out from the sitting room and limning his features, but she remembered the late marchioness's portrait in the gallery, her dramatically beautiful face against a velvety black background.

"You resemble your mother a great deal."

"I do."

"I wouldn't have been able to tell that you were related to your father."

Instantly she regretted her statement. Before her London Season, Lady Balfour had given her an important piece of advice: *Never comment on likeness or the lack thereof.* With marriage what it was among the upper crust, there was no telling who might have fathered a lady's third or fourth or fifth child.

But he was the firstborn, the heir.

"I am my predecessor's son," he said calmly.

"Of course you are. I only meant to say that the resemblance is slight."

There was a beat of silence. He tilted his chin at the telescope. "It's Io, by the way."

It took her a moment to understand that he was talking about the moon that cast a shadow on Jupiter. She examined the image in the telescope again. "Because it's the closest to Jupiter?"

"Yes."

"Do you have any formal training in astronomy?"

"No, but I did read mathematics and physics at university."

He had been at Cambridge; that she knew. But she drew a blank when she tried to come up with the name of the public school he must have attended. "And before university, you were at . . ."

"Here. I was tutored at home."

He had so many friends, she'd assumed that they must have been accumulated from his days as a pupil. She couldn't imagine someone who enjoyed the company of others as much as he being stuck home, with no other children nearby for playmates.

"Why? I thought you said you did not suffer from any illnesses."

"My mother preferred to keep me at Huntington."

She almost asked, *Was she very attached to you?* But the measured, neutral tone with which he'd spoken of his parents did not convey any particular closeness.

"I see," she said instead, fiddling with the knobs. "By the way, are there any other eyepieces? And would you mind explaining to me the best ways of using them?"

*T*his was the peril of being close to another person: One became seen for what one was.

Felix preferred to view his biography as beginning with

the day he inherited his title, when his sleek new persona was first forged.

In this, he was greatly helped by the facade of devotion his mother presented in public—of course the son of a woman who so genuinely adored him would embody all the virtues of manhood. He was also greatly helped by the fact that most people preferred to take one another at face value—a well-turned-out chap of pedigree, manners, and hospitality must be just that, the epitome of gentlemanliness.

He'd always known he was nothing of the sort. As did Louisa. But it was one thing to let her see the flaws that he in fact considered strengths—cunning, unscrupulousness, a willingness to break rules—quite another to expose his actual weaknesses, the old pains and yearnings that had never completely dissipated into the ether.

To allow her access to the one soft spot on the dragon's underbelly that no fire or adamantine scales could protect.

The eastern sky was turning paler when they stowed the telescope and came back inside.

"Did you already know that I get up in the middle of the night to use the telescope?" she asked, as they passed into her bedroom.

"I've seen you."

On those occasions Lady Tremaine had caught him coming back into the house at odd hours, he had been on the grounds, standing in the shadows, gazing up at his wife's balcony, and her solitary figure at the telescope.

She hopped onto the bed and sat at its edge, leaning forward slightly, her elbows on her knees, her interlinked fingers beneath her chin.

It was the way a young girl would sit. Her face, of course, appeared open and sweet. Her dressing gown was cream colored, trimmed with bands of small, embroidered daisies. Taken altogether, the wholesome innocence she exuded would have been too much, if it weren't for the devious gleam in her eyes.

His breath caught. "You look expectant."

"I've never seen you naked," she said, the way another wife might accuse a husband of offenses such as insobriety or spendthriftness.

He raised a brow. "And you think you will now?"

Her tone was imperious. "I had better."

That she was fiercely drawn to him was what made his sense of vulnerability bearable.

He had thought so an aeon ago, when his only vulnerability was having made his interest known with his offer to buy her body. He was infinitely more unprotected these days, led about by his needs, master of neither his thoughts nor his actions—a condition made tolerable only because she was just as enslaved by the pleasures of their marriage bed.

He kicked off his shoes. "Don't I do well enough by you with my clothes on?"

"Very well. I particularly liked the sensation of all that Harris tweed against my thighs. In fact, I demand that when we make love outside, you keep your clothes on—that's how it was in my dreams, and I am nothing if not a stickler for erotic details."

He began unbuttoning his shirt. "But I should disrobe when we make love in safe, boring places?"

"Sometimes a lady is in a mood for skin."

"Are you ever not in a mood for skin?"

"Yes, sometimes I just want your head on a pike," she answered without blinking an eye.

Her words sent a shiver of fear through him—she did not even know the worst about him. Yet.

He peeled off his shirt and approached the bed. "Then I wouldn't be able to do this."

He kissed her below her ear.

She let out a shaky breath. But the next moment, she was pointing at his trousers. "I'll bet if you'd gone to school, you'd have been able to better remain on task."

"Well, next time I see my Old Etonian friends, I'll ask whether they strip more efficiently than I do."

"I am convinced they do. I will advise my sisters not to accept anyone without a public school ed—"

He let his trousers drop. She fell gratifyingly silent. Then she licked her lips and looked into his eyes. "Good. Now put it to use."

He did, making love to her with the devotion and fervor of a new convert, building ramparts of pleasure to keep out fears and consequences, and hoping that he was creating something more substantial and permanent than castles in the sky.

It was two nights later, as her husband tried to elucidate the Newtonian mechanics behind Urbain Le Verrier's prediction of the position of Neptune, then still undiscovered, that Louisa's ignorance revealed itself to be as high and thick as the Wall of Jericho.

"I'm sorry," she said sheepishly. "I didn't understand a thing you just said."

He threw up his hands in mock exasperation. "That was probably the best explanation anyone has given on the subject in the past forty years. Do you mean to tell me that you failed to appreciate my brilliance?"

"Utterly."

"Well, that will not do, will it?"

"You could teach me Newtonian mechanics," she said tentatively, not at all certain how he would react to such a request.

He shook his head. "That would be like teaching you to do a handstand on a galloping horse, when you don't even know how to ride."

Her hopes shriveled.

But before she could say anything to shield herself from embarrassment, he went on. "I would have to start you with the fundamentals and assume that you know nothing beyond elementary arithmetic."

"But I can solve—" She stopped, self-conscious. "Saying I can solve paired equations now would be like telling a safari hunter that I once stepped on an ant, wouldn't it? Or that I once caught a mouse in a trap?"

"You once caught a mouse? I run from those satanic creatures."

She had the urge to giggle at the image he brought to mind, but suppressed her mirth. She did not want to be disarmed by his humor—it would be even more difficult to be wary when she was dissolving in laughter.

Instead, she cleared her throat. "Will you actually teach me?"

For a moment he seemed disappointed that his joke wasn't better received. She felt a strange pang in her chest. She had to remind herself that with him, there was no such thing as simply wishing to please her. Always he aimed to exert more control, to reap more power.

He tapped a pencil against the barrel of her telescope. "See, this is why so many gentlemen never marry. You get yourself a pretty wife, you spend half of your waking hours pleasuring her; then you spend the other half eradicating her ignorance. Soon your estate smolders in neglect and your personal hygiene suffers. Your tenants complain, your staff depart, and your wife won't let you near her anymore because you are poor and malodorous."

Something about his tone—a barely perceptible

melancholy—made her want to reach out for his hand. But it was probably her mind playing tricks on her. She needed to defend against him, not comfort him.

"I had eleven pounds and eight shillings of emergency money set aside," she said briskly. "I will earmark it for soap, so you never need to reek, no matter how poor you become."

He looked at her a moment, his expression inscrutable. "Well, in that case, I must test you to see exactly how under-educated you are. Then we will need to spruce up the schoolroom—a dismal place. After that, I will try to teach you, provided you can refrain from seducing the professor."

A tactical retreat, she thought. She'd done the same herself, steering a conversation into the somewhat less complicated realm of the bedchamber. She fluttered her eyelashes. "Will you rap me on the hand with a yardstick if I do try to seduce the professor?"

"Of course," he said. "I might even have to bend you over the table and spank you."

"Oh, my." She touched her throat. "I suppose I had better let you know that I've never been in the presence of a learned professor without somehow becoming naked in the process."

That had led to a very good time in bed, including a few playful thwacks on her bottom. But now it was the middle of the next afternoon, his lordship was sequestered with his secretary, and she was alone in the schoolroom, looking about.

She wouldn't go so far as to call it dismal, but compared to the rococo airiness of his apartment, it was undoubtedly dull and uninspiring, all dark panels and somber drapes. Much of one wall was taken up with a big blackboard. Near the windows stood a lectern; in the middle of the room, a desk and a chair.

Inside one glass-fronted cabinet was a rock collection, with each mineral's name, provenance, and date of sampling recorded in a meticulous hand. Her attention snagged by the sparkling interior of a geode, she didn't realize for some time that all of the rocks came from locations on the estate, in the neighboring countryside, or from parks in London during the Season.

She had assumed that since he'd never had to submit to the fixed schedule of a school, he might have visited interesting, glamorous places when other boys were stuck in drafty classrooms. But if anything, his childhood had been almost as geographically circumscribed as her own.

It was disconcerting to think of him not as a man who marshaled wealth, beauty, and cleverness to obtain everything his heart desired, but as a possibly lonely little boy who could no more control the events of his own life than he could change the tilt of the Earth's axis.

She shook her head: She was reading too much into a room that he hadn't visited in a decade. If anyone was born able to manipulate, it would be him. His nannies probably ran themselves to the ground to please him. His parents would have lavished him with presents. And what father wouldn't be thrilled to have sired such a son?

All the same, she left in a pensive and perhaps mildly forlorn mood.

Felix felt as if he were in the middle of a long stretch of a high wire, unable to go back to where he'd started, nor reach the relief of the far end—if there was such a thing as the relief of the far end.

He needed a safety net: If she were already in love with him, then perhaps it wouldn't be so terrible if he were to fall off his shaky perch.

Looking back, it was shocking that he hadn't been particularly concerned about the state of her heart. Whether she loved him had been immaterial; it had been enough for him to hold her mesmerized and unable to escape.

Now he was the one mesmerized and unable to escape.

As much as he pleased her in bed and as much as she couldn't seem to get enough of him, like a racetrack, the bed was a closed venue. All the distances covered, all the thunderous finishes, and still they were in the exact same place as before.

He needed to do something that would open the terrain, that would in fact break through the confines. The decision to invite her to his observatory was not made lightly. It was a door that, once opened, could not be so easily closed again, the door to almost the entirety of his private life, something he shared with no one else in Society.

Even after the decision had been made, he still hesitated: It would be no different from the gifts he'd presented to his parents, in the hope of pleasing them and pleading his case.

The weather, overcast when it wasn't actively raining, gave him a valid enough excuse to postpone the visit night after night.

But eventually the sky cleared.

He walked into the drawing room ten minutes after she withdrew from the dinner table. She was at the rosewood secretary, writing a letter. A day rarely went by without a letter from her to her family. In the predawn hours, sometimes he would check the salver that held all the correspondence that was to go out on the early post, weigh her letters in his hand, and wonder what lies and omissions undergirded the narratives within.

She looked over her shoulder. "Finished with your cognac so soon?"

"I have something I'd like to show you, if you are not busy."

"What is it?"

"The best private telescope in England—we've talked about it before."

She blinked, and turned around more fully. "You want me to see it *now*?"

Belatedly he remembered that she had asked about his telescope once and only once. What if she was no longer interested? "If you'd like."

"Would I have to travel for it?"

"A short way."

She turned the fountain pen in her fingers. It felt as if it were his heart that she held, tilted one way, then the other.

It occurred to him that she was stalling, as if she, too, were hesitant. He couldn't see why: It was not her intentions and her offerings out in the open, with rejection a very real possibility.

After an eternity, she blotted her letter and capped her pen. "Yes, I would like that," she said. "Lead the way."

*H*e led her by the hand.

Though they made love night and day, they rarely held hands.

The warmth of their interlaced fingers made it difficult for Louisa to remain wary.

The entirety of his demeanor, since the end of the house party, made it difficult to remain wary. He was a solicitous husband, an attentive and insatiable lover, not to mention the perfect mentor, whose encyclopedic knowledge of the night sky paved the path for her growth as an amateur astronomer.

Sometimes the terrible days at the beginning of their marriage seemed to have taken place aeons ago, when dinosaurs still roamed the earth. It was only the depth and bleakness of her erstwhile misery, the memory of which still made her cringe, that still fed her caution.

A diet that was apparently less than plentiful, for as she glanced at him, walking beside her, she did not want to doubt his motive, but to kiss him on his cheek—or some other such silly, girlish gesture.

"Why now?" she made herself ask, as they climbed yet another set of stairs. "Why do you want me to see your telescope tonight, out of the blue?"

If she did not protect her heart, who would?

"I was waiting for a clear night."

"I mean, why do you want me to see your telescope at all?"

He looked at her askance. "Because I have ulterior motives?"

She felt a little sheepish at her suspicions being so plainly identified. "Don't you?"

"Of course," he said, his tone glib.

This time he gazed straight ahead and she could not quite judge what he meant.

They came to a vertical ladder. He went up to open the trapdoor, then came down again so she would have someone beneath her while she climbed.

The cupola at the top of the manor was sizable when viewed from ground level. Up close it was huge—only the house's spectacular size prevented it from overwhelming the whole structure.

"My observatory," he said, once he'd climbed up and closed the trapdoor.

She should have realized it was the cupola, since she never saw a dome anywhere from inside the manor. But could any telescope be big enough to need such cavernous housing?

"Ready?" he asked.

She hesitated once more. It was not the telescope she was not ready for; it was always him. "Oh, why not?"

He took her hand again—not interlacing their fingers this time, only holding her wrist. All the same, it was nearly impossible to think of anything else except the sensation of his touch. Lowering, really, considering that he touched her in far more unspeakable ways and far more unspeakable places on a daily, sometimes hourly basis.

"Now look up."

Belatedly she realized that they had come to a stop, but she was staring down at those fingers that encircled her wrist. She pulled her hand free and tilted her head up.

And emitted a choked sound. "My God. My God!"

She had never before taken the Lord's name in vain, at least not aloud. An absolute beast of a telescope lens loomed above her. "Please forgive my language. What . . . what's the aperture size?"

"Sixty-four inches."

It was almost incomprehensible that such a marvelous monstrosity could exist. She laughed—the sound oddly unfamiliar in her ears, as if she hadn't heard it in a very long time—and kept laughing, too awed and astounded to say anything else.

He tugged at her elbow. "Come see more of it."

She followed him reluctantly, not wanting to let the telescope out of her sight. But inside the observatory, she was even more dumbstruck. Yes, the aperture was magnificent, but she had not imagined the telescope would be more than forty feet in length. And this leviathan was mobile, by the look of it, mounted on a system of rails and manipulated by an intricate arrangement of pulleys, in order to track across the sky and maximize its utility.

She caressed the thick barrel incredulously. "You had this built?"

"It took five years."

She placed her cheek on the cool steel casing of the barrel. "That long?"

"Not the actual construction, but it took many tries to arrive at a design that would allow me to realign the telescope by myself."

She glanced toward him. "I admire that. I admire that tremendously."

He shrugged, almost as if the compliment didn't sit well with him.

"I know this will sound silly," she asked, still breathless, "but is this the biggest telescope ever?"

"No." He smiled. "The Earl of Rosse's telescope at his castle in Ireland measures seventy-three inches across. I have visited it. It is truly a juggernaut. But mine has the advantage of being mobile."

She kept feeling the barrel up and down, the sheer size of the thing. "I can't get enough of it."

"Yes, I know. You said so every night last week."

Her face grew warm at his teasing. "Ha. I will never be impressed with your puny instrument again, now that I've seen this monster."

"Well, good luck getting this monster inside your—"

She gasped.

"—house." He laughed. "What? What did you think I was going to say? I had to have the roof specially reinforced, and we assembled the monster piece by piece right here. It isn't going anywhere."

She whacked him on the arm.

Faintly she realized that they hadn't been so easy or playful with each other since their wedding night. But she couldn't seem to care too much.

"Let me see if the Stargazer can show you something good," he said.

He consulted two notebooks, changed the telescope's coordinates, then sat down before the eyepiece to ascertain that he had what he wanted. "I'm sure you won't need me again after tonight, now that you have met your one true love," he said, yielding his seat, "but I hope you'll remember me fondly."

Impulsively, she gripped his shoulder as she passed him. He glanced at her as if startled.

Their eyes remained locked for several seconds before she, a bit awkwardly, let go of him to see what he had found for her.

*B*efore the eyepiece she gave a trembling, almost orgasmic sigh. "Is it—my goodness—it is Neptune? It really is blue, like the ocean."

Her pleasure was bittersweet in Felix's chest. He watched her. He had been watching her ever since they met and he suspected that he would go on watching her for the foreseeable future.

When she had admired Neptune as much as her heart desired, they went outside the observatory. It was a magnificent, moonless night, the stars a million gems carelessly strewn across a swath of black velvet, with the hazy stream of the Milky Way flowing from north to south.

She tilted her head back; the Swan and the Lyre dominated the zenith of the sky.

"Deneb, Vega, Altair." She whispered the names of the stars that made up the Summer Triangle.

The strand of pearls twined into her hair glowed, tiny stars in their own right against the rich darkness of her hair. The soft blue lisse of her skirts billowed in the night breeze, a nimbus of captured starlight. Her sleeves, made of translucent gauze, were rings of fairy dust pooled around her upper arm.

"Thuban. Polaris. Capella." He joined her in the naming of old friends, faithful companions of his nocturnal life.

She took his hand in hers. Next came something even more amazing: She rested her head on his shoulder.

He reciprocated by putting his arm around her waist, the chaos in his chest expanding to the size of the universe.

A sensation of agony, almost.

He could no longer deny it: He was hopelessly in love with her.

*L*ouisa fought against the words that kept rising to the tip of her tongue.

This is the most perfect night of my life. You are the most beguiling man I have ever met. And I have this most terrifying urge to tell you that I love you. That I have loved you all along.

"Do you have a favorite star?" he murmured.

She was thankful to give an answer that had nothing to do with the impulses of her heart. "Algol."

"The Demon Star?"

The star's luminosity varied every few days, which fascinated her. "Yes. What about you?"

"The North Star, always."

How odd that he should prefer something constant and stalwart, while she was drawn to the mysterious and ever shifting.

In the case of Algol, there was a scientific reason for its inconstancy: The star was most likely a binary system, the weaker star of which periodically passed before the brighter star, reducing its luminosity as seen from Earth.

But what was his reason for being unpredictable? When would his thoughtfulness and consideration again be eclipsed by an inexplicable onset of distance and coldness?

Keep your secret a little longer—it is something that cannot be unsaid.

*T*hank you for a memorable evening," she said, as they entered her bedroom.

"Is it?" Felix searched her face, hoping for something that would make him feel less desolate.

Such a lonely feeling, being hopelessly in love.

Once he had told her that he found her more opaque than he'd expected, when it came to matters not directly related to physical desires. It was only truer now. If she were a book, then there were crucial passages written in languages entirely alien to him.

She pushed him into bed. "Of course. I love a monster instrument. And I love even better going from one monster instrument to another."

He was rock hard. But her decided preference for his body he already knew—they had been ragingly in lust with each other from the beginning. But what of her mysterious heart and her enigmatic soul?

"Is that all you need to be happy, a pair of monster instruments?" He could not help himself.

The look she gave him was as veiled as the surface of Venus. She lifted his hand and sucked on his index and middle fingers, the inside of her mouth soft and moist. He grimaced with the jolt of pleasure.

"I also have your pretty face and your vast fortune. So, yes, my happiness is complete."

She kissed him, lips, teeth, and tongue. Climbing atop him, she opened his shirt to the waist, nibbling each inch of torso she uncovered. But her eyes were on him, watching.

Could she detect it on his face, his need to intermingle their molecules and meld their atoms? Could she see through to all the deep, secret, cobwebbed places in his heart?

She undid his trousers. Her lips followed her hands, her tongue swirling about him in scalding, indecent ways. His hips flexed involuntarily, even as despair swamped him. She took him deep into her mouth; his grunt of pleasure echoed against the walls.

"I love the size of you," she declared, "the texture of you, the taste of you."

And the rest of me?

He shut his eyes tight against the pleasure, against the pain, against the possibility of betraying all the yearning in his soul.

CHAPTER 15

$\mathcal{L}$ouisa did not gain access only to the Stargazer; her husband also issued her carte blanche to visit his study anytime she liked.

Huntington had a library worthy of its stature, but the true treasures of its collection were to be found in his study. There were scientific classics from the age of antiquity, first-edition copies of Newton's great works, and every issue of the journal *Nature* from the past fifteen years. The study also boasted a wealth of astronomer's aids, from *Uranometria* and *Atlas Coelestis* to the just-arrived *New General Catalogue*, an exhaustive survey of 7,840 star clusters and nebulae. And last, but certainly not least, copious volumes of his own notes, and cabinets upon cabinets of photographs he had taken of the Stargazer's view of the sky.

Until now, they'd spent most of their waking hours apart, time in bed and before her telescope notwithstanding. But with the study at her disposal, that changed. When she had discharged her own duties, she took to reading in a corner of the study, a pile of books in her lap, another pile on the floor, writing down anything she didn't understand in a notebook.

When the weather was fine and at times even when it rained, they went for walks in the afternoon. After dinner each night he apprenticed her in the operation of the Stargazer—the levers and pulleys used in changing the beast's direction and angle required both muscle and delicacy. She learned how the prism attached to the Stargazer split the incoming light into its rainbow patterns, with bright lines corresponding to emission of light by atoms and dark lines corresponding to their absorption. And he taught her the steps involved in photographing the patterns onto silver-coated daguerreotype plates, to be developed for detailed analysis later.

Sometimes she found herself thinking that she was a happily married woman: both on the surface and quite some distance beneath the surface.

If she kept digging down, of course, at some point she came into contact with a barrier and signs that warned, *This close but no closer.*

And not just from her side of the barrier.

As kind and helpful as he had been of late, the way he sometimes looked at her, it was almost as if he didn't trust *her.*

"Finding anything in my notes?"

She looked up to see the man too much on her mind closing the door of the study behind himself. He was still in his riding clothes, having gone out to inspect the new roofs on the tenant houses that had recently been completed.

"They are excellent notes," she said. "Very detailed. Very legible."

He had teased her about the near illegibility of her handwriting, warning her that when she solved mathematical problems under his tutelage, her penmanship had better not give him trouble, or he would mark everything as incorrect and then rap her on the hand with a ruler.

"What do you think of my prediction of the ninth planet's position?"

She moved a finger down the smooth edge of the pages. Despite the clear readability of his letters and numbers, she didn't know enough mathematics or physics to understand much. She just liked to huddle with his notes because *he* had set them down in his beautiful hand. Because if he loved nothing else, he loved his work. And if she could become part of his work . . .

"It's absolutely wrong. Should be at least another half astronomical unit farther out."

"Really, my young virtuoso of Newtonian mechanics?"

"Find the planet and prove me wrong."

"I will, tonight itself."

She smiled, closing the notebook, only to remember that she was practically covered in them. There were notebooks on her lap, next to her on the chair, on both armrests, behind her head, and at her feet—she'd wanted to feel as if she were in his embrace. "You won't. It will rain tonight. You will better spend your time in my bed."

He looked at her oddly, almost as if he were displeased by that invitation. "Still haven't tired of me yet?"

His question unnerved her. "Any day now," she said, deliberately flippant. "So you'd best take advantage of my lust while it lasts."

He picked up a newspaper that had been set down on top of a low shelf and brought it to his desk. She gazed at him as he began to read while still standing—the beautiful profile, the strong shoulder, the long, sinewy arm—but only a moment; she didn't want him to catch her staring.

So she stared at the cover of the notebook instead. *Planet IX, volume 2.* After a few minutes, he left the paper and returned a book to its place on the shelves just behind her chair.

Her heart began to pound as his hand cupped her face and turned her enough for him to kiss her. "Finally," she murmured. "I was wondering whether I'd expressed my carnal needs forcefully enough."

"Worry not. You always express your carnal needs loud and clear."

It further unnerved her that she couldn't tell whether he wanted to reward or punish her for being so forward.

He rounded to the front of her and shoved aside all the notebooks from her person with a carelessness that was completely at odds with the thousands of meticulous hours that must have gone into the work. Next thing she knew, her skirts were bunched at her waist. He sank to his knees, pushed her thighs apart, and pulled her to the edge of the seat.

She began to tremble almost from the moment his mouth descended on her. And she did not stop trembling until long after he was finished.

Only to tremble again when he rewarded—or was it punished?—her the exact same way that night.

*S*he was recovering from a case of sniffles brought on by a sudden onslaught of autumnal weather. Her nose was red. The rest of her face, too, was somewhat ruddy. And the somber blue of her cloak did her complexion no favors, making her appear even more splotchy.

All this Felix perceived. But he could *see* only loveliness, endless, endless loveliness.

Love was not blind, but it might mimic a deteriorating case of cataracts.

"No luminiferous aether?" she asked, half frowning, smoothing the thick blanket on her knees with her gloved hand. Outside the carriage, the day was cold and drizzly, as it had been since the middle of October. "But that's the medium in which light travels, isn't it? What next, no gravity either?"

Sometimes he wondered what she'd made of him lately. He was afflicted with a deep possessiveness intermingled with an equally deep frustration that he could not move an inch closer to her heart, even with the help of his telescope. She might not be able to identify exactly what ailed him, but as much as he tried to keep it to himself, she had to have sensed, to some degree, his inner disequilibrium.

"You can verify gravity," he answered, "even if you cannot see, hear, or touch it. Luminiferous aether, on the other hand, is entirely conjecture. Why can't light simply travel through a vacuum?"

They were approaching the nearest town: The renovation of the schoolroom was almost finished and she wanted her own supply of notebooks before her lessons began. He was beginning to wonder about the wisdom of those lessons: In his vanity, he had wanted to be the one to reveal to her the scope and majesty of his favorite disciplines, but now the lessons seemed simply the next thing that would not garner him her heart.

"So that's what your correspondence with the American professors is about, disproving the existence of aether?"

He had familiarized her with his various scientific inquiries and correspondences in the hope that she might yet fall in love with what he did, if not who he was. When had he come to be made of foolish hopes? Or perhaps more accurately, when had he come to be once again made of foolish hopes?

"We discussed the specifics of their experiment. If aether exists, then one should be able to measure its relative motion to our planet as it moves through all the surrounding aether. If you are interested, there is a lecture coming up in London on refining the measurement of the speed of light, and that should address some of the issues surrounding whether aether plays a—"

The carriage had slowed to a crawl as it neared the high street. Her attention was squarely on him. Then it wasn't.

She stared beyond his shoulder, her expression one of both confusion and consternation. He turned around to see what had caused such a reaction on her part.

His gut tightened. Miss Jane Edwards, Lord Firth's sister, emerged from a milliner's shop, arm in arm with a man. The man opened an umbrella, his face turned toward Miss Edwards and away from Felix. But Felix didn't need to see the man's face to know that he could not be Lord Firth, unless Lord Firth had added two stone in weight and four inches in height.

"That is Miss Edwards," said Louisa, as their carriage began to pull away.

"So it is," Felix replied, hoping he was as good an actor as he used to be. "I wonder who is the man—not Lord Firth, to be sure."

Louisa, her lips curled in distaste, still stared after Miss Edwards and her companion, who climbed into a carriage of their own that drove off in the opposite direction.

"I suppose he could be a cousin or an uncle," she answered. "Wait—Lord Firth once told me that neither of his parents had siblings who survived childhood."

Felix could almost hear his heart plummet.

Her brow furrowed. "But then again, Miss Edwards had a different mother. And her mother could very well have living male relatives."

He nodded, trying to look only marginally concerned.

She shook her head. "I'm sorry; what were you saying about London?"

"That there is a lecture that we can attend that might address the paucity of proof for the existence of aether."

Could this really be the end of the matter?

"That does sound interesting," she said, her tone making it plain that her thoughts were still largely preoccupied with something else.

He held his breath. Should he say something to distract her, or should he absolutely refrain from such a tactic, lest he appear to be deliberately changing the subject?

She stared out the window for a few seconds. They passed an ironmonger's shop, a penny bazaar, and a bakery.

Abruptly, she looked back at him. "By the way, I never asked you, but how did you come to know that Miss Edwards and her brother are lovers? I would imagine it isn't something they would let anyone, even the servants, witness."

Now he prayed that he was as good a liar as he believed himself to be. "When I was still at university, years ago, I was invited to shoot grouse in Scotland one year. Lord Firth and Miss Edwards happened to be at the same shooting party.

"You know I keep a somewhat irregular schedule. So at half past three one morning, I opened my door, intending on an hour or so of observation outside, with a portable telescope I'd brought. And whom should I see stepping out of Miss Edwards's room down the hall, still fastening his trousers, but her half brother."

She grimaced. "Right, of course."

Then, unexpectedly, she kissed him on his cheek. "Thank you," she said, with a rather weak smile. "I would hate to have married him."

*O*nce upon a time, all he wanted was to reduce her to a state of unbearable sexual arousal.

Then, possible revelations on Miss Edwards's part would have earned a shrug from him, plus a redoubled effort to cheat, lie, and steal his way to what he wanted. The Felix

Wrenworth of that era would scarcely recognize himself today, a man in love, a man who blanched at the thought that his bride would think less of him.

Yet it was now that Miss Edwards cropped up, a reminder from the gods that acts of hubris never went unpunished.

By the next afternoon he had collected various intelligence concerning her reason for being in Derbyshire. He didn't particularly like what he learned, but the silver lining was that Miss Edwards was expected to leave the country before the end of the year.

He didn't anticipate that Miss Edwards would call on his wife, but he didn't want to take that chance. Nor did he want to take the chance that Louisa might run into Miss Edwards again, this time without him. Thank goodness he had happened to mention the lecture in London. He would bring that up again. It should not be too difficult to persuade Louisa to attend an astronomical lecture. And once they were in London, he'd keep her there until they must return to host the Christmas house party.

By then Miss Edwards would be gone and he would be safe.

CHAPTER 16

The travel plans fell into place with surprising speed, once Lord Wrenworth recommended that they could first visit the Cantwells in their new house before heading off to London.

Louisa could not turn down such an opportunity. She missed dear Matilda. She missed everyone. She even missed Julia's indignant yowl as Cecilia dragged her by the ear from one room to the next.

She anticipated a wonderful time with her family, and perhaps a wry amusement watching her husband resume the mantle of The Ideal Gentleman, a phenomenon she had not witnessed in weeks upon weeks.

She did have a wonderful time with her family at the bright, tastefully furnished new house. And she did derive a wry amusement watching The Ideal Gentleman take the Cantwell women by storm again, leading Cecilia to opine that while she believed women the far superior gender, her brother-in-law made an outstanding representative for his sex.

What Louisa had not expected was the butterflies in the stomach that she experienced watching him wield that glossy allure of his, with an occasional sidelong glance at her as if to say, *Remember this?*

She did remember this feeling of being a coconspirator, of being in on a delicious secret that she would always keep to herself.

But he didn't stop there. Even when they were in the privacy of their own room, he remained utterly winsome—droll, naughty, and faultlessly considerate. It made her realize that she had never experienced a direct charge of his monumental charm. Gone was the undercurrent of tension that had made her just slightly nervous since the night of the telescope. This particular incarnation of her husband wanted only to show her a marvelous time.

Part of her realized that his charm was being deployed with military precision, and the rest of her didn't care. He'd been so good for so long; why should she cling to those most awful of memories? Why shouldn't she stop doubting and let herself enjoy her good fortune?

London made it even easier to have a marvelous time. The great metropolis provided endless diversions. Besides attending the Royal Astronomical Society lectures and purchasing Christmas presents for her family, they spent long, leisurely afternoons at book dealers', explored a fascinating exhibition of adding machines, and frequented music halls, the newer venues where a man could take his wife without worrying about her respectability.

Apparently her husband had, in his younger days, been to music halls of the more risqué variety, too.

"There was this one particularly memorable song. Do you know, according to its lyrics, what English gentlemen like to do?" he asked mischievously as they lay in bed together one night.

Louisa moved her head closer to his on the pillow. "What?"

"Play cricket, box, and torture cocks," he said with a straight face.

"Oh, that is horrible!" she exclaimed. "Tell me another one."

Which made him kiss her, chortling. And they stayed up deep into the night, laughing over all manner of naughty things.

When he got up to go to sleep in his own bed, she almost told him to stay. She didn't, though she did take hold of his hand when he leaned down to kiss her good night—and only slowly let go.

At some point, she must think of the future. It was all very well and good to wall off her heart and plant signs that said, *This close but no closer*. But what if her husband had reformed? He had said nothing one way or the other, but his actions spoke loud and clear for themselves. In every sphere of their life together he had become an admirable partner; it seemed almost unfair to continue to withhold her greater affection from him for choices during one aberrant fortnight months ago.

It would be so much easier to thrive in this marriage without the constant weight of her cautions and suspicions.

Deep down, she *wanted* to trust him.

And always had.

*O*utside, wind howled and rain lashed at the window shutters. But inside, Felix and Louisa were warm and snug under the covers. The lamps and sconces of the room had been extinguished, but a fire still roared in the grate and its coppery light danced on the walls and glowed upon her smooth cheeks.

They lay on their sides, facing each other. He caressed the indentation of her waist. Her hand had been roving over his buttocks only a minute ago, quite freely and greedily, but now those same fingers played with her hair, making her look sweet and girlish.

"It's been a while since I asked you this question, but I'm in the mood for it again," she said. "So . . . why did you marry me?"

With a thud of his heart, he recognized the significance of the question. Much of her distrust must have arisen from the fact that from her point of view, he appeared to make major decisions for no logical reason—the foremost of which being, of course, his marriage.

Asking him to explain himself meant that she was willing to reexamine her prejudices against him.

If only he didn't actually deserve those prejudices.

He pushed away the thought—some things she didn't need to know.

"I didn't want you to have to marry your butcher," he began with a partial truth. "You didn't sound as if you were too thrilled with the idea."

She made a face. "So you were just being charitable?"

"Hardly. Every day of my bachelorhood, women married for reasons that did not thrill them and I did not make them my concern. You mattered because I didn't want you to be nice to the butcher in bed. And since you insisted only a man who married you could have the privileges I wanted . . ."

She grazed the ends of a strand of hair against her jawline. "What if I tell you that you showed your hand far too soon? If I couldn't find another means of support, eventually I would have agreed to your initial offer—it was hardly certain that Mr. Charles would have been willing or able to take in Matilda."

He had her brush the palm of his hand with the same strand of hair; it tickled pleasantly. "I took that into account. If not the butcher, there would still be a lawyer, an accountant, or a greengrocer waiting somewhere in the wings, with matrimony on his mind. What man with an ounce of sense wouldn't want to marry you?"

She looked away for a moment, as if embarrassed by his compliment. "If I understand you correctly, you married me because you wanted me too much to take the risk that someone else might come along and waltz me to the altar."

"And if your next question is why, if I wanted you so much, I stopped sleeping with you right after our wedding night, the answer is, I didn't like realizing just how much I wanted you."

It was the closest he had ever come to admitting this particular wrinkle of his psyche.

She considered his confession, her index finger resting against her cheekbone. "Does that mean you've since learned how to want me less?"

He took a deep breath—it still went against every grain of his temperament to concede such knowledge. "No. I became mortal and learned to live with it."

She bit a corner of her lower lip, then reached out and touched his cheek. "Thank you, Felix."

His breath caught. He had asked her to use his given name, but she never had, until this moment. He placed his hand over hers. "What for?"

"Now things actually make sense. I prefer a husband whose actions I can interpret and understand—at least somewhat."

She nestled closer to him and kissed him on the mouth.

Later, when he kissed her good night upon leaving her bed, she reached up and touched his cheek once again. "Sweet dreams, Felix."

*T*hey had meant to slip in and out of London undetected by Society, but Louisa could not refuse an invitation from Lady Balfour, who also happened to be in town, for an afternoon tea party held to celebrate a niece's birthday.

Louisa arrived at the party by herself, with a promise from

Felix to come as soon as he was finished with his solicitors. Not five minutes after she sat down, she looked up and saw someone she had never seen under Lady Balfour's roof: Miss Jane Edwards.

"I do believe you have already met Miss Edwards, Lady Wrenworth?" Lady Balfour loved to call Louisa by her new honorific. "Miss Edwards and Mrs. Summerland have become rather fast friends, you see, since they met in the Ladies' Literary Club."

Mrs. Summerland was another one of Lady Balfour's daughters. Louisa pulled together a stiff smile for Miss Edwards. Miss Edwards, however, shook Louisa's hand most amiably. And she didn't stride off after that convivial greeting, but stayed by Louisa's side.

Lady Balfour left after a few minutes to greet a pair of late arrivals.

Miss Edwards leaned forward. "My congratulations on your marriage, Lady Wrenworth," she said warmly.

Louisa had trouble believing this was the same icy woman she had once fancied for a sister-in-law. But then again, now that Louisa was married, she was no longer a competitor for Lord Firth's affection.

"Thank you," she said carefully, trying not to imagine what Miss Edwards and her half brother did in private.

"I would like to take this chance to apologize," Miss Edwards said with great sincerity, "for my earlier rudeness. I hope you will forgive a sister's protective instincts."

Louisa kept her expression bland. "I'm sure I do not understand."

"Please excuse my bluntness. But you see, Lady Wrenworth, for much of the past Season, I was worried that you might be after my brother only for his income, and not because you cared particularly for him. And for that reason, I'm afraid my conduct was less affable than convention dictated."

Louisa didn't quite know what to say, given that Miss

Edwards was largely correct in her conjecture. "Well, I did think Lord Firth a very fine, upstanding man."

She had, but no more.

"Yes, that he is," Miss Edwards concurred proudly. "The finest man and the best brother there is."

Louisa could only nod.

"The poor darling." Miss Edwards sighed fondly. "He was heartbroken over your engagement, Lady Wrenworth. For days on end he lamented that he should have been more outspoken with regard to his sentiments and that he should not have decided to wait until the end of the Season to propose to you. And that was when I became terribly ashamed of my behavior. Perhaps he would have had a better chance with you had I been more civil."

Louisa was less shocked by the revelation of Lord Firth's matrimonial intentions than by Miss Edwards's regret that they never came to pass. She didn't sound the least bit jealous that her brother was in love with someone else. "I'm . . . I'm afraid I had no idea."

Miss Edwards shook her head. "He can be too taciturn at times, my brother."

She was about to say something else when a tall, handsome man came up to her with a cup of tea.

"Oh, thank you, my dear." Miss Edwards clasped his hand. "Lady Wrenworth, may I present my fiancé, Mr. Harlow."

Miss Edwards, engaged? But of course, he was the man Louisa had seen with Miss Edwards earlier. Louisa coughed up a line of congratulations.

"My aunt lives not very far from Huntington," Mr. Harlow said. "In fact, we were in the area recently, visiting her. Beautiful place, but alas, the rain never let up the entire time we were there."

While he spoke, Miss Edwards gazed upon him with what could only be termed rapture—a sight that made Louisa queasy.

"I'm sorry," Miss Edwards said with a broad smile after her fiancé retreated. "I must look so idiotic. I have been in love with Mr. Harlow since we were both toddlers. But it has taken him a while to realize I'm the right girl for him. We became engaged only last month."

Louisa tried to remember the loverlike gestures on Miss Edwards's part that had sealed her belief that the woman was indeed her brother's mistress. Had there not been lips-to-ear whispers and other touches that had indicated a far greater intimacy than was normal between siblings?

To her horror, she realized that she had never actually seen Miss Edwards's lips touch her brother's ear: Miss Edwards had whispered to Lord Firth behind her fan, and Louisa, fresh from Felix's shocking revelation, had convinced herself that there must be unseemly physical contact behind those ostrich plumes.

And as for Miss Edwards standing with her breasts pressed into Lord Firth's arm—to Louisa yet another piece of evidence—dear God, but hadn't there been a large party moving through the crush that was the Fielding ball? It had been the crowd squashing Miss Edwards's chest into her brother's person, not a gesture on Miss Edwards's part to exhibit ownership over the latter.

Louisa began to hurt between the eyes, a severe pain that radiated across her forehead and spiked deep into her cerebrum. She tried not to think, but the inevitable conclusions tumbled into place one after another, like a chain of dominoes.

If Miss Edwards was telling the truth . . . if Miss Edwards had been in love with Mr. Harlow her whole life . . . and she thought that her brother was the best man there was . . . and Lord Firth thoroughly regretted not having made Louisa his wife . . .

Many, many times she had told Felix she did not trust him. But never had she suspected him of such an egregious, utterly immoral fabrication that could have ruined the reputation of two innocent people, had Louisa been any kind of a tattletale.

And he had lied again the day they had seen Miss Edwards and Mr. Harlow together. He had once again slandered Lord Firth's and Miss Edwards's good names—and she had believed him, because he had looked her in the eye while he lied.

She stared at Miss Edwards's happy countenance, barely able to concentrate on her moving lips as the latter enthusiastically furnished Mr. Harlow's myriad virtues and accomplishments.

So that was why Felix had ushered her away from Huntington. How stupid of her not to understand it for the manipulation it had been. How stupid of her to even think of doing away with her defenses. And how stupid of her—even in her state of numbness she felt the pinch in her chest—to have begun to look forward to a future in which she never needed to doubt him again.

And there he was, being shown into the parlor, searching for her. He even smiled. The moment he realized to whom she was speaking, however, his expression turned into a rigid mask, as if he were a defendant facing an adverse verdict. Or a patient awaiting a fatal diagnosis.

He knew. And he was as guilty as the serpent in the Garden of Eden.

*E*verything outside was shrouded in fog, indistinct, chimerical forms. The only reality existed within the confines of the town coach, within its velvet-upholstered seats, mahogany panels, and suffocating silence.

Louisa sat opposite Felix, her face turned toward the window, her hands hidden in the folds of her short mantle; the opalescent beads that trimmed her skirts shimmered and shuddered with each sway and jostle of the vehicle.

"You told me they were an incestuous pair, Lord Firth and

Miss Edwards," she spoke at last, her jaw clenched. "Did you lie?"

"I did," said Felix. His voice sounded as hollow as he felt.

He wanted to add, *I'm sorry*, but somehow he couldn't. *I'm sorry* was what one said when one accidentally bumped into someone, or ran out of a guest's favorite vintage. Before a disaster of this magnitude, *I'm sorry* was about as useful as a spoonful of water poured on a burning house.

"Care to give your reason? I can't wait to hear it."

He wished she'd screamed, or clawed at his face. Her coldness made him quake inside. "There was nothing wrong with Lord Firth," he said, keeping his voice free of inflection. "Mr. Pitt disobeyed his parents by paying court to you, but Lord Firth was his own man. His finances were sound and his character was sterling. There was no chance of your becoming my mistress as long as Lord Firth remained a viable candidate for your hand."

He never thought it would sound good, this explanation. But still, its egregiousness stunned him. He had never been uglier.

Her expression only turned tighter. "Did you not think of the possible consequences for them? I could have passed on this falsity. It could have spread beyond my immediate circle. In time it might have taken on a life of its own and made pariahs of Lord Firth and Miss Edwards."

What could he say? There was no defense for his lies. "I calculated that there was no one in whom you could confide, and not necessarily because of the salaciousness of the charge, but the source of it. You knew that no one would believe it of you were you to say that The Ideal Gentleman had told you such a thing—it was for the same reason I dared to propose that you become my mistress."

His name and his persona carried power. She had been a nobody, and her sponsor only the wife of a baronet. Society would have chosen to question her sanity, rather than his character.

"How exceedingly clever you are. And how frightfully accurate your reasoning," she said, her voice as flat as his. "I should be flattered that you would resort to such extraordinary tactics just to sleep with me. I wonder why I am not."

"It was wrong of me."

"*Wrong* of you? It was wrong of me the time I slapped Julia hard enough to loosen one of her teeth when I caught her deliberately trying to trigger a seizure on Matilda's part. She was only six, with no real understanding of what she was doing. I should have explained, rather than hit her.

"What *you* did was hideous. Even if I were to accept that you were able to predict with perfect exactitude my silence concerning the matter, and that Lord Firth's and Miss Edwards's reputations were never in any danger of besmirchment, do you think I can overlook what you did to me?"

How stupid he had been to think that he would prefer her openly furious. Her anger burned him like live coals shoved into his lungs.

"As much as it scandalized me, I did not scorn you for trying to make me your mistress. It was immoral and opportunistic, but I thought at least you were honest about what you wanted. I thought you meant to compete on an even playing field. And now I find out that the whole thing was rigged and The Ideal Gentleman had all the scruples of a common cardsharp." She closed her eyes for a moment. "I could live with a scoundrel, but I cannot stand a cheater."

*W*hen they arrived at their town house, he followed her into her room.

She turned around sharply. "What do you want, Lord Wrenworth?"

The formality of her address—the depth of the chasm that separated them—made him dizzy.

"Louisa—"

"There is a time and place for that name—and the time is now behind us," she said, chilling him to the bone.

"Don't say that. We have taken vows before God. We have committed to a lifetime together. And I know it does not mitigate everything, but part of the reason I offered you marriage in the end is that I did not wish your life diminished by the lies I told."

"So if I had become your mistress instead, disqualifying myself to ever become another man's properly wed wife, you would not have considered my life diminished?"

"I . . ." He felt like a man who had been pushed off the edge of a cliff, arms flailing to catch anything that might stop his free fall. "Louisa, please listen to me. What I've done, I've done—I cannot go back in time to make changes. But I'm not the same man I was."

"How have you changed? And if you have changed, why did you not come and tell me yourself what you had done? Instead, you made up fresh nonsense concerning Lord Firth fastening his trousers as he came out of his sister's room in the middle of the night. Then whisked me away from Huntington to avoid discovery. And that's why you have been so nice and sunny to me since, to distract me from all the clues to which I should have paid better attention."

"I didn't want you to think ill of me. I . . ." He almost could not bring himself to say it. A lifetime of worshiping at the altar of strength and he was very nearly too weak to move the words past his lips. "I love you."

She stared at him. For a moment hope spread unchecked in his heart that perhaps those very words, those sentiments that had been so difficult for him to express, would make her understand how important she was to him, how he could not possibly have brought himself to admit to his misdoings for precisely the fear of this rupture between them.

"I am not particularly altruistic," she said quietly. "But between the time I turned sixteen and the time I became your fiancée, I did not spend one penny of my allowance. That and whatever I could strip from the household budget went to the emergency fund I'd set aside for Matilda. And when I went to London, I was fully prepared to marry a man I did not love, so that I could care for her as long as she lives.

"I daresay romantic love isn't the same thing as sisterly love, but all love should meet a minimum standard. A lover should take my wishes into consideration and have a care for my well-being. When have you ever thought about me, except so that you may better gratify yourself—either to make you feel more powerful or to make you feel less out of control?"

He could say nothing, could feel nothing except an ever-rising panic.

"I'm weary," she said. "Please grant me some privacy."

He did not want to be banished. Even if he didn't know how to plead his case, even if—

He closed the distance between them, pulled her into his arms, and kissed her on her cheek, her jaw, her lips.

She struggled. "What are you doing?"

But he was much stronger than she. He maneuvered her backward until she was pinned between his body and a long-case clock. He would not let her dig a moat around herself and keep him out. He would not accept that she no longer wanted him to touch her. And he would not—

A resounding thwack. A burning sensation on his cheek.

He stared at her in incomprehension.

"Get out!" she shouted.

"I don't want you to be angry," he said dumbly. "You said that when we are in direct physical contact, you cannot remain angry at me."

"I don't care what you want," she answered, her teeth gritted. "I deserve to be angry and you do not deserve anything. Now get out."

$\mathcal{L}$ ouisa did not go down for dinner that evening. When her supper was delivered, along with it came a vase of golden tulips, which in the language of flowers meant, *I am hopelessly in love with you.*

When the footman who brought the tray had left, she shoved the vase behind a wardrobe, where it could not stray into her line of sight. Five minutes later she moved it *into* the wardrobe. After another three minutes she yanked it out of the wardrobe and opened the window to defenestrate the whole thing.

She recovered her self-control just in time—the vase was costly, the tulips probably just as costly this time of the year, and the gossip generated by such a wanton gesture of rage would dog her for years to come. Taking a few deep breaths, she walked out of her room, marched the tulips to a room at the end of the corridor, and left them on the mantelpiece.

Coming back into the corridor, she stopped. Lord Wrenworth stood outside his door, watching her. He would have seen the exile of his flowers—the exile of his sentiments.

She returned to her room without another glance at him.

CHAPTER 17

$\mathcal{F}$elix returned to Huntington alone.

Louisa had left London the day after she ran into Miss Edwards, but he had several appointments to keep—and she'd made it all too plain that she wished to be left alone.

The last time he had traveled by himself in the private rail coach had been before the wedding. He'd had *Messier's Catalogue* on his person, and a smile on his face, thinking of the laugh she'd get from the dress dummies on the belvedere.

Now all he had were her words burning in his ears.

Hideous. Cheater. Common cardsharp. When have you ever thought about me, except so that you may better gratify yourself?

There was a part of him that squirmed at the reiteration of these accusations. It wanted to defend him by pointing out that she was far better off than she had ever been—or would have ever been had she married anyone else. Now she possessed a fortune of her own, never needed to worry about the welfare of her family again, and could deploy the finest private telescope in all of England anytime she wanted.

But he could not deny the truth of the charges she'd leveled at him. Until now, whatever he had done for her, he had done for himself, whether it was to give her five thousand pounds a year—for his vanity—or to allow her access to his telescope—for his heart, in the hope that she would reciprocate his sentiments.

The entire aim of his adult life had been getting what he wanted, exactly the way he wanted it; so it was hardly surprising that his character would be marked by a keen attentiveness to himself. But what made his soul recoil was a dawning understanding that his love, so important and fearsome for him, was actually a remarkably shallow thing, little more than a will to possess.

Or at least so it would seem, viewed through her eyes, through the prism of all his lies and distortions.

He fought against successive waves of despair. He would not give up. He would make her understand. He would use every advantage at his disposal and he would—

It was only as the train approached its next stop that he realized what he was doing. He was still trying to turn the situation to *his* benefit, when what he ought to do was first become the kind of man who deserved her.

In his prior transformation from a young, orphaned boy to The Ideal Gentleman, his entire aim had been strength—strength enough to bend the will of others and strength enough to always hold the upper hand.

But now he would need to acquire humility. Or, if not that, at least the ability to truly put her needs above his own.

This brought a new surge of uncertainty. What if he became that better man, but she could not see it? What if she would only ever perceive him through the prism of his prior lies and distortions?

He pressed his fingers into his temples. He would simply have to accept failure as a possibility, that whatever he did might be futile. That her heart might always remain closed to him.

Now, given all that—or perhaps despite that—what could he do for her?

*T*he day after his return to Huntington, Louisa received a note from her husband, informing her that the schoolroom was completely ready and he awaited only her pleasure to begin the lessons.

She tossed the note into an empty drawer.

At dinner that night—the only time they were in the same room, and with so many epergnes and vases between them that she was in little danger of actually seeing him—he asked whether she'd received his note.

"Yes, I have," she answered.

Iterations of the same note, however, kept arriving. She kept shoving each day's rendition into the drawer.

But after a week or so, she found herself going up to the renovated schoolroom. She could not recognize the place. The walls were now a pale celery green, the curtains a daffodil yellow. The ceiling, which had seemed so oppressively low before, had been repainted into a trompe l'oeil image of library shelves going up and up, reaching toward an oculus from which pink-cheeked cherubs peered down, as if they, too, were interested in quadratic equations.

Now there were two sets of a desk and chair, one set the same as before, except repainted and refinished. The other set—larger, more ornate, a professor's perch—she recognized as having been moved from the library. On this desk there were a stack of notebooks with dark blue covers and a rectangle of white space in the middle—like all his other notebooks.

The one on top was labeled, *Lecture Notes: Fundamentals of Algebra*. She opened it to his familiar, handsome penmanship. His lecture plan was lucid and easy to follow, illustrated with plenty of examples. The notes were already halfway through lecture twenty-three.

The next notebook was *Homework*. For each lecture, there would be two full pages of homework. She would need to copy the problems into a notebook of her own, as he had not left room for her to work on the page.

She did not look into a third notebook, *Tests and Examinations*, but only rubbed her fingers along its spine and corners.

She remembered what it was like to be covered in his notebooks, notebooks still neat and clean, but with the pages having been ever so slightly warped by dried ink. Such a luxurious sensation to be surrounded by all that learning, all that data, all that *him*.

It was only when she looked up from the notebooks that she saw the tulips on the bookshelves. Golden tulips, freshly come to bloom.

I am hopelessly in love with you.

She was out the door the next moment, as if a ghost had breathed on her neck.

*D*ecember was upon them all of a sudden.

Mrs. Pratt had barrels of dried currants and candied peels at the ready, to undertake the huge quantity of Christmas cakes her stillroom manufactured and dispensed each yuletide to all tenants on behalf of the marquessate. Mr. Sturgess oversaw the production of ginger brandy and lemon gin. M. Boulanger muttered of not only chestnut-stuffed geese, but of capons, herons, and pheasants in the tradition of his native Poitou; a roasted suckling pig with pineapples, as was served in the Sandwich Islands; or perhaps even a boar's head in the manner of Oxford.

Louisa carried with her a large notebook filled with lists and determinedly saw to one item after another.

One morning, she and Mrs. Pratt, who employed an even more impressive notebook, sat down with the guest list for the Christmas house party and discussed the needs of each person on the list in order to begin the assignment of rooms.

Most of the guests had stayed at Huntington before, and Mrs. Pratt already had dossiers on their habits and requirements. The notable exception was Louisa's family.

Louisa turned to the page in her own notebook on which she'd jotted down those particulars that needed to be mentioned. But before she could start, Mrs. Pratt said, "Here are my notes on the Cantwell ladies. The lamp wicks in Mrs. Cantwell's room must be trimmed each evening, before she retires, as she needs a light on the entire night—either that, or she should be supplied with a long-burning taper. Miss Cecilia cannot sleep on a feather mattress, as it makes her sneeze impossibly. Being a late riser and generally irritable in the morning, Miss Julia would prefer to have her room not face east. Miss Matilda needs to room with one of her sisters in case she has a sudden attack, but not with Miss Julia, as the latter has never had the responsibility of handling a seizure of Miss Matilda's by herself."

Astonished, Louisa looked down at the identical items on her list. "Did . . ."

She meant to ask whether she had somehow spoken to Mrs. Pratt and then entirely forgotten about it. Mrs. Pratt answered, "Yes, ma'am, his lordship did give me these instructions."

His visit to her family had lasted little more than a week. How did he know so much?

"Was that all the instruction his lordship gave?"

"No, ma'am. I also have here that Miss Cantwell is allergic to all shellfish, that Mrs. Cantwell will not eat anything orange in color, that Miss Cecilia and Miss Julia should preferably not be seated close to each other, as they have a tendency to quarrel."

Louisa fidgeted in her seat.

"Is there anything you'd like to add, ma'am?" asked Mrs. Pratt.

Louisa looked down at her list. "Just that Miss Julia must have porridge for breakfast every morning. And that my mother does not mind her food being orange if the hue comes from saffron. She quite admires saffron and the distinction it confers."

When Mrs. Pratt had left, Louisa found herself climbing the stairs up to the schoolroom again. It was a clear day, and sunlight streamed in from the south-facing windows. The room very nearly sparkled.

And there again, on the bookshelf, a bouquet of golden tulips, as fresh and lovely as a breath of spring.

She realized, only after she'd been at it for a while, that she was standing before the bookshelf, stroking the cool, smooth petals.

Felix found her in the gallery, before a portrait of his mother. She cast one swift look in his direction, as his footsteps echoed in the long, cavernous space, but offered no greeting when he came to stand next to her.

She had become thinner, paler, her cheekbones prominent, her eyes almost too large. The only dimension on her person that hadn't shrunk, at least not while she was fully clothed, was that of her bosom, as full and buoyant as ever, cantilevered by those bust improvers for which he harbored such a great fondness.

He felt a completely inappropriate desire to smile, accompanied by a sharp pinch in his chest.

"I understand you have been making guest room assignments with Mrs. Pratt," he said. "In case you haven't done so, I'd like Lady Tremaine placed on the top floor, away from the other guests. I'd promised her a house full of handsome men. Should she choose to take a lover, a room wedged in between the Denbighs and the Hollisters would not offer enough privacy."

She made no response. His heart felt as if it had been made into a pincushion.

"I can speak to Mrs. Pratt directly, if you do not wish to concern yourself with the matter."

"Do you—" She stopped, as if shocked that she was speaking to him. "Do you count yourself among the handsome men on offer?"

"No," he said. "I only want you."

Her throat moved. "I will speak to Mrs. Pratt about it."

"Thank you."

Silence expanded to fill all available space, making the gallery feel closed and stifling. He watched her unsmiling profile, then followed her line of sight to his mother's equally unsmiling face. Something clanked inside him: the realization that like his father, he, too, was now married to a woman who wanted nothing to do with him.

He let the initial panic pass. It was what it was; the only thing that mattered now was what he could do for her.

"She was not happy here," he heard himself say.

Surprise flickered at the corner of her lips.

"She was in love with someone else, a poor man," he went on, relating the story that had come to him so long ago, and which, in the twenty years since, he'd never repeated to a single soul. "But her father kept her under house arrest until she acquiesced to marrying my father. My father loved her greatly, but her pain and anger were so great she could not see past it to any possibility of joy ever again.

"I don't believe she realized that, in her wrath, she was punishing herself as well. But she did, for years upon years, till the day she died."

Don't do that to yourself; don't let go of your *capacity for joy*, was what he could not quite bring himself to say.

She moved to a nearby globe and touched the lapis ocean. Slowly she spun the globe.

"I'm sure you find my daily notes repetitive, but I'd like to see you at something you love. If you do not wish for me to instruct you, we can find you a tutor."

She kept spinning the globe; continents flew by under her palm.

"If we were in London, we could probably have someone of impeccable credentials by the end of the week." Was he rambling? He could not tell. "It will take longer to find a qualified person willing to rusticate eight months out of the year at Huntington, but I will make it happen if that's what you want."

The globe went around a good dozen times before she said, "I am not in the habit of spending money for a tutor when I have a husband who can instruct me free of charge."

If she had left the connecting door open at night, he could not be more thrilled. "When should we start?"

"After the guests depart. And after you have removed those tulips from the schoolroom."

With one finger, she stopped the spinning globe. And then she turned and walked away.

CHAPTER 18

When the Christmas guests arrived, The Ideal Gentleman returned.

On the first night of the yuletide house party, Louisa stood at the edge of a fully populated room and watched her husband with a pang in her chest. It unsettled her to realize that part of what she felt was nostalgia—for her spring and summer, for those days and months when his smiles would send her lurching from arousal to panic and back again.

When life had been so much simpler and easier, and she'd suspected him of nothing more than arrogance and sexual deviance.

Or so it felt. A glorious, lost era of being enthralled by his frank wickedness. Of not seeing that when he broke the rules, he broke all the rules. And of not yet knowing that when he schemed for her, he also schemed against her.

Could he tell, with his occasional glances at her, that she'd been second-guessing the wisdom of agreeing to the lessons? Could he understand how it had shocked her to the core that it wasn't just conventional sexual mores he eschewed, but fundamental principles of fairness and sportsmanship? It would never have occurred to her to disparage another debutante for her own competitive advantage, not even with an epileptic sister as an excuse.

I love you, he'd said. Once upon a time there had been no words she wanted to hear more. Yet his action had made her feel stripped of all humanity and individuality—reduced to a trophy, something for him to hoist aloft in triumph.

She did not want to be loved like that, with her heart an objective to be captured for his satisfaction.

And yet she'd said yes to the lessons that would put them in close proximity day after day, allow him to dazzle her, and lead her to mistake the pleasure she derived from learning for pleasure she derived from his company.

Even with all her illusions gone, there was a part of her— a forceful, potent part of her—that longed to return to his side. To touch and kiss him, and make love endlessly. To let the delights of his bed tip her into forgetfulness, perhaps even oblivion.

He chose that moment to look again in her direction. Their gazes held. She looked away, flushing hotly.

Half an hour later, as the ladies bade good-bye to the gentlemen and made ready to retire, for the first time since she slapped him, he set his hand on her person and kissed her on her cheek.

"Good night, Lady Wrenworth."

Her cheek tingled until well past midnight.

A week before Christmas Eve, a freezing rain fell. Louisa's husband strongly cautioned all the guests to remain indoors, to minimize the risk of unpleasant spills. With the usual shooting crowd and the usual walking crowd all stuck inside, Louisa couldn't seem to take a step outside her own rooms without running into someone with whom she must make pleasant small talk.

Late in the morning she found herself climbing up to the schoolroom. At least there she could be sure of being alone. Or so she thought, only to see Felix standing before the window, his hands in the pockets of his trousers, looking down.

He turned around.

Several of the wall sconces had been lit, but it was the kind of overwhelmingly dreary day that seemed to sap all warmth and brightness from such minor flames. The room felt grey and anemic, and yet he . . . he seemed to be illuminated by mysterious sources, bright and vivid against a receding backdrop.

She should have uttered an apology and made herself scarce; instead, she entered and closed the door behind her.

"Anything I can do for you, my dear?" he asked.

She cast about for something to say that wouldn't make it seem as if she had been drawn in despite her better judgment. "I understand Mr. Weston and Mr. Harris have gone out, against your advice."

"And taken two of my best horses with them, those young hooligans."

"Will they be all right?"

"I certainly hope so. It would be hazardous to send out a search party in this weather." He moved to the desk and closed a notebook that had been lying open. "If you'd like to use the schoolroom, I will be glad to see myself out."

She chose not to give a direct answer, but pointed her chin at the notebook. "Were you in the middle of something?"

"Trying to time a particular lesson."

She noticed only then that the standing blackboard to the side of the desk was full of equations and that he held a watch in his hand—he seemed to have already devoted a monumental number of hours to these not-yet-begun lessons. The awful tug at her heart was one of both pain and painful pleasure.

"And does this particular lesson require you to study the weather?" she said, trying not to betray the more turbulent of her emotions.

"It might, when you are solving problems at the board." He pointed to the bigger blackboard that hung on the wall.

She approached the newly repainted blackboard and examined its currently spotless surface. When she solved those future problems, would he be standing next to her, his scent of summer rain distracting her from what she needed to do?

It was some time before she realized that she had put her hand on the blackboard to feel its texture, in a motion that might be termed a caress. In the silence, there was only the pitter-patter of the rain and his irregular intakes of breath.

She pressed her lips together and dropped her hand. Without turning around, she asked the question that had troubled her for days. "When we spoke in the gallery some time ago, you said something about your mother. That she did not quite understand that, in her wrath, she was punishing herself as well."

A beat of silence. "What of it?"

"She was punishing herself *as well*, you said. So whom else did she punish?"

A longer stretch of silence. "She would have preferred to punish her father, I believe, for forcing her into a marriage she did not want. But he died almost before her honeymoon ended, so it was my father who bore the brunt of her anger, for his mistake of taking his suit to her father when she'd already refused him."

She picked up a piece of chalk from the trough beneath the blackboard. "What did she do? Ignore him?"

He sighed. "Has anyone ever told you that you are an immensely good person, my love? That your idea of punishment amounts to no more than a pointed spurning? My father's punishment was the belief my mother instilled in him that I was most likely not his flesh and blood—an idea made plausible by the fact that I resembled him not at all."

She clutched the chalk in her hand. She could not accept cruelty of such magnitude, of deploying one's own child as an instrument of vengeance.

And him, caught in the middle of his mother's rage and his father's misery.

As she turned around to face him, someone rapped at the door, startling them both.

"My lord!" came Mr. Sturgess's urgent voice. "Mr. Harris's horse has returned to the stables without him, sir."

*H*arris was stuck in a ditch, with a broken rib and a fractured elbow. Weston wasn't so lucky: He and his horse were both found at the bottom of a ravine.

And Felix, after shooting one of his favorite horses, descended into the ravine with a rope tied around his waist. When he reached the stoutly built Weston, he had to secure the latter—about two stone heavier than himself—on his back and climb up.

It was pitch dark when the rescue party finally arrived back at the house. Louisa came running out of the front door, and it was worth the entire day of blistering cold to see the anxiety in her eyes.

She went right past him. And then, almost comically, she stopped and pivoted on her heels. "There is a bath waiting for you. Go. The surgeon and I will see to Weston."

He saw his reflection as he crossed the entry hall mirror. No wonder she hadn't recognized him immediately: He'd lost his hat, his hair was plastered to his head, and his face was dirty, his riding coat and trousers torn, drenched, and coated with mud.

The bath had been drawn in her tub—the best one in the house. He sat down, wincing at the pins-and-needles sensation in his lower extremities, still numb from the cold.

His valet left with his ruined clothes. He closed his eyes and leaned his head back. The water was heavenly, though it did sting the myriad scratches on his person, and the steam called notice to minor lacerations on his face, nicks that he had barely felt earlier, because he'd been so cold.

The door opened.

"I won't need anything for at least another quarter hour," he said. "You may see to your other duties."

"I have already seen to my other duties."

Louisa.

He opened his eyes. She carried a pot of tea and a plate of fresh buttered buns.

"Would you like anything?" she asked.

Yes, you.

And not even for lovemaking, but just to hold, for safety and comfort.

"Or should I ring the kitchen for something else?"

"No, thank you. I ate plenty on the way back."

When he'd arrived at the waiting wagonette with Weston, who had turned unconscious from the pain of being maneuvered down a bumpy slope to the designated meeting place, there had been food and drink waiting: mulled ale, whiskey-spiked coffee, and curried pastries, all carefully packed to preserve their heat in the weather.

"The pair of grooms who were with you told me all about your heroics. I hope you didn't do it just to polish The Ideal Gentleman's halo. You could've killed yourself," she said, her tone unusually harsh, as she set down the tray on a footstool within his reach.

"I was quite ready to let someone else undertake the heroics, but the two grooms with me were both afraid of heights."

Ten grooms and stable hands had fanned out in five teams in the search for Weston's whereabouts. It was sheer chance that the team Felix had joined had stumbled across him.

She lowered herself to one knee and examined his badly scratched right hand. "Why didn't you have anyone see to it?"

"You said there was a bath, so I came."

If she'd said he had to go back out and dig a ditch, he would have, too.

"What happened?"

"I had to remove my gloves to climb up. Then the rope slackened and I lost my foothold. So I grabbed the nearest thing, which turned out to be a rather thorny bush."

Her expression was pinched. He could not tell whether she was actually concerned for him or merely going through the motions.

She tilted his still-cold hand toward the light, looking for any splinters that might be stuck under the skin.

"I removed them all. They put me on the wagonette for the return trip—with a hot-water bottle in my lap, no less. There was a lantern nearby and I had plenty of time to pluck out the thorns."

She straightened. "Wait."

It was a request that required no response from him, but he answered all the same. "I will," he told her. "I will keep waiting."

*O*utside the bath, Louisa leaned against the wall for a moment.

Ever since he left the house, her stomach had churned with anxiety. Hour after hour passed. Even after a messenger came and relayed the news that Mr. Weston had been found and everyone was headed back, she remained on tenterhooks, pacing in the entry hall, rushing outside at the slightest noise.

Only to miss him completely when he actually did come back, looking like a chimney sweep who had been caught in the rain.

As soon as she'd seen Mr. Weston settled, surrounded by the surgeon, the physician, two nurses, and Mrs. Pratt, the housekeeper, she'd left to see to her husband. She'd expected to encounter the chimney sweep again, but the man in her bathtub was as beautiful as ever, if somewhat bruised and battered.

I will keep waiting.

She made herself push away from the wall and retrieve the items she needed. On the way she encountered a gaggle of ladies, all anxious to learn of their host's condition. News of his intrepid rescue of Mr. Weston had spread throughout the house—tomorrow it would be carried in dozens of letters to all corners of the empire.

Steam rushed out when she opened the door of the bath. It was only as she approached the tub that she could see him clearly: the breadth of his shoulder, the column of his neck, the muscularity of his arms, stretched out along the rims of the tub.

His eyes were closed, his eyelashes spiked with moisture. But as she neared, he opened his eyes and regarded her with so much gladness that she could not hold his gaze. Nor did she know where else to look—glistening skin and strapping build seemed to be everywhere in her vision.

She sat down on a footstool, lifted his hand, and dabbed it with an alcohol-soaked handkerchief. He gritted his teeth but made no complaints.

"You will be given a hero's welcome tomorrow," she said as she unrolled a length of white gauze. "That is, unless you decide to go down to dinner tonight, ravishingly bandaged."

"And that does not sit well with you?" he asked, ever perceptive. "An unscrupulous man like me becoming ever more celebrated?"

"You did save Mr. Weston today."

She was more proud than she wanted to let on. But it was not an unalloyed pride. Mixed into it was a queer envy: an envy of those who knew him only as The Ideal Gentleman and did not ever question his glittering perfection.

She would have been happy to feel nothing but pure admiration. To not be constantly torn between the gravitational pull of his person and the restraint of her well-justified caution.

As she finished bandaging his hand, he rubbed his thumb along the edge of her palm, sending a shock of sensation up her entire arm. She pulled her hand away and busied herself dousing a fresh handkerchief in alcohol.

But now she had to clean the cuts on his face. She patted around one scratch on his cheek, taking care not to look into his eyes.

"When I slipped and it seemed Weston's weight might plunge both of us back down the ravine, my mind went blank," he said. "The moment it became clear that we would be all right, I thought of you."

She cleaned another scratch and remained silent.

"If nothing else, I've almost half a term's worth of lecture notes ready to go," he went on. "It would be a shame to waste all that preparation."

She turned his face, looking for untended cuts. "The Ideal Gentleman always gets what he wants, doesn't he? And now he wants my heart."

He waited until she'd finished disinfecting a welt at his temple to take her chin in his hand, to make sure she was looking into his eyes. "The Ideal Gentleman might have always had what he wanted, but I have not. I know perfectly well what it is like to wish for affection and receive none in return."

His gaze was sincere, transparent almost. She remembered what he'd told her earlier, the poisonous estrangement among all members of his family.

"I won't deny that if I were to have your heart, it would make me the happiest man in the world," he continued. "But in the meanwhile, what I really want is for you to profit from our association."

"By any definition, I have already profited handsomely from our association."

"That's for your family. I want *you* to have everything you have always wanted in life, everything you have ever dreamed about."

"And you will be content to just give and take nothing in return?"

He raised himself and kissed her at the corner of her mouth. "I won't be just content. I will consider it a privilege."

CHAPTER 19

$\mathcal{L}$ ouisa's lessons began on the second day of the New Year, after their guests had departed.

Since she'd last visited the schoolroom, a bronze model of the solar system had been placed on top of one of the shelves. The easel-like blackboard next to her husband's desk had been painted with a grid of lines. And though the golden tulips were gone, there was now a large mixed bouquet on the deep windowsill, a splash of color against the greyness of yet another winter day.

In a fawn tweed coat with leather patches on the elbows, the professor arrived exactly on time. He opened his lecture notes, checked his supply of chalk, and tapped one piece of chalk against the painted lines on the easel blackboard. "We'll start with the Cartesian grid."

$\mathcal{W}$ hen Louisa was called to the small blackboard and asked to find various coordinates on the grid, she'd been all too conscious of the shape of his hand at the top of the easel, the way his hair curled at his nape as he reached in to take another piece of chalk, and the scent of the fancy soap they'd been given at Christmas, which made him smell as if he had just taken a stroll, in the snow, across an entire slope of pine and spruce.

But this physical proximity, as dangerous as it was, was not the reason she had resisted and then postponed the lessons for as long as she had. She'd been afraid he might prove to be a good teacher; as it turned out, he was an exceptional one.

A love for his subject, a deep understanding of its intricacies, a logical, orderly progression of topics, and a delivery as charismatic and mesmerizing as any rallying speech from *Henry V.*

She sat spellbound by this other side of him, the antithesis of the largely smoke-and-mirrors Ideal Gentleman. This was a man who had arrived at his knowledge and competence the honest way—no tricks, no shortcuts, no manipulation of the perception of others.

A man of substance.

An hour flew by.

She left the schoolroom with four pages of sprawling notes and returned to her rooms to see her obviously flushed face in the mirror. It was another hour before she was sufficiently recovered to tackle her homework.

And when she had done so, for reasons that did not exactly make sense, she walked out to her balcony, removed the cover from her telescope, pushed it out to the balustrade, and pointed its nine-and-a-half-inch aperture toward the Roman folly in the distance.

There were once again dress dummies on the belvedere. No, not dress dummies: a single dress dummy, clad in a tweed coat much like those her husband wore around the estate, with a boutonniere pinned to the lapel.

And the boutonniere was none other than a sprig of golden tulip.

I am hopelessly in love with you.

*S*he was the perfect student.

She was always on time, always ready to learn, and always willing to ask questions. Her notes looked like those of a monkey attempting cuneiform, but her homework was always impeccably neat and almost always completely correct. In fact, she missed only one problem, on the third day of their lessons, and it had vexed her so much that it hadn't happened again.

However, Felix, by the end of their second lesson, already regretted that he hadn't hired a tutor for her instead.

She had the most potent gaze in the world.

He could not fault her for looking at him as he described how to graph an equation or calculate the slope of a line—after all, she was supposed to pay attention. And it wasn't as if she licked her lips, played with her hair, or toyed with the buttons on her blouse. To the contrary, she was indisputably prim and proper, her pen flying across her notebook, her expression serious, sometimes frowning slightly, as she took in his explanations.

And yet, ten minutes into a lecture he would be tumescent. And at the end of a lesson he would be ragingly erect.

It was in the slight part of her lips as she stared at him, the heightening of the color in her cheeks as the minutes passed, the way her left hand gripped onto the edge of her small desk during the latter part of a lesson, as if she were trying to physically restrain herself.

He had to relieve himself with his hand after every lesson. And sometimes another time after she came to show him her homework. During their lessons, he would write problems on the big blackboard for her to solve, and he would find himself standing far too close to her, watching her, and barely holding himself back from pushing her against the blackboard and having his way with her.

All the same, when she asked, after the lessons had gone on for a fortnight, whether she could have two lessons a day, he said yes.

And then immediately locked himself in his bedroom, desperate for relief.

*I*f he were actually someone hired to tutor her, Louisa would have been doomed.

The purposeful, fluid movements of his wrist as his chalk dashed across the blackboard held her rapt. His perfect freehand circles and parabolas sent frissons of pleasure through her. The talk of quadratic equations, matrices, and inverse functions were so much erotic poetry that set her belly aflutter. And if he even so much as hinted at trigonometry, well, she burned.

If he ever noticed her lust simmering underneath her scholarly attention, he did not remark upon it. And did not let it impair his effectiveness as an instructor.

"As you can see, the relative thinness or fatness of an ellipse is determined by the ratio of distance from focus to distance from directrix, or eccentricity, represented by the Greek letter epsilon."

She held her breath as a remarkably symmetrical oval appeared on the blackboard, complete with two foci and two directrixes.

"The very nature of the ellipse, the fact that it closes on itself, sets the value of its eccentricity between zero and one, for the foci are never points on the ellipse, and the distance from focus can never be greater than the distance from directrix. But watch what happens when *e* is equal to one."

A parabola rose above the x-axis, its two arms perfect mirror images of each other. An unwanted heat began to pool inside her belly.

"Every point on the parabola is equidistant from the focus and the directrix. Now, when *e* exceeds one, however, a hyperbola results."

An elegant *x* materialized, centered on the origin, its four arms extending into infinity. Despite her better intentions, she found herself breathing more rapidly.

"All three of these forms, along with the circle, can be formed by intersecting a plane through a solid cone, as Apollonius of Perga discovered centuries before Christ."

A fire roared in the room. Afternoon sunlight streamed in from the windows. It was warm. Prodigiously warm. He unbuttoned his morning coat and proceeded to peel it off. Louisa stared.

"Most of his books have been lost. But *Conics*, which survived, is still considered one of the greatest scientific works of the ancient world and . . ."

It had been weeks since she last saw his naked form, the moisture on his skin gleaming in firelight. She wanted to run her hands over him as he whispered the impassioned corollaries of non-Euclidean geometry. Perhaps he would push her onto his desk, sweeping aside all his notebooks as he did so. And she would plunge her hands into his hair—

"Lady Wrenworth," someone called her, seemingly from the bowels of the manor.

She made no reply. The staff could get by on their own for another half hour.

"Lady Wrenworth!" the voice snapped, along with an explosive noise that almost made her jump out of her chair.

He had slammed a yardstick against the corner of her desk. Her heart thumped with the unexpected ferocity of it.

"Yes?" she squeaked.

He slid the yardstick across the palm of his left hand, a rather malevolent gesture.

"My dear," he said calmly, "I spend hours every day preparing for these lectures. I have a right to expect respectful attention."

She swallowed. "I apologize. It won't happen again."

He was unappeased. "I doubt that. It isn't the first time I've caught you at it. It isn't even the first time today."

Her cheeks scalded. She hung her head.

He sighed softly. "Perhaps I should dismiss class early today, since you cannot seem to concentrate."

Her gaze flew up. "No, no, please don't."

"Then what should I do?"

His voice was most reasonable, yet her knees quaked. Her heart quaked, too, violently. She was the one who had once boasted to him of her ability to endure the deprivation of what she truly wanted. If that were still the case, then she should be able to modulate her voice to something that mimicked his appropriateness, and tell him to continue with the lesson, from the point where the value of the eccentricity exceeded one.

"You should punish me as you see fit, my lord," she heard herself say, half in dismay, half in . . . anxiety, as if afraid he wouldn't.

He leaned against the edge of his desk and crossed his arms before his chest. "When I misbehaved as a child, my tutor would send me to that blackboard"—he indicated the bigger blackboard on the wall—"and make me stand facing it, while he read a magazine."

She pulled her lips and did as she was told. She supposed some part of her must have hoped that he would tell her to bend over his desk, as they'd laughingly discussed during a different age of the world altogether.

The blackboard was full of ellipses, parabolas, and luscious hyperbolas. She felt as lonely as she ever did in this marriage, standing with her nose almost touching the chalk marks, while the clock on the mantel ticked second by second.

Without being conscious of it, she counted the seconds— fifty-two, fifty-three, fifty-four, fifty-five—as if that would give structure and meaning to an otherwise blank, miserable stretch of time.

"What was it that so diverted you, Lady Wrenworth? You were glassy-eyed, to say the least." His cool voice came from behind her—directly behind her.

Her misery evaporated all at once, replaced by that state of shattered nerves she'd come to know all too well around him. She picked up a piece of chalk and wrote her answer on the blackboard.

You.

His hand cupped her face. "That is not appropriate for the middle of a lesson."

She closed her eyes, leaned against him, and lifted her arm to wrap around his neck.

The next second, her skirts were shoved up, her bustle knocked aside, her drawers pushed down not only without ceremony, but with hardly even any acknowledgment that they were ever there.

And then he was inside her, hard and thick.

It was the most incredible, most delicious sensation, like being pounded by a runaway train. The force of his thrusts flattened her. It nearly lifted her off the floor. With one hand on her abdomen, he pulled her toward him, so that he came in farther, deeper, harder.

She cried aloud, her pent-up desires igniting into a

fracturing climax, barely noticing that he was shuddering into her, caught in a climax of his own.

Minutes passed before she realized that she was still crushed against the blackboard, and that she had smeared a large portion of his graphs with her torso and her face. But she didn't care, because by that time he had started to move again inside her, slow, deliberate, gorgeous strokes that drove everything out of her mind except the pure, undiluted pleasure.

*A*fterward, he turned her around, kissed her, and wiped the chalk dust from her face. Then he kissed her again. "I would clear the chalk from your blouse, too, but that would require me to do unspeakable violence to your chest."

She looked down and slapped her hand a few times across her own sternum. A cloud of chalk dust rose between them, surely the most romantic sight in the world, far better than morning mist on the Seine.

When he would have pulled her into his arms again, she walked away, retook her seat, and opened her notebook. He realized after a second that she expected him to pick up where they'd left off.

After a couple of false starts, he did. The class concluded twenty-five minutes late. But other than that, everything proceeded normally: She had a few questions at the end of the class, and then she thanked him and quietly showed herself out.

By the time dinner came around, it was as if nothing had happened. They spoke of the estate, her family, and the weather as it related to the hours of nighttime observation that could be reasonably expected.

Later, however, as he stood in his room, trying to decide whether their lovemaking in the afternoon marked the end of his abstinence or whether it had been simply an aberration, the connecting door opened and she walked in.

His pulse accelerated. "Evening, my dear."

"We are married, Felix," she answered. "You should call me Louisa."

His pulse accelerated further. "Is there a time and a place for it, specifically?"

"Here. And now." She came toward him and kissed him on his chin. "But it's only so that I can concentrate in class. We wouldn't wish to waste your time or disrespect all your wonderfully prepared lectures."

"No, we wouldn't," he answered, cupping her face and kissing her on the mouth.

"So we will take care of all these distractions outside the schoolroom," she said as he lifted her up to carry her to his bed.

He laid her down and kissed her again. "And we will take care of them thoroughly and tirelessly."

After that, neither of them said anything for a very long time.

*H*ave you forgiven me?" he asked, much later.

"Yes." Louisa combed her hand through his hair. "Or at least enough to once again use you for your young, firm body and your pretty, pretty face."

He smiled and rested his palm against her cheek. "I'd like you to be happy here. I want to see you discover new stars and whole new galaxies. And I'm still waiting for you to win unimaginable sums playing cards with my friends."

This last made her laugh a little. "What about you? Don't you want anything for yourself?"

"I've been satisfying my whims my entire adult life. It will not injure me to put aside my self-consideration for a while."

"I can't imagine you saying anything like this six months, or even three months ago."

"I know," he said simply. "Stay with me tonight."

"All right." She'd always meant to, from before she'd opened the connecting door.

"I love you," he told her, just before he fell asleep.

She remained awake for at least another hour, thinking of him, thinking of their future.

CHAPTER 20

*L*ouisa considered it a testament to their dedication that they succumbed to "distractions" during lecture only three more times in the four weeks since they were first overcome. She made speedy progress. At this rate, according to Felix, she'd be ready to tackle trigonometry by the beginning of April. And even with all the fuss of a London Season—their first together as a couple—that promised to be unusually busy, he was confident he could give her a taste of calculus by the end of the year.

They also resumed working together in his study. The weather was becoming less wet and they were often up in the middle of the night to carry out observation. The household was accustomed to such shifts in the master's schedule; breakfast was laid out at ten, instead of eight, and everything else carried on as before.

On this particular morning, he arrived in the breakfast room looking gloriously hale, approached her chair, and whispered in her ear, "I always think I cannot love you more if I tried, but I always do."

Oddly enough, these late breakfasts became his preferred place for telling her that he loved her. It didn't happen daily or semiweekly or on any other kind of regular basis, but only as the mood struck him. In this way, he was still unpredictable: Before this day, more than a week had passed since his last avowal of love.

I feel exactly the same, she almost answered, but caught herself just in time.

It was as if she were waiting for something, a sign from above, a final reassurance, before she was ready to admit the nature of her sentiments.

Hundreds of snowdrops had sprung up, seemingly overnight, on the still-dormant lawn. They were admiring those messengers of spring when Sturgess came into the breakfast room and presented a silver salver to Felix.

The latter glanced at the calling card. "I take it the gentleman is not anyone you recognize?"

"No, sir," said Sturgess.

Felix broke the seal on the note and began reading. His expression changed almost instantly. Dropping the note, he picked up the card and gave it a hard perusal.

"What is it?" she asked, alarmed by his unusual reaction.

"A Mr. Aubrey Lucas, applying to visit the grave of the late marchioness," he said flatly, handing her everything.

The note was simple. Mr. Lucas identified himself as an old friend of the late Lady Wrenworth. He stated that he had been in the civil service in India for many years and had only now returned to England to retire. He would very much like to pay his last respects to the late marchioness in honor of their friendship. Would the present marquess be so generous as to give permission and have a manservant conduct him to the grave site, where he might lay a wreath?

"Show Mr. Lucas to the green drawing room," Felix instructed Sturgess. "Look after his comfort, and tell him that Lady Wrenworth and I will be glad to receive him and conduct him to the late marchioness's final resting place."

Sturgess bowed and left. Louisa looked up from the note. "Are you thinking what I'm thinking?"

"Probably. Certainly she didn't form many friendships after her marriage, male or female. A life of vengeance doesn't leave much room for finer things."

"What are you going to do?" She was both curious and worried.

"Meet him, of course." He took up the card again, and turned it over a few times in his fingers while he finished his coffee.

When he looked up, he said, "I take it you are not hungry anymore, my love?"

Indeed she wasn't.

*L*ouisa half expected a dashing young man of Felix's age. Failing that, she thought she'd see a commanding figure, tall, handsome, and ramrod straight.

Mr. Lucas was of medium height, round, and stooped. His hair might have been golden once, but was now an indistinct shade of grey, his eyes a faded blue. His clothes were a decade behind fashion. He moved somewhat jerkily and spoke a little too fast, giving the impression of someone always on the edge of nervousness.

Traces of boyish good looks were still detectable when he occasionally broke into a self-conscious smile. But Louisa could not imagine that he was anywhere near as beautiful as the late Lady Wrenworth, even if one took away thirty years of aging in the harsh climate of the subcontinent.

Could he really be the one for whose loss two generations of Wrenworth men had paid so dearly?

She glanced at her husband. He was being the perfect host. "When did you leave for India, sir?" he asked amiably.

"Oh, must have been December of fifty-nine."

Six months before Felix was born. Six months after Mary Hamilton married Gilbert Rivendale.

"Was it a difficult decision to leave?" She took it upon herself to ask that potentially significant question. It wouldn't do for it to look as if Felix were grilling him.

"I was the fourth son of a baronet, Lady Wrenworth. It was largely a foregone conclusion that I'd have to venture abroad to seek my fortune." He smiled ruefully. "I'd have gone sooner, but I was a young man madly in love and couldn't bear to tear myself away."

Louisa stirred her tea. "And Mrs. Lucas, did she not accompany you today?"

"There is no Mrs. Lucas—I never married." Mr. Lucas raised his teacup to his lips and gazed wistfully at Felix. "Forgive me, sir, but you are the very image of your late mother. How beautiful she was, how devastatingly lovely."

"Did you know her well, by any chance?" Felix's voice was slick as marble, but behind his urbane smile, Louisa detected ripples of tension.

"I hardly know how to answer that question, sir." Mr. Lucas shook his head. "We exchanged correspondence—I still keep every one of her letters—but we rarely had the opportunity of speaking to each other. She was well guarded and I didn't see her as much as I would have liked to."

"I see," Felix murmured.

"That does not mean that I didn't gain any insight into her character," Mr. Lucas said staunchly. "As I'm certain you can attest, sir, she was the sweetest, kindest angel God ever put on earth."

For an instant Felix froze. That moment passed, however, before it even registered on Mr. Lucas. "Yes, indeed. Now, sir, if you are finished with your tea, I would be happy to show you the way."

*L*ouisa, for all that she was the mistress of Huntington, had never been to the private cemetery. It was small and without ostentation, the marble grave markers laid out in neat, well-tended rows.

From a package he carried, Mr. Lucas carefully extracted a dried and faded wreath and placed it on Mary Hamilton Rivendale's tombstone.

"Amaranth. Her favorite flower," Felix said in a low voice.

Mr. Lucas looked up, his eyes misty. "Yes. I had the wreath made shortly after she passed away—and I always hoped that one day it would find its way to her even if I couldn't."

A silence fell. Mr. Lucas's gaze returned to the tombstone, as if he could penetrate the layers of marble and earth to the bones below of the woman he loved. Felix watched him. Louisa watched her husband.

A few moments later, he asked, "Would you like to see some of her favorite places around Huntington, sir?"

Louisa tried to conceal her astonishment.

Mr. Lucas's face lit. "Would it not be too much trouble?" He almost squeaked in his excitement.

Felix was solemn. "No. Not at all."

They went on a grand tour. There was the small stone bridge that spanned Huntington's trout stream, where the late Lady Wrenworth had set up her watercolor easel on many a sunny spring day. There was the pier at the far end of the lake, where she liked to read on summer afternoons under a large canopy. There was the cloistered ornamental garden she had designed herself, and greenhouses filled to the brim with exotic flowers of all descriptions, her true legacy to Huntington.

What stunned Louisa was not so much the tour in itself, but how her husband conducted it. He spoke at length of his mother, fluently, easily, as if that woman had never caused him a shred of pain in his entire life. He described her daily habits, her improvements to Huntington, and her many charitable works. He painted a picture of a grand lady who lived a life above any mortal reproach.

Mr. Lucas listened with the rapture of an aspiring young soldier before a celebrated war hero, holding fast to Lord Wrenworth's words as if they were so many gleaming pearls. He devoured the locales they visited, looking about them as if he could transport himself back in time, to the side of his beloved, if only he stared fiercely enough.

They ended the tour back in the house, the formal, majestic portion of it, where Mr. Lucas was shown an elegant parlor where every stitch of needlework had been done by the late marchioness's own hand. Gingerly, he touched his fingers to the meticulous embroidery, to the fastidiously and beautifully rendered irises, roses, and tulips.

The very last place he was taken to was the gallery, so he could see the three large portraits of her on the wall and the dozen or so photographs in a glass-topped display case.

Once again, they watched in silence as Mr. Lucas stood lost before the images.

"She never changed," he said at last. "Still as beautiful as the day I first saw her."

For Louisa, however, the hardening of the late marchioness's eyes was plainly visible as the years went on. A grim, humorless countenance stared back at them from the last photographs taken of her, in her midthirties.

"Was . . . was her passing difficult?" Mr. Lucas asked diffidently.

"No. She caught a chill and developed acute pneumonia. It was swift."

"She must be lovingly remembered," Mr. Lucas said softly, his eyes never leaving the portraits.

"The entire county turned out for her funeral," said her son.

Unlike Louisa, Mr. Lucas did not notice the deft sidestepping. He took out a large handkerchief and dabbed surreptitiously at the corners of his eyes.

An invitation was issued for luncheon, but Mr. Lucas declined with much effusive gratitude for their time and trouble. Louisa suspected that the emotional man was in great need of solitude. They let him go, and watched on the steps before the house as he drove his rented dogcart out of sight.

Her husband headed straight into the house. "I could do with some whiskey."

She did not follow him immediately, except with her eyes, her heart swelling with a ferocious tenderness for this man. His mother had to be one of the most difficult and unhappy subjects of his life. But he had burnished Mr. Lucas's angelic image of the late Lady Wrenworth, because he recognized that the illusion was what sustained Mr. Lucas, because the belief that he had had the love of a wonderful woman was all Mr. Lucas had to comfort himself in an existence that found neither fortune, fame, nor a family of his own.

She might attribute Felix's sweetness to her to the fact that he wanted something from her. But this . . . this was pure kindness, without anything to be gained on his part.

The sign she had been waiting for, it had come.

She ran into the house, found him in his study, leaped on him, knocking over the whiskey he was pouring, and kissed him with all her might.

"I love you. I love you. I love you." Her words emerged breathless, almost hiccupy.

He pulled back and gazed at her in astonishment. Then he kissed her hard. "Say that again."

"I love you. I love you. I love you."

Her words were largely muffled by his lips.

He broke off the kiss. "I hope you aren't saying it out of some misplaced sense of my nobility. You saw the man. I could hardly send him home with a broken heart."

"No. I haven't any misplaced sense of your nobility, Felix. I know exactly who you are and I love exactly who you are."

He stared at her for a second before pulling her into his arms again. "That's good enough for me. Now tell me some more; count all the ways you love me."

EPILOGUE

*L*ouisa finally visited the Roman folly in person the following August.

Her jaw dropped the moment she stepped onto the belvedere. "You said this location was remote. There is a village right there. I can see into the windows of the cottages."

"I realized that only when I came to place the dress dummies here before our wedding," her husband answered, grinning. "It wasn't as if I visited frequently—silly place."

"How come you never said anything to me?"

"You were willing to make love in the Greek folly in the middle of an outdoor party. You don't lack for courage—or perversity."

She hit him on the arm. "That was at night. I am much more respectable during the day."

"We don't have to do anything naughty. We can just enjoy the view."

She linked her fingers with his. The view was quite ordinary, but the day was warm and lovely and she was inexpressibly happy.

"Still over the moon about your comet?" he asked, smiling at her.

"It will always be my first."

It had been an accidental discovery, as she compared photographs taken of the same patch of sky on successive nights. Together they did the work afterward, comparing the timing and trajectory of the comet to those that had been observed before, eliminating the possibility that it was one of those on a returning trip—and that was when she first learned that Felix had discovered other comets before.

But now it was confirmed: a previously unknown astronomical body. She hadn't stopped smiling since the letter from the Royal Astronomical Society arrived.

And she couldn't help wrapping her arms around him. "Oh, all right, why not? We came all the way here. Let's give the villagers an eyeful."

He guided her to a corner of the belvedere where it would be difficult for anyone below to see anything. "I know I love you for a reason. I will love you even more when they come for you with pitchforks."

She laughed, cupped his face, and looked into his eyes. "And I could never be this happy with anyone else."

Read on for a special preview of the next
historical romance by Sherry Thomas.
Coming soon from Berkley Sensation.

PROLOGUE

1891

On a storm-whipped sea, some prayed, some puked. Catherine Blade wedged herself between the bed and the bulkhead of her stateroom and went on with her breathing exercises, ignoring the fifty-foot swells of the North Atlantic and the teetering of the steamship.

A muffled shriek, faint but entirely unexpected, nearly caused her pooled chi to scatter. Really, she'd expected more reserve from members of the British upper class.

Then something else. A blunt sound, as if generated by a kick to the back of the neck. She checked for the box of matches she carried inside her blouse.

There was no light in the corridor—the electricity had been cut off. She braced her feet apart, held on to the doorknob, and listened, diving beneath the unholy lashing of the sea, the heroic, if desperate, roar of the ship's engines, and the fearful moans in staterooms all along the corridor—the abundant dinner from earlier now tossing in stomachs as turbulent as the sea.

The shriek came again, all but lost in the howl of the storm. It came from the outside this time, farther fore along the port promenade.

She walked on soft, cloth-soled shoes that made no sounds. The air in the passage was colder and damper than it ought to be—someone had opened a door to the outside. She suspected a domestic squabble. The English were a stern people in outward appearance, but they did not lack for passion and injudiciousness in private.

A cross-corridor interrupted the rows of first-class staterooms. At the two ends were doors leading onto the promenade. She stopped at the scent of blood.

"Who's there?"

"Help . . ."

She recognized the voice, though she'd never heard it so weak. "Mrs. Reynolds, are you all right?"

The light of a match showed that Mrs. Reynolds bled from her head. Blood smeared her face and her white dressing gown. Next to her on the carpet sprawled a large, leather-bound Bible, likely her own: the weapon of assault.

The ship plunged. Mrs. Reynolds's body slid on the carpet. Catherine leaped and stayed her before her temple slammed into the bulkhead. She gripped Mrs. Reynolds's wrist. The older woman's skin was cold and clammy, but her pulse was strong enough—she was in no immediate danger of bleeding to death.

"Althea . . . outside . . . save her . . ."

Althea was Mrs. Reynolds's sister, Mrs. Chase. Mrs. Chase could rot.

"Let's stop your bleeding," she said to Mrs. Reynolds, ripping a strip of silk from the latter's dressing gown.

"No!" Mrs. Reynolds pushed away the makeshift bandage. "Please . . . Althea first."

Catherine sighed. She would comply—that was what came

of a lifetime of deference to one's elders. "Hold this," she said, pressing the matchbox and the strip of silk into Mrs. Reynolds's hands.

She was soaked the moment she stepped outside. The ship slanted up. She grabbed on to a handrail. A blue-white streak of lightning tore across the black sky, illuminating needles of rain that pummeled the ankle-deep water sloshing along the walkway. It illuminated a drenched Mrs. Chase, dressing gown clinging to her ripe flesh, abdomen balanced on the rail, body flexed like a bow—as if she were an aerialist in midflight. Her arms flailed, her eyes screwed shut, her mouth issued gargles of incoherent terror.

A more distant lightning briefly revealed the silhouette of a man standing behind Mrs. Chase, holding on to her feet. Then the heavens erupted in pale fire. Thunderbolts spiked and interwove, a chandelier of the gods that would set the entire ocean ablaze. And she saw the man's face.

What had the Ancients said? *You can wear out soles of iron in your search, and you would come upon your quarry when you least expect.*

The murderer of her child.

A dagger from Catherine's vambrace hissed through the air, the sound of its flight lost in the thunder that rended her ears. But he heard. He jerked his head back at the last possible second, the knife barely missing his nose.

Darkness. The ship listed sharply starboard. Mrs. Chase's copious flesh hit the deck with a thud and a splash. Catherine threw herself down as two sleeve arrows, one for each of her eyes, shot past her.

The steamer crested a swell and plunged into the hollow between waves. She allowed herself to slide forward on the smooth planks of the walkway. A weak lightning at the edge of the horizon offered a fleeting glow, enough for her to see his outline.

She pushed off the deck and, borrowing the ship's own downward momentum, leaped toward him, one knife in each hand. He threw a large object at her—she couldn't see, but it had to be Mrs. Chase, there was nothing else of comparable size nearby.

She flipped the knives around in her palms and caught Mrs. Chase, staggering backward—the woman was the weight of a prize pig and the ship had begun its laborious climb up another huge swell.

She set Mrs. Chase down and let the small river on deck wash them both toward the door. She had to get Mrs. Chase out of the way to kill him properly.

More sleeve arrows skimmed the air currents. Fortunately for her, his sleeves were sodden and the arrows arrived without their usual vicious abruptness. She ducked one and deflected another from the back of Mrs. Chase's head with the blade of a knife.

Catherine kicked open the door. Sending both of her knives his way to buy a little time, she dragged Mrs. Chase's inert, uncooperative body inside. A match flared before Mrs. Reynolds's face, a stark chiaroscuro of anxious eyes and bloodied cheeks. As Catherine set Mrs. Chase down on the wet carpet, Mrs. Reynolds, who should have stayed in her corner, docilely suffering, found the strength to get up, push the door shut, and bolt it.

"No!" shouted Catherine.

He wanted to kill her almost as much as she wanted to kill him. One of them would die this night. She preferred to fight outside, where there were no helpless women underfoot.

Almost immediately the door thudded. Mrs. Reynolds yelped and dropped the match, which fizzled on the sodden carpet. Catherine grabbed the matchbox from her, lit another one, stuck it in Mrs. Reynolds's hand, and wrapped the long scrap of dressing gown around her head. "Don't worry about

Mrs. Chase. She will have bumps and bruises, but she'll be all right."

Mrs. Reynolds gripped Catherine's hand. "Thank you. Thank you for saving her."

The match burned out. Another heavy thump came at the door. The mooring of the dead bolt must be tearing loose from the bulkhead. She tried to pull away from Mrs. Reynolds but the latter would not let go of her. "I cannot allow you to put yourself in danger for us again, Miss Blade. We will pray and throw ourselves on God's mercy."

Crack. Thump. Crack.

Impatiently, she stabbed her index finger into the back of Mrs. Reynolds's wrist. The woman's fingers fell slack. Catherine rushed forward and kicked the door. It was in such a poor state now that it could be forced out as well as in.

As she drew back to gather momentum, he rammed the door once more. A flash of lightning lit the crooked edges of the door—it was already hanging loose.

She slammed her entire body into the door. Her skeleton jarred as if she had thrown herself at a careening carriage. The door gave outward, enough of an opening that she slipped through.

His poisoned palm slashed down at her. She ducked, and too late realized it had been a ruse, that he'd always meant to hit her from the other side. She screamed, the pain like a red-hot brand searing into her skin.

The ship plunged bow first. She used its motion to get away from him. A section of handrail flew at her. She smashed herself against the bulkhead, barely avoiding it.

The ship rose to meet a new, nauseatingly high wave. She slipped, stopping herself with the door, stressing its one remaining hinge. He surprised her by skating aft quite some distance, his motion a smooth, long glide through water.

Then, as the ship dove down, he ran toward her. She

recognized it as the prelude to a monstrous leap. On flat ground, she'd do the same, running toward him, springing, meeting him in midair. But she'd be running uphill now, and against the torrent of water on deck. She'd never generate enough momentum to counter him properly.

In desperation, she wrenched at the door with a strength that surprised her. It came loose as his feet left the deck. She screamed and heaved the door at him.

The door met him flat on at the height of his trajectory, nearly twelve feet up in the air, and knocked him sideways. He went over the rail, past the deck below, and plunged into the sea. The door ricocheted into the bulkhead, bounced on the rail, and finally it, too, hit the roiling waters.

The steamer tilted precariously. She stumbled aft, grasping for a handrail. By the time the vessel crested the wave and another lightning bolt split the sky, he had disappeared.

She began to laugh wildly—vengeance was hers.

Then her laughter turned to a violent fit of coughing. She clutched at her chest and vomited black blood into the black night.

CHAPTER 1

The Lover

For someone who had lived her entire life thousands of miles away, Catherine Blade knew a great deal about London.

By memory she could produce a map of its thoroughfares and landmarks, from Hyde Park in the west to the City of London in the east, Highgate in the north to Greenwich in the south. On this map, she could pinpoint the locations of fashionable squares and shops, good places for picnics and rowing, even churches where everyone who was anyone went to get married.

The London of formal dinners and grand balls. The London of great public parks in spring and men in gleaming riding boots galloping along Rotten Row toward the rising sun. The London of gaslights, fabled fogs, and smoky gentlemen's clubs where fates of nations were decided between nonchalant sips of whiskey and genteel flipping of *The Times*.

The London of an English exile's wistful memory of his gilded youth.

Those memories had molded her expectations once, in distant days when she'd believed that England could be her answer, her freedom. When she'd painstakingly made her way through Herb's copy of *Pride and Prejudice*, amazed at the audacity and independence of English womenfolk, the liberty and openness of their lives.

She'd given up on those dreams years ago. Still, London disappointed. What she had seen of it thus far was sensationally ugly, like a kitchen that was never cleaned. Soot coated every surface. The grime on the exterior walls of houses and shops ran in streaks, where rain, unable to wash off the encrusted filth under windowsills, rearranged it in such a way as to recall the tear-smudged face of a dirty child.

"I wouldn't judge London just yet," said kindly Dr. Rigby, whom she'd "met" in Shanghai three months ago, before the start of her journey.

She smiled at him. It was not London she judged, by the foolishness of her own heart. That after so much disappointment, she still hoped—and thus doomed herself to even more disappointment.

"There they are," cried Mrs. Chase. "Annabel and the Atwood boys."

It was impossible to know Mrs. Chase for more than five minutes—and Catherine had known her five weeks, ever since Bombay—without hearing about her beautiful daughter Miss Chase, engaged to the most superior Captain Atwood.

Such boastfulness was alien to Catherine, both in its delivery—did Mrs. Chase not fear that her wanton pride would invoke the ill will of Fate?—and in its very existence.

Parental pride in a mere girl was something Catherine had never experienced firsthand.

At her birth, there had been a tub of water on hand—to drown her, in case she turned out to be a girl. In the end, neither her mother nor her amah had been able to go through with it, and she'd lived, the daughter of a Chinese courtesan and the English adventurer who'd abandoned her.

She'd been a burden to her mother, a source of worry and, sometimes, anguish. She'd never heard a word of praise from her amah, the woman responsible for her secret training in the martial arts. And the true father figure in her life, the Manchu prince who'd brought her mother to Peking and given her a life of security and luxury—Catherine had no idea what he thought of her.

And that was why she was in England, wasn't it, one last attempt to win Da-ren's approval?

On the rail platform, a handsomely dressed trio advanced toward them, a young woman in a violet mantle flanked by a pair of tall men in long black overcoats. Catherine's attention was drawn to the man on the young woman's left. He had an interesting walk. To the undisciplined eye, his gait would seem as natural as those of his companions. But Catherine had spent her entire life in the study of muscular movements and she had no doubt that he was concealing an infirmity in his left leg—the strain in his back and arms all part of a mindful effort to not favor that particular limb.

He spoke to the young woman and a strange curiosity made Catherine listen, her ears filtering away the rumble of the engines, the drumming of the rain on the rafters, the clamor of the crowd.

". . . you must not believe everything Benedict says, Annabel," he said. His head was turned toward the others, the brim of his hat and the high collar of his greatcoat obscuring much of his profile. "My stay on the subcontinent was marked by nothing so much as uneventfulness. The most excitement I had was in trying to keep a friend out of trouble when he fell in love with a superior's wife."

She shivered. The timbre of that quiet voice was like the caress of a ghost. No, she was imagining things. He was dead.

A pile of bones in the Taklamakan Desert, bleached and picked clean.

The other man was adamant. "Then explain why your letters came only in spurts? Where were you all those months when we hadn't the least news of you?"

Miss Chase, however, was more interested in the love triangle. "Oh, how tragic. Whatever happened to your friend? Was he heartbroken?"

"Of course he was heartbroken," said the man who refused to limp. "A man always convinces himself that there is something unique and special about his affections when he fancies the wrong woman."

Catherine shivered again. An Englishman who'd spent time in India, whose brother suspected that he'd been farther afield than Darjeeling, and who had a lingering injury to his left leg—no, it couldn't be. She had to have been a more capable killer than that.

"You wouldn't be speaking from experience, would you, Leighton?" said Miss Chase, a note of flirtation in her voice.

"Only in the sense that every woman before you was a wrong woman," answered the man who must be her fiancé, the most superior Captain Atwood.

A shrill whistle blew. Catherine lost the conversation. Mrs. Reynolds reminded her that she was to entirely comply with Mrs. Reynolds's desire to put her up at the Brown Hotel. Catherine suspected that Mrs. Reynolds, out of gratitude, planned to find Catherine a respectable husband. A tall task: She herself had never come across a man willing to marry a woman capable of killing him with her bare hands—and easily, too.

Except *him*.

Until he changed his mind, that was.

The welcome party was upon them. Greetings erupted, along with eager embraces. Miss Chase's fiancé stood only a few feet away. Catherine looked toward him, her heart beating fast without a shred of reason.

He had a face that was almost ridiculously beautiful, exactly the kind of progeny one visualized—but didn't usually get—when an extremely lovely woman married an equally handsome man. A face that would have been considered too pretty were it not for a long scar on his jaw. And there was something hard-edged and cynical about the otherwise amiable smile he directed at his future mother-in-law, who fussed over him as if he were her own firstborn son.

Catherine had never seen this man before.

Of course. What was she thinking? That the lover who had betrayed her, and whom she had punished in turn, would be miraculously alive after all these years?

Then he glanced at her and she gazed into the green eyes from her nightmares.

If shock were a physical force like typhoons or earthquakes, Waterloo station would be nothing but rubble and broken glass. When remorse had come, impaling her soul like a device of torture, she'd gone looking for him, barely sleeping and eating, until she'd come across his horse for sale in Kashgar.

It had been found wandering on the caravan route, without a rider. She had collapsed on the ground, overcome by the absolute irreversibility of her action.

But he wasn't dead. He was alive, staring at her with the same shock, a shock that was slowly giving way to anger.

Somebody was saying something to her. ". . . Lieutenant Atwood. Lieutenant Atwood, Miss Blade. This is Miss Blade's very first trip to England. She has lived her entire life in the Far East. Lieutenant Atwood is on home leave from Hong Kong, where he is serving with the garrison."

Benedict Atwood was several years younger than Catherine, a jollier, brawnier version of his brother. "Please tell me that I did not overlook your society while I was in Hong Kong, Miss Blade," he said. "I would be devastated."

She made herself smile, in a properly amused manner. "No need for premature devastation, Lieutenant. I rarely ventured into Hong Kong. Most of my life has been spent in the north of China."

"And may I present Captain Atwood?" Mrs. Reynolds went on with the introductions. "Captain Atwood, Miss Blade."

Leighton Atwood bowed. Leighton Atwood—a real name, after all these years. There was no more of either shock or anger in his eyes, eyes as chilling as water under ice. "Welcome to England, Miss Blade."

"Thank you, Captain." Words creaked past her dry throat.

Then she was being introduced to Annabel Chase. Miss Chase was young and remarkably pretty. Wide eyes, sweet nose, soft pink cheeks, with a head full of shiny golden curls and a palm as plain as a newborn chick.

"Welcome to England, Miss Blade, I do hope you will like it here," Miss Chase said warmly. Then she laughed in good-natured mirth. "Though at this time of the year I always long for Italy myself."

Something gnawed at the periphery of Catherine's heart. After a disoriented moment she realized it as a corrosive jealousy. Miss Chase was not only beautiful, but wholesome and adorable.

Every woman before you was a wrong woman.

Of course. A woman such as Catherine was always the wrong woman, anywhere in the world.

"Thank you," she said. "It has been a remarkable experience already, my first day in England."

*C*atherine could not stop looking at her erstwhile lover. She glanced out of the corner of her eyes, or from below the sweep of her lashes. She pretended to examine the interior of the private dining room at Brown Hotel: the crimson-and-saffron wallpaper, the moss-green curtains, the large painting above the fireplace—two young women in white stolas frolicking against a dizzyingly blue sea that reminded her of Heavenly Lake in the Tian Shan Mountains— and then she would dip her gaze and let it skim over him.

His hair was cut short, no hint of the curls through which she'd once run her hands. The lobes of his ears still showed indentations of piercings, but the gold hoops he'd worn were long gone. And the deep tan that had fooled her so completely as to his origins had disappeared, too—he was quite pale; pallid, almost.

He did not return her scrutiny, except once, when his brother seated himself next to her. He had glanced at her sharply then, a hard, swift stare that made her feel as if someone had pushed her head underwater.

"Tell us about your life in China, Miss Blade," said Benedict Atwood. "And what finally brought you home to England?"

"My mother died when I was very young." At least this part was true. Her next few sentences would be well-rehearsed lies. "I lived with my father at various localities in China, until he passed away several years ago. I suppose some would call him idiosyncratic—he did not seek the company of other English expatriates and rarely spoke of his life before China."

Leighton Atwood did not roll his eyes, but the twist of his lips was eloquent enough.

She made herself continue. "Sometimes I, too, wonder why I didn't venture out of China sooner—I'd always wished to see England and in China I would always remain a foreigner. But the familiar does have a powerful hold. And part of me was afraid to find out that perhaps in England, too, I would always be a foreigner."

There was the faintest movement to his left brow. She

could not interpret whether it expressed further scorn or something else.

"But that is nonsense!" exclaimed Benedict Atwood. "You are home now. And we shall all of us endeavor to make you *feel* at home, too."

She smiled at the young man. He looked to be the sort who was easily impressed and easily delighted. But his sincerity was genuine enough. "Thank you, Lieutenant."

"I quite agree with Lieutenant Atwood," declared Miss Chase. "I think it's marvelous that you have come. You must not hesitate to let me know if there is anything I can do to help you become better settled."

The girl was so fresh, so unsullied, a lovely, innocent Snow White—with Catherine very close to becoming the fading, malicious Queen. When she smiled this time, her face felt as if it were made of stone. "Thank you, Miss Chase. You are too kind."

"Now would you believe me, Miss Blade, when I tell you that you would meet with a most unambiguous welcome?" said Dr. Rigby.

She glanced at Leighton Atwood. He was all languid, indeed, lethargic elegance, if such a thing existed. What happened to the young man who rode the length and breadth of East Turkestan, slept under the stars, and hunted her suppers?

"I understand that you and Miss Blade"—did she detect a slight hesitation, the space of a heartbeat, before he said her name?—"met in Shanghai, Dr. Rigby."

"We certainly did," Dr. Rigby replied.

"Oh, how did you meet?" asked Miss Chase, greatly interested.

"Outside the ticket agent's at Mortimer *hong*. Miss Blade saved me from losing my wallet."

Mrs. Chase wore a look of smug satisfaction. Miss Chase started. Now it was out in the open: Catherine had not been introduced to Dr. Rigby by a known third party; therefore what everyone knew of her was only what she chose to tell them. Leighton Atwood looked meaningfully at his brother.

"It sounds like a wonderful coincidence," Benedict Atwood said in oblivious cheerfulness.

"It was a stroke of luck for the rest of us, too," said Mrs. Reynolds firmly. "Miss Blade kept us alive when we were set upon at sea."

"Set upon?" exclaimed Miss Chase. "Surely not by pirates?"

"Only the most awful Chinaman," answered Mrs. Chase. "Oh darling, forgive us for not telling you sooner. It was a terrible ordeal. We thought we'd spare you the knowledge of it, if we could."

That said, Mrs. Chase launched into a luridly detailed account: her first glimpse of the insolent Chinaman, his aggressive interest in her, her virtuous attempt to avoid his distressing attention, and her last-resort plea to the captain to cast him ashore.

Miss Chase listened with wide eyes. Benedict Atwood abandoned his lunch entirely. Dr. Rigby was discomfited by Mrs. Chase's enthusiasm in the telling. Mrs. Reynolds looked outright troubled—so Catherine was not the only one to suspect that there might have been a sexual liaison involved.

Lin's appearance during the storm had been a shock. But Da-ren had warned her before she departed that news of the jade panes had reached ears other than his own. The Dowager Empress herself wanted the treasure; she would dispatch an agent of her own.

Mrs. Chase was now vividly re-creating the night of the storm off the coast of Portugal. The Atlantic that had the ship in its hungry maw. The hapless vessel, pitching and bobbing like a piece of refuse at high tide. The intruder in her cabin, subduing her, hauling her outside to set her on the railing above the roiling black waters, tormenting her with visions of her own death.

She ended with a coy, "Then I knew no more."

"But what happened?" Miss Chase and Benedict Atwood cried in unison.

"Miss Blade saved us," said Mrs. Reynolds quietly. "I couldn't. But she ventured out into the storm and brought back my sister. And when the man almost beat down the door, Miss Blade saved us once again."

"Was the man brought to justice?" asked Benedict Atwood.

All eyes were now on Catherine. She shook her head. "He fell overboard."

"That's justice enough for me," said Mrs. Reynolds.

"Hear, hear," said Benedict Atwood.

"And were *you* all right, Miss Blade?" asked Miss Chase. She had one hand over her heart, the other laid over Leighton Atwood's sleeve.

He had been gazing into his goblet, but he looked at Catherine now. Pain suffused her, pain complicated with a twist of pleasure, like a drop of blood whirling and expanding in a glass of water.

"I was fine. Mrs. Reynolds was the one who suffered injuries."

When Mrs. Reynolds had satisfied everyone that despite the bandages under her turban, she was quite all right, Benedict Atwood turned to Catherine. "But to single-handedly fight off a villain, Miss Blade, how did you manage it?"

"I had the advantage of surprise on my side," Catherine replied modestly, "a great deal of luck, and the experience of taking a pot to a miscreant's head once in a while."

"My goodness, Miss Blade," Benedict Atwood laughed. "Do remind me to remain in your good grace at all cost."

Leighton Atwood's lips curled in an ironic smile. "Yes, indeed. Do remind us."

"She is a rebel, a rule-breaker,
and above all, a romantic."
—Lisa Kleypas

FROM

SHERRY THOMAS

Author of *Private Arrangements*

Beguiling the Beauty

When the Duke of Lexington meets the mysterious
Baroness von Seidlitz-Hardenberg on a transatlantic
liner, he is fascinated. She's exactly what he's been
searching for—a beautiful woman who interests and
entices him. He falls hard and fast—and soon proposes
marriage.

And then she disappears without a trace . . .

For in reality, the "baroness" is Venetia Easterbrook—
a proper young widow who had her own vengeful reasons for instigating an affair with the duke. But the
plan has backfired. Venetia has fallen in love with the
man she despised—and there's no telling what might
happen when she is finally unmasked . . .

penguin.com